Maurice Procter and The Murder Room

⟩⟩⟩ This title is part of The Murder Room, our series dedicated to making available out-of-print or hard-to-find titles by classic crime writers.

Crime fiction has always held up a mirror to society. The Victorians were fascinated by sensational murder and the emerging science of detection; now we are obsessed with the forensic detail of violent death. And no other genre has so captivated and enthralled readers.

Vast troves of classic crime writing have for a long time been unavailable to all but the most dedicated frequenters of second-hand bookshops. The advent of digital publishing means that we are now able to bring you the backlists of a huge range of titles by classic and contemporary crime writers, some of which have been out of print for decades.

From the genteel amateur private eyes of the Golden Age and the femmes fatales of pulp fiction, to the morally ambiguous hard-boiled detectives of mid twentieth-century America and their descendants who walk our twenty-first century streets, The Murder Room has it all. **⟩⟩⟩**

The Murder Room
Where Criminal Minds Meet

themurderroom.com

Maurice Procter 1906–1973

Born in Nelson, Lancashire, Maurice Procter attended the local grammar school and ran away to join the army at the age of fifteen. In 1927 he joined the police in Yorkshire and served in the force for nineteen years before his writing was published and he was able to write full-time. He was credited with an ability to write exciting stories while using his experience to create authentic detail. His procedural novels are set in Granchester, a fictional 1950s Manchester, and he is best known for his series characters, Detective Superintendent Philip Hunter and DCI Harry Martineau. Throughout his career, Procter's novels increased in popularity in both the UK and the US, and in 1960 *Hell is a City* was made into a film starring Stanley Baker and Billie Whitelaw. Procter was married to Winifred, and they had one child, Noel.

Philip Hunter

The Chief Inspector's Statement (1951)
  aka *The Pennycross Murders*
I Will Speak Daggers (1956)
  aka *The Ripper*

Chief Inspector Martineau

Hell is a City (1954)
  aka *Somewhere in This City*
The Midnight Plumber (1957)
Man in Ambush (1958)
Killer at Large (1959)

Devil's Due (1960)

The Devil Was Handsome (1961)

A Body to Spare (1962)

Moonlight Flitting (1963)
    aka *The Graveyard Rolls*

Two Men in Twenty (1964)

Homicide Blonde (1965)
    aka *Death has a Shadow*

His Weight in Gold (1966)

Rogue Running (1966)

Exercise Hoodwink (1967)

Hideaway (1968)

Standalone Novels

Each Man's Destiny (1947)

No Proud Chivalry (1947)

The End of the Street (1949)

Hurry the Darkness (1952)

Rich is the Treasure (1952)
    aka *Diamond Wizard*

The Pub Crawler (1956)

Three at the Angel (1958)

The Spearhead Death (1960)

Devil in Moonlight (1962)

The Dog Man (1969)

The Pub Crawler

Maurice Procter

An Orion book

Copyright © Maurice Procter 1956

The right of Maurice Procter to be identified as the author of this work
has been asserted in accordance with the Copyright, Designs and Patents
Act 1988.

This edition published by
The Orion Publishing Group Ltd
Orion House
5 Upper St Martin's Lane
London WC2H 9EA

An Hachette UK company
A CIP catalogue record for this book is available from the British Library

ISBN 978 1 4719 0251 2

www.orionbooks.co.uk

chapter

one

Detective Inspector Robert Fairbrother was starting up the steps of City Police Headquarters at one minute to nine on Saturday morning when he met Detective Superintendent Belcher hurrying ponderously down.

"Good morning, sir," he said. "Forgotten something?"

"You're nearly late," Belcher snapped. "Can't you get up when the sun's shining?"

"I've been up hours, sir," was the smiling reply. "What's the matter? Something happening?"

The superintendent glared impatiently toward the end of the street, where the heavy traffic of Crown Row was rolling past. "It's a job," he said. "You'd better come with me." As he spoke a plain black C.I.D. car turned the corner from Crown Row, coming from the direction of the police garages. Detective Sergeant Nolan was at the wheel, and Detective Constable Adkin was sitting beside him.

The car came diagonally across the street and drew up at the curb. Belcher, six feet two inches of bone and fat, and sometimes disrespectfully known as The Belly, went down the steps and steered a torso of planetary rotundity toward the waiting vehicle. When he had made his grunting entry, Fairbrother got in and sat beside him. There was not a lot of room for the inspector, but he moved his wide shoulders ruthlessly and made room, and Belcher grunted again in inarticulate acknowledgment of his right to do so.

"What's the job?" Fairbrother asked when the car was in motion.

"Murder. Reported as such, anyway."

Fairbrother whistled. "Who? Where?"

"Sam Gilmour. At the bottom of his own cellar steps. Head bashed in. His daughter found him when she came downstairs this morning."

"Motive robbery?"

"It looks like it. The till's been rifled."

"What about his rare coins?"

"Don't know yet," Belcher replied.

Fairbrother was silent, thinking about Sam Gilmour, innkeeper and well-known numismatist. The inn was a small one, on the edge of a very rough district, but it was one of the few "free" houses in the city and it dispensed a great deal of liquor to the turbulent elements who frequented its bar and taproom. There would be a worth-while amount of money in the till. The murder, Fairbrother reflected, was probably the work of an ungrateful customer.

That was the obvious view. But Sam Gilmour had been a numismatist. He had been an acknowledged expert in his uncommon hobby. His collection of rare coins had taken many years of careful gathering, and was reputed to be worth a small fortune. Policemanlike, Fairbrother supposed that many of the coins would be gold ones: tempting plunder for a murderous thief.

It was a short ride to Gilmour's place. Without noise or fuss, the C.I.D. car made rapid progress along Ridge Street and into Timberhall Lane, all the time moving away from the city's shopping, financial and administrative district, toward the industrial area which closely girdled it. Timberhall Lane was an arterial road cutting through this belt. Traffic sped along it, making haste to get into the sweeter air of the suburbs.

In Airechester as in other large cities, between the smart business hub and the factory belt, slums had survived, or had been recently created. There was a slum here along Timberhall Lane, less than half a mile from the town's big stores. Its presence was proclaimed by the sudden change in the appearance of the road-side shops. Small and shabby they were: fish-and-chips shops, tripe shops, second-hand shops, pawnshops, so-called medical stores, snack bars with dirty windows, and empty shops whose windows were boarded up. On the right of the road the slum stretched away for a considerable distance, taking its name from one of its thoroughfares, Champion Road.

Gilmour's place was a few yards from Timberhall Lane, on a corner along a street which cut through a warren of poor dwellings, workshops and small warehouses into Champion Road. That was Bagdad Street, called Bag Street by the police. The inn itself had a brighter appearance than most of the public houses in the district. Its doors and window frames, and its swinging sign, were newly painted green. There was no picture or device on the sign, but only the name: "The Starving Rascal."

A policeman in uniform stood beside the open door of the inn. Another P.C. and a sergeant were behind the bar, standing with conscious rectitude well away from the beer pumps. "This way, sir," the sergeant called when Belcher guided his globular stomach into the lounge bar.

Lounge bar it was called, but it was not a place of thick carpets and potted palms. The bar, the stools, and the table tops were of plain dark-brown wood. The tables had strong iron legs, and they were bolted to the composition floor. The pictures on the walls were girlie advertisements for champagne cider and similar drinks. The four beer pumps had blue-and-white handles. But the place was clean and the girlie pictures were attractive, and on the shelves behind the bar was a bright display of bottles which promised drinks for the most exacting connoisseur of spirits and liqueurs.

The seals upon most of the bottles were still intact. The customers of that place did not care much for fancy drinks. There was no such thing as a cocktail shaker on the premises.

The shelves behind the bar were narrow, so the till was placed on the bar itself, near the middle. The cellar steps, with a door at the top, were behind the bar and handily placed for bringing up cases of bottles. The cellar door, which opened outward, was quite near to the till.

The cellar lights had been switched on. Followed by his three

3

subordinates, Belcher went down the steps. The body lay at the foot.

Sam Gilmour had been about sixty years of age, thickset, and still powerfully muscled. One rucked sleeve of his beige cotton house jacket showed a thick, strong forearm. His gray head was a mass of blood. He had not killed himself by falling down the stone steps. There was no doubt that he had been murdered. The weapon of murder, a heavy coal hammer, lay on the floor beside him. There was blood on the hammer head.

"A mug's job," said Belcher.

"It looks like it," Fairbrother agreed. "Or else some crafty type arranged it for us to think so."

Belcher shook his head. Such subtlety in murderers did not accord with his experience. He saw the crime as the work of a petty thief, a novice perhaps, who had entered the Starving Rascal, or concealed himself there, for the purpose of rifling the till. He had committed murder to do it, and murder or serious assault had been his intention. It was not the crime of a man who had struck in rage or fear after being caught in the act of stealing. He had crept unsuspected upon Sam Gilmour, to strike him down from behind.

"None of your fancy stuff," said Belcher. "Some miserable little tea-leaf did this. There'll have to be a round-up. Where's the telephone here?"

He went up the steps. At the top he met Dr. MacKay, the divisional police surgeon.

"Morning, Doctor," he said. "Tell us when he was killed."

The doctor nodded, his glance already on the body. He went down the steps. Belcher stood for a moment, staring thoughtfully at the open, empty till; then he went in search of a telephone.

In the cellar, MacKay stood looking at the body. "Well, I can assure you he's dead," he said dryly.

He squatted beside the battered head and looked at it, with the three detectives watching him closely. He reached out to touch, and Fairbrother said: "We haven't taken photos yet, Doctor."

MacKay nodded. He lifted the head gently, and looked at the face. "A bruise or two," he said. "Tumble marks." He carefully replaced the head in its original position, then without moving

4

the torso he tested for *rigor*. He made sure that he replaced each limb and each finger exactly. Then he stood up and produced his thermometer. He stared around. "Not very cold down here, is it?" he said.

On the right at the foot of the steps was an opening which gave access to the coal cellar. On the left was the main cellar, a long room where there were barrels of beer on trestles, and many cases of bottles. A thermometer hung from a nail on the further wall. Fairbrother went to it and read the temperature. "Exactly fifty-five degrees," he reported.

The doctor nodded again. "I believe that some brewers advise a certain fixed temperature for keeping their beer," he said. "British bellies can't do with icy ale."

As he spoke he began to take the temperature of the body. "I think your inquiries will tell us that this cellar is kept at fifty-five degrees by a thermostat," he went on. "In the meantime, we'll assume it to be a constant temperature."

He held up his thermometer and looked at it, then he put it away. With a very handsome fountain pen he made a note on a prescription pad. He began to calculate. The detectives waited.

At last he put away his pen and his pad. "In my opinion he's been dead at least nine hours," he said. "I may be able to get closer to the time after the post-mortem, if we can find out when he last had a meal."

"Nine hours will do to be going on with," Fairbrother said. "There would be customers in the pub till half past ten or so. We'll check on that, of course. That gives us the time of death between ten-thirty and midnight."

MacKay gazed at the body. "A pity," he said. "From the look of him he should have lived to be a hundred. Dr. Lang will be along from the laboratory, I suppose. You'll hear what he says about it." He looked at the bloodstained hammer with cool curiosity. "I don't think there's any doubt about the weapon," he said in his dry way, "but we'll verify that later. I'll see the body again at the mortuary. Good morning to you."

Fairbrother followed him up the steps. The photographers and fingerprint men were arriving. The inspector stopped for a few words with them. He saw Belcher having a final word with the departing MacKay. The superintendent beckoned.

5

"It seems to me that this lout was in an awful hurry," he said. "Why didn't he try and hide the hammer, in the hope that we'd think the death at least was accidental?"

Fairbrother smiled. "Not much hope of that, had he?"

"Maybe not, with you around. Look here, the daughter's upstairs. You'd better go and get her story. Take Adkin with you. He can do shorthand."

Fairbrother said "Yes, sir," and turned to go back to the cellar. But Adkin, nicknamed the Echo, was already at his elbow. On the plainclothesman's head was the only surviving bowler hat in the Airechester police. He had a red, vulgar face and popping blue eyes, but he lacked neither intelligence nor application. Fairbrother disliked him, and was aware of it, and for that reason treated him with rather more consideration than he did other subordinates.

The two men went upstairs. "She'll be in a bad way," said Fairbrother. "We'll have to handle her with gloves on."

"Handle her with the cooin' doves on," said the Echo.

On the landing at the head of the stairs, all the doors were closed. Fairbrother selected one which he thought might be the living room. He tapped gently on the door, and waited. Presently the door was opened by a pretty girl in her early twenties.

Fairbrother was observing the signs of grief on her face even as he introduced himself and his companion. She had been weeping. She still had a crumpled handkerchief in her hand.

"Sorry to intrude upon you at this time, Miss Gilmour," he said. "We naturally have to get the facts as soon as possible. I must ask you some questions, but I'll try not to distress you. May we come in?"

"Yes, come in," the girl said, turning back into the room. The two men followed her. Fairbrother already had his hat in his hand: Adkin removed his bowler. The plainclothesman's eyes bulged more than ever as he studied the girl's figure. Then he saw Fairbrother looking at him, and his expression became wooden.

Fairbrother glanced round the pleasant room. Then he strode to the window and looked out, as if he hoped that there might be a view. All that he could see was the grimy frontage of the Champion Foundries across the street. He turned his back to the window, and stood politely until the girl invited him to sit down. He sat on the settee which was under the window. Adkin, pulling a notebook from his pocket, went to sit beside him. By this routine move they compelled the girl to sit facing them, and facing the light.

"We'll begin with a few particulars about yourself, Miss Gilmour," the inspector said, when Adkin had opened his book. "What is your full name?"

"Gay," she said.

"Just Gay Gilmour?"

She did not answer. Fairbrother waited a moment, then he went on: "Would you care to tell me your age?"

"I'm twenty-two."

"You live here, at the Starving Rascal?"

"Yes."

"Do you work full time here, for your father?"

"Yes. I'm a barmaid, sort of."

"There are—there were just the two of you living here?"

"Yes."

"What time did you discover your father's, er, death?"

"It would be about twenty to nine."

"How do you remember the time?"

"Because I was late. Breakfast is usually at half-past eight, prompt. It was ready at twenty-five to nine this morning. I hadn't heard Sam stirring, but his sciatica had been bothering him lately, and he's had breakfast in bed once or twice. So I went to his door and knocked and called out, but he didn't answer. I looked in. He wasn't there and his bed hadn't been slept in. I thought that was strange. He wasn't in the bathroom, so I went downstairs. There was nobody about and there didn't seem to be anything wrong, except that the till was open. I couldn't understand it. Then I opened the door to the cellar. The light was on, and I saw him."

The girl paused. She seemed to be trying to control her feelings. Considering her, Fairbrother came to the conclusion that she was more than pretty. She was of medium height, with an excellent shape. There was a tautness about her figure and legs which suggested that she would never run to fat. Her shoes, and the way she wore her clothes, indicated that she had dress sense. Her face, which had at first seemed merely pretty, upon closer

7

inspection had a certain firmness which showed character. Her blond hair was fashionably arranged and, he thought, her hazel eyes would normally sparkle with health. He decided that it would be no great exaggeration to call her beautiful. He was certain that the reporters would.

"What did you do then?" he asked.

"I ran halfway down the cellar steps, then I got frightened. I turned and ran to the front door, and out into the street. Some men were across the road at the foundry, getting some sort of machine off a lorry. One of them was a young man who comes in here sometimes. Bill Knight, they call him. I ran to him and told him, and he came back with me. I stood at the bar while he went down to look at Sam. He came back and told me to go upstairs. He said he'd attend to everything."

"Was it he who called the police?"

"I suppose so."

"How long was he down the cellar?"

"Not more than a minute."

"Where is he now?"

"He had to go back to his work. He came up here and said a policeman had come, and he said I knew where he'd be if I wanted him."

"A very thoughtful young man. Bill Knight."

"He's a very nice young man," the girl said warmly.

Fairbrother smiled at her. "I never thought for a moment that he wasn't. Tell me, when did you last see your father alive?"

"When I went out last night, about half-past ten. It was the Licensed Victualers' dance, you see. As soon as we stopped serving at ten o'clock I went upstairs to get changed. The taxi came at half-past. I said good night to Sam and Abe Farley, and went in the taxi."

"Who is Abe Farley?"

"He's our part-time waiter. He just works evenings for us."

"Was anyone else on the premises when you left?"

"No, unless there was still somebody in the taproom. Abe was sweeping up, and Sam was polishing the glasses."

"I see. Who was the taxi driver?"

"I don't know his name. It was a Blueline taxi."

"Who were you with at the dance?"

8

"I met Bill Knight there. I stayed with him the whole time. I talked to other people, of course."

"Excuse me asking, but did you meet Mr. Knight by arrangement?"

"No. He hadn't told me he was going. I was surprised to see him there."

"Was he surprised to see you there?"

"No, I'd told him I was going."

"Was he at the dance before you, or did he come later?"

"Before, I think. I met him as soon as I got there."

"Did he bring you home?"

"Yes. It was a fine night, and we walked."

"What time did you get home?"

"I don't know for sure. About half-past one."

"Did you come indoors as soon as you got home?"

"We stood talking about five mintues, then I came in."

"Mr. Knight didn't come in with you, then?"

"No. I left him at the door. The front door."

"Was the door locked?"

The girl seemed surprised. Then she saw the reason for the question. "Yes, but it wasn't barred," she said. "Sam had left it on the latch, so's I could get in with my key. I barred it when I got inside."

"And did you have to unbar it to get out this morning?"

She thought about that. "Yes, I did unbar it this morning. I remember I was in such a state that my fingers were all thumbs."

Fairbrother nodded. "When you got in at half-past one, did you notice anything out of the ordinary?"

"Only that the light over the bar was on, instead of the stair light. I thought Sam had forgotten it."

"Was the cellar door closed?"

"I think it must have been. I would have noticed if it had been open."

"Was the till open?"

"I don't know. I never looked at it. I switched off the bar light and went straight upstairs, and straight to bed."

"You didn't go to your father's room at all?"

"No. I thought he was in bed, asleep."

"Of course. You didn't see or hear anything at all suspicious?"

"No, I didn't," the girl said. Her lip trembled. Fairbrother refrained from uttering words of sympathy. He did not want her to break down.

"Miss Gilmour," he said gently. "When I asked you your name, you did not give me an explicit answer. Is your full name Gay Gilmour?"

There was a long pause. Fairbrother waited patiently. Then the girl said: "My real name is Gay Harper. But Sam Gilmour was my father."

The inspector sought in his mind for tactful words to bring elucidation. "You mean your mother and father, er, weren't married to each other?"

"I'm not illegitimate, if that's what you're thinking. My mother was married to a man called John Harper. He was a solicitor, much older than my mother. She ran off with Sam Gilmour. They lived together in London for about six months, then they quarreled. It was a silly quarrel, Sam always said. My mother came back to Airechester and lived with her parents. Though he knew she was expecting a baby, John Harper asked her to return to him. She did so, a month before I was born. Then Sam asked her to return to *him*. But John Harper had been so good and kind she wouldn't leave him again. I was born while my mother was living with her husband."

"So John Harper is your putative father?"

"I don't know what that means. I think he's my legal father, but not my real one."

"Is he still alive?"

"Yes. He comes here sometimes. My mother died when I was four years old. Daddy—John Harper—and Sam were both at her bedside when she died. After that, Daddy let Sam come and see me sometimes. He used to bring me presents. He'd been a professional footballer, and he was the trainer for Airechester United."

"Was he still the trainer when he bought this pub?"

"Yes. He'd saved some money, and one of the directors of the club lent him some more. He paid the director back, and then he retired from football."

"When you were a little girl, I suppose he told you to call him

Sam, and that's why you still do. And I notice that you still call John Harper your Dad."

"Yes, he's my Daddy."

"When did you come to live with Gilmour, then?"

"When I was nine. Daddy developed very bad eye trouble, and he had to retire from business to go to live with his sister. She'd never liked my mother and she wouldn't have me, so Sam persuaded Daddy to let me go to him. I've lived here at the Starving Rascal ever since."

"Sam and John became quite friendly, then?"

"Yes. Daddy isn't a man to hold a grudge."

"Were you legally adopted by Sam?"

"No. At least I don't think so. No, I'm sure Sam never adopted me. He would have told me."

"Well, it's quite a story. Who gave you all the details?"

"Daddy, when I was eighteen. Then I asked Sam about it, and he said it was true."

"Quite a story," Fairbrother repeated. But he was wondering who would inherit the public house, and the coin collection.

It was time that he asked about the coins. He did so.

"They're in a little room we call the study," the girl replied. "It's locked."

"It might not be, now," said Fairbrother. And to Adkin: "Go and see if you can find out anything about Mr. Gilmour's keys."

Adkin said: "Righto, the keys," and went downstairs. Gay Gilmour led the way to the study. The door was not locked. Fairbrother said: "Excuse me," and entered first.

The room was in semi-darkness, with curtains drawn across the window. The inspector switched on the light, then he stood just inside the doorway and looked around. There was a roll-top desk and a chair beside the window. The remainder of the wall space, up to a height of six feet or so, was taken up by coin cabinets. Each cabinet had a number of shallow drawers, and each drawer had a lock. But many of the drawers were open, and some of them had been pulled right out and left lying on the floor. All the drawers on the floor were lined with black velvet, with circular depressions for coins. They contained no coins.

Fairbrother turned to look at Miss Gilmour. He was a man

11

who would suspect anybody and everybody in the early stages of an investigation. But the girl's dismay appeared to be genuine.

"Oh dear!" she said, looking from the drawers to the cabinet from which they had been taken. "The best coins!"

"Gold ones?"

"Most of them," she replied.

Adkin returned, carrying a bunch of small keys. "Under a table in the bar," he said. "The bloke must have thrown 'em away as he was leavin'." He stared into the study. "Well, well! He's been at the coins. That should help, if he tries to get rid of 'em."

Fairbrother frowned. The remark, made in the presence of the girl, was only slightly indiscreet but wholly unnecessary. "Everybody out of here," he said, holding out his hand for the keys. "I'm going to lock this place up."

They stepped out onto the landing. Fairbrother, after several attempts, found the correct key and locked the door. He went to the head of the stairs and bawled: "Sergeant Preston!"

"Yessir!"

"Have you a man who isn't busy?"

"Yessir."

"Send him up here, will you?"

A young P.C. in uniform came up the stairs. Fairbrother took a straight-backed chair from the living room and put it beside the study door. "Sit down there and cool your feet," he said to the constable. "Nobody goes through that door without permission from myself or Superintendent Belcher."

"Very good, sir," said the P.C. stolidly. Then he said: "I'm Early Turn, sir. I haven't had me breakfast yet."

"I'll see that you get a relief," said Fairbrother.

"I'll give him some breakfast," said Miss Gilmour. "It'll keep me occupied for a little while."

Fairbrother smiled, and so did the P.C. Breakfast on the spot meant that he could sit and cool his feet for the remainder of his tour of duty.

"You haven't time to feed bobbies," Fairbrother said to the girl. "I have a lot of things to ask you yet."

He had indeed. For an hour he had the girl trying to recall the names of people who had been in the Starving Rascal last night, and the night before, and the night before that, and recently. He tired her out.

"You'd better try to eat something now," he said at last. "If you can't eat, have a cup of tea and a couple of aspirins."

He left her then, and went downstairs, with the Echo in close attendance. He gave Sam Gilmour's keys to Belcher, and told him about the empty coin drawers. "We'd better give that room the once-over before we start to list the stolen stuff," he said.

Belcher nodded. "I'll see to it. And I'll put the word out. All Districts. Anybody in this country who wants to sell some foreign coins is going to have a very warm time."

Fairbrother turned away. Belcher said: "Where are you off to now?"

"I'm going to see this lad Knight, who informed the police. He was at a dance with Gilmour's daughter last night."

"You think he might have something to do with this job?"

"I don't think anything yet. Just suspicious, that's me."

"Just the spirit of Christmas, that's you," said the Echo, but this time he said it to himself.

One of Belcher's rare smiles appeared. Fairbrother was his best man. He had "brought him up" as a detective. For years he had steadily taught the younger man to question human nature and human motives until it was an even-money bet that he couldn't be deceived by anybody. The superintendent's nod of dismissal was almost affectionate.

Fairbrother and Adkin went across the street and walked into the clangor of the Champion Foundry, where grimy, muscular men labored like hellions in a smoky inferno. It was a piecework place. The men there really did work.

The two detectives stood for a minute or two, looking on and keeping out of the way of busy men. Then a foreman approached, with his head at a questioning angle.

"Police," said Fairbrother. "I'd like to speak to Bill Knight."

"Oh, aye," said the foreman, with the alacrity of a man who is suddenly interested. He walked away bellowing the name, and was lost to sight in the fiery haze of the place. Fairbrother reflected that all the foundrymen would now know about the murder across the street, unless Knight was an unnaturally taciturn man.

13

Presently a man came toward the detectives. "This'll be him," the inspector murmured. "A big lad!"

"A proper boyo!" said Adkin.

Knight was tall, and extraordinarily well-built. He was too well-built to have an elegant shape. Pads of muscle made his shoulders seem to slope too much, and he had the very slight stoop—by no means a round back—of one type of strong man. His limbs were columns of muscle—his bare, grimy wrists and forearms were like those of a Michelangelo statue—but any suggestion of the ape was denied by his well-shaped head set firmly on the thick pillar which was his neck. His face, too, was without brutal characteristics. It was a short face with blunt features, but the short nose had fine nostrils, and the mouth was firm. His hair was dark, with a slight wave in it. His eyes too were dark, and very steady as he gazed at the two policemen. He seemed to be about twenty-three years of age.

"I'm Knight," he said. "You wanted me?"

"Just a few questions," said Fairbrother. "I want to know what happened this morning. Tell me in your own way."

Knight did so, briefly and adequately. He corroborated Gay Gilmour's story. Fairbrother asked him about the dance the night before, and again his story tallied with Miss Gilmour's.

"A dear do, wasn't it?" Fairbrother suggested. "Twelve-and-six a ticket."

"A bit dear," the young man agreed.

"What made you go?"

"Nothing made me. I wanted to go."

"To meet Miss Gilmour?"

Knight gave him a very cool, level glance. He did not reply.

"What do you do here?" the inspector pursued.

"I'm a laborer."

"How long have you worked here?"

"Three weeks."

"H'm. You don't sound like Airechester to me. Where are you from?"

"Sheffield."

"Ah, you've worked in the steel trade before?"

"Yes, in a forge," said Knight. He made a small gesture which seemed to imply contempt. "Not this sort of stuff."

14

"You left Sheffield three weeks ago?"

"No. Four months ago."

"You've been in Airechester four months?"

"No. Three weeks."

"Where were you in the meantime?"

"I can't tell you, sir," was the reply. The tone was civil, but quite firm. The "sir" took Fairbrother by surprise.

"Why can't you tell me?"

"I can't. Not today, anyway. I might tell you tomorrow."

And tomorrow, Fairbrother thought, he might be a hundred miles away, hiding in the murk of some other foundry in some other city. Who said "sir" to police officers? Jailbirds did, sometimes. And here was a man who refused to account for three recent months of his life.

"Where are you living?" the inspector demanded.

"Hudson House, Champion Road."

"That's Mrs. Byles's place," said Adkin.

Worse and worse, Fairbrother thought. A common lodging house in the city's most disreputable thoroughfare, run by a whiskey-soaked hag whose children—some of them, anyway— were known to the police as thieves and prostitutes.

"What are you doing in that buggy hole?" he wanted to know.

"It isn't buggy. I wouldn't stay in a place where they had bugs."

"Well, it doesn't look so clean to me."

Knight did not reply. His cool glance told the inspector to mind his own business.

A good detective has to remember to ask all the questions which should be asked. He also has to know when to stop asking questions. If Knight had a criminal record, that could soon be discovered without alarming him. Even if his name were not Knight, a description of his remarkable physique would soon bring his photograph and record from the Sheffield police. "All right," said Fairbrother. "You can go back to your work now. I shall want a statement from you, later."

"I daresay you will," Knight said tonelessly. "You'll know where to find me."

"You can be sure I will," said Fairbrother.

15

When the two policemen were outside, Adkin asked: "Are you goin' to search his lodgin's, sir?"

"I suppose so," the inspector replied. "But first I've got to make sure that he doesn't run away from us. He may be in the clear on this job, but I'm not satisfied with him. I think he's hiding something."

"Sure he is. I thought he was laughin' up his sleeve."

"Let him laugh. You go back into the pub and watch this side of the building. Don't let him see you if he looks out of his loading bay. I'll go round to the works entrance."

They parted. Fairbrother went to the time office at the works entrance. He flashed his warrant card to the timekeeper. "Do you know Bill Knight who works here?" he asked.

"The big fellow? Yes, I know him."

"Well, if he goes out of here before knocking-off time, or if he comes and talks about getting his money, will you phone the police? He's an important witness, and we don't want to lose touch with him."

The timekeeper was interested. "You think he might go on his travels, eh? I'll give you the wire if he comes out this way."

Fairbrother thanked the man, and returned to the Starving Rascal. Belcher was no longer there. The hunt was up, and the superintendent had returned to Headquarters to direct it. For the next few hours, the C.I.D. would be busy in hostels, common lodging houses, furnished rooms, tenements and all places where known thieves, suspected thieves, associates of thieves and seedy transients might be found. All likely persons would be questioned. A few "clients" would be brought in for further interrogation, and the corridors of the police building would ring with the protests of injured innocence. Informers too would be busy, making surreptitious telephone calls, asking for this or that police officer and passing on their bits of rumor or information. And as usual when a murder or a big robbery caused the police to cast an unusually wide, fine net, the catch would include half-a-dozen wife and draft dodgers and wanted criminals. Their fishing in murky waters was seldom unrewarded.

Fairbrother noticed that Adkin was at his post. He went upstairs. Two C.I.D. men were in the study, dusting for fingerprints. The uniformed constable was still sitting there. He was smoking a cigarette and reading a newspaper. He tried to hide the cigarette when he saw Fairbrother.

The inspector frowned. He had forgotten to get the man a relief. His last meal had probably been at five o'clock in the morning before he set out to parade for Early Turn.

"You should be getting hungry," Fairbrother said, and the reply was a cheerful affirmative. He went downstairs and phoned one Smithson, the duty inspector for the division.

"I've got a man of yours here, doing guard duty for me," he said. "Number four-two-seven, I don't know his name. He hasn't had his break yet. Can you send him a relief, and arrange for a further relief at two o'clock?"

"Certainly, old man," Smithson replied. "How's the job going?"

"Well, it's keeping me busy. I'll say that much."

"I guess so. Your client will be around, somewhere. He'll be one of our own hand-reared rats. Incidentally, I have a raw recruit out in that neck of the woods."

"In Champion Road? You're taking a chance, aren't you? Somebody might get wise and cut his throat."

"Not this boy. He can look after himself. He breaks six-inch nails as if they were candles."

"What's he after?"

"He's crawling round the pubs. On betting jobs. He's doing all right, too. We've got two pubs all set, ready for a raid. We'll do half-a-dozen if they don't spot him."

Fairbrother was silent, thinking of the police custom of occasionally taking a recruit, fresh from his course at a training school, and putting him out on plainclothes work. This work was usually something connected with illegal drinking or betting. Well, here was a policeman who had never walked the streets in uniform, a stranger in the town, an undercover man already established in the district where the murder had been committed. A novice, but a trained novice. He would at least be trustworthy, and he would do as he was told. He *might* be an extremely valuable man.

"How would it be if you held your hand?" the C.I.D. man suggested. "Your man might be more useful to me."

"Of course. That's why I mentioned him. I mean to say, what's the use of wasting him on betting jobs when he might help us to clear a murder? He'll be ringing in tonight. I'll have a talk with him."

"Where is he working, or pretending to work?"

"He's working all right. Champion Foundries."

Fairbrother caught his breath. "What's his name?" he demanded.

"Knight," said Smithson. "William Knight."

chapter

two

Bill Knight was a disappointed man when he received his first instructions after reporting for duty as a college-trained policeman. He was asked to establish himself in what was apparently a festering slum, and ordered not to set foot in Police Headquarters again until a most distasteful mission was accomplished. He told himself that he had joined the force and endured the training for the purpose of being a policeman, not a sneaking spy. He hoped some day to be a detective, but not that sort of detective. The idea of hobnobbing with innkeepers and their customers in order to betray them to his superiors was repugnant to him. It wasn't as if they had asked him to work on a crime. His outlook was still that of a civilian rather than a policeman—he was not yet "police minded"—and he was like the majority of the population in regarding ready-money betting as no more of a crime than legal betting on credit. He thought it was better that a man should gamble with what he had rather than with what he did not have; with this week's wages rather than with next week's. He said as much to Inspector Smithson, who seemed to be a reasonable man.

"Policemen don't make the law, and they don't question it," said Smithson. "They only administer it. There's too much betting in pubs around Champion Road."

Bill was about to reply that the law was an ass, but that a policeman need not be. He was also considering putting in his resignation and going back to his old job in Sheffield. Smithson could tell almost exactly what was in his mind, and he knew exactly what to say to a recruit of this caliber. It had been said before, many times.

"You said you could do it," was his reminder.

Bill looked at him. "I never said I could do *that*."

"Of course you did. It's a lawful order, for you to obey. You took an oath."

Bill stood in thought. His expression was bitter. "How long will it go on?" he asked.

"A month or five weeks, happen. You'll have to watch your step. I'm sending you into a very rough part of town. I've talked to your physical training instructor at the school. He says you can do your stuff, all right. Otherwise I wouldn't risk putting you in that district. You're a picked man, let me tell you."

So Bill accepted his orders. He was told to get a job and live on his earnings. His police pay would be saved for him, so that there would be no income-tax complications; so that the Pay-as-you-earn clerk at his place of work would not notice anything odd about his code number. He carefully cleared his baggage of everything which might indicate a connection with the police, and he left it at a public convenience in City Square. From there he went to the Employment Exchange, and talked to a clerk at the counter. In Sheffield he had been something better than an unskilled laborer, but "laborer" was to be his description for the next few weeks.

"What sort of laborer?" the clerk asked guardedly.

"In a forge," said Bill. "Or in a foundry if you have no forges here."

The clerk was delighted to meet someone different from the professional light-job seekers who were the bane of his life. "A foundry," he murmured, turning busily to his files. "I think I can fix you up."

Presently he read out the names of half-a-dozen firms who wanted men. One of them caught Bill's attention.

"Champion Foundries, did you say?" he asked. "Is that anywhere near Champion Road?"

19

"It isn't in Champion Road," said the clerk reassuringly. "It's in Timberhall Lane."

"And how far is that from Champion Road?"

"Not far," was the reluctant answer. "Three or four hundred yards."

Bill pretended to consider. "All right, I'll try that one," he said.

"Right," said the clerk. He reached for a green card. "Ask for Mr. Oates. I'll give him a tinkle and tell him you're on your way."

At the foundry, Mr. Oates looked at Bill and seemed pleased. The mention of Sheffield, and the one great steelworks which had employed Bill, pleased him even more. He asked a few questions about this and that, and was satisfied. The promise of ability was the only reference he required. Bill had got himself a job. He could start in the morning.

Bill wandered away in search of lodgings. He had decided that if he must go through with this despicable spying assignment, the only thing to do was actually to live in or near Champion Road. He strolled along notorious Hamburg Street, and almost changed his mind about that, but soon he found himself in a wide thoroughfare which had a cleaner air. This effect was an illusion achieved quite simply by the many open spaces. Houses stood back, behind plots of land which had once been lawns. The lawns of sixty or seventy years ago were now areas of flourishing weeds or sour, hard-trodden earth. There were terraces of large Georgian houses, brick-built in Flemish bond, in all stages of repair or disrepair. Many were in ruins. More were derelict. Some had been turned into small clothing factories, workshops, or warehouses. Some provided so-called furnished rooms. Some had been converted into flats. A few were still brave in the paint and pride of Victorian gentility.

This, Bill perceived, was Champion Road.

He wandered on, looking this way and that along the side streets. On the other side of the road, going toward South Street, were streets of terrace houses which had once been the dwellings of black-coat workers of the humbler sort, but now they were obviously teeming slums. No lodgings there, he decided.

He studied the wayfarers. For a byway in an English provincial city they were curiously diverse. He saw several Negroes, a turbaned Sikh, a Pole with a face like Lenin, a tall Jewish youth with a schoolbag slung from his shoulder, two sturdy, bushy-haired Polish girls, and two men who looked like brothers, with faces as Irish as the hills of Donegal. He passed a Jewish clothier and his assistant at the door of their tiny factory. One was saying something to the other in a Yorkshire accent. And, Bill thought with some surprise, of course they were Yorkshiremen, just as much as he was.

He came to a corner where there were buildings of a different sort. A pub, and some little shops, and among them a double-fronted house in Victorian Gothic, and behind them real ware-houses and factories of a blackened and dilapidated sort, and among these a labyrinth of yards and alleys and narrow cross-streets, stretching away toward Timberhall Lane. He guessed that he had almost completed a circular tour, and that he was now within five or ten minutes' walk of Champion Foundries.

He came level with the Victorian house. It stood back some five feet from its own building line. It was next door to a small tailoring establishment, and between the two buildings was a long court or yard which apparently served them both.

There were three steps up to the front door of the house, and on the top step sat an eighteen-year-old girl. She wore a very ordinary blue-and-white cotton dress, no stockings, and scuffed shoes of blue suede. But she had a splendid strapping physique, and her face was attractive, with a flawless youthful complexion.

The girl smiled at Bill. On an impulse, he stopped and spoke to her. "Excuse me. Is there any place around here where I can get some decent lodgings?"

The girl's smile widened. "Yes," she said. "Here."

He looked at her. Her medium-blond hair was straight and sleek, and it suited her rather long, softly-rounded face. It looked clean and well-combed. Her bare legs were clean, and so were her ankles. She bore his scrutiny with equanimity.

He looked up at the house. The windows were not too grimy for that city and climate. The lower halves of the ground-floor windows had been covered with green paint a long time ago, and there were no curtains. Upstairs, there were old-fashioned lace curtains, and he thought that they were yellowed with age rather than dirt.

21

"It's not as bad as it looks," the girl said, rising from the doorstep. "Come in, I'll show you round."

He followed her, into a hallway which smelled strongly of carbolic. She walked on the bare boards with a straight back and a little swagger which suggested that she had been to the pictures and seen Miss Marilyn Monroe.

"Dining room," she said, with a movement of her left hand. Bill looked through an open doorway and saw more bare boards, with two long, bare tables and a score of plain wooden chairs. It was a large room. The walls were covered with paint which had faded to an indeterminate drab color. The fireplace was a chipped and cracked marble monstrosity, and it was filled with empty cigarette packets and discarded wrapping papers. On the opposite wall was a big, old-fashioned kitchen stove, with a bright fire in its grate. Near the fire, a shabby, middle-aged man sat nodding on a chair. One of the lodgers apparently. He had a marked foreign appearance, with a flat face and mongoloid eyes.

The tables were clean-scrubbed, but the floor was gray-black. Bill looked at it doubtfully.

"It's mopped every day with disinfectant," the girl said.

There was another room across the hallway. The door was closed. "A bedroom," the girl said in explanation. Then she pointed forward. "Along there is the kitchen, where we live."

In the kitchen a woman's voice was raised suddenly and coldly in some sort of reproof. It subsided as abruptly as it had begun.

"That's Ma," the girl said calmly. She led the way up the stairs, which were also bare boards. The handrail was of mahogany supported by fine bronze filigree.

At the head of the stairs there were five doors on a landing. The girl went to the furthest door, and showed him what had been the master bedroom of the house. Now it contained eight single beds. Each bed had a chair beside it, a large chamber pot beneath it, and a large, padlocked wooden box at its foot. There were four washbasins and two mirrors in a corner. There was no other furniture in the room.

Bill surveyed it. The room was tidy and it smelled clean. This was where he ought to be if he wanted to make friends and influence people. No sooner had he thought of that than he rebelled against it. "It's like a doss house," he said bluntly.

22

The girl nodded. "But it isn't," she said. "Ma won't take fellows for less than a week. Payment in advance if she can get it."

"That won't do for me," said Bill. "I want a room of my own."

"All right," the girl said. She turned, and he followed her back along the landing, and up another, narrower flight of stairs. At the top there was another landing with a passage running from it. There were three doors on the landing. She opened one of the doors and showed Bill a small bedroom.

"How about this?" she asked.

The room was shabby. The iron bedstead, the chair, the yellow chest of drawers, with mirror, were all shabby. The window was quite large, but the curtains were frayed. The piece of coconut matting beside the bed was worn thin. The doors of the built-in wardrobe cupboard had not been varnished for thirty years. Bill frowned at it all, but he could not truthfully say that he thought the place was dirty. There was the familiar carbolic smell, and there were no signs of vermin. The bedsheets seemed to be clean. He tried the bed with his hand. It was hard, as he had expected. But he supposed that it was as good as anything he would find in that neighborhood.

"What about baths?" he asked. "Mine's a dirty job."

"We have two baths," the girl said proudly. "One bathroom's on this floor, right next door."

Next door, the washbasin was more brown than white. The water closet was cracked, but it worked. The enamel on the bath had flaked off in places, but there was hot water. A man could have a bath and a shave.

"Not bad," said Bill cautiously. "How many people use this bathroom?"

"Only me and our Rosem'ry," the girl replied. She smiled, and pointed to the room opposite the one which would be Bill's. "That's where we sleep."

Bill looked along the passage, which appeared to have a turning. "What's round the corner?" he asked. "Another doss-house bedroom?"

"No. There's just a locked door. It leads to an empty workshop."

The girl was patient, though she obviously had very little interest in the matter of unused doors.

"They say this house once belonged to a merchant or something like that," she explained. "His house and his warehouse were in the same building, like. There were connecting doors on every floor, but now the others are blocked up. The other part of the building is let off, when there's a tenant. A printer had it, but he's moved, and now it's empty."

Bill turned to the bedroom again. "How much a week?" he asked.

"You'll have to talk to Ma," she said. She leaned against the doorpost and smiled at him. "Eeh," she said. "You're a big 'un, aren't you? I'll bet you're strong."

"Fairly," he admitted. Then he said politely: "You're no waster yourself."

"I'm strong for a girl, but I'll bet you could pick me up with one hand. I wouldn't have a chance against you."

"In that case," he said, "you'd better not tempt me."

She giggled. Evidently this was the sort of conversation she enjoyed.

"I'll bet you wouldn't take much tempting," she said. "Are you married?"

"No."

"That's what they all say. I'll bet you're married. Have you left your wife?"

"I'm not married."

"Bet you are!"

"Well," he said, "I don't have to prove it to you, do I?"

She was not abashed. Apparently she was used to plain words clearly uttered. But his remark ended the talk. "I'll take you down to see Ma," she said.

They went down to the kitchen, which was large enough to serve also as a living room for the family. There was the same general shabbiness as elsewhere in the house, and the same sort of cleanliness. The only floor covering was a worn hearthrug in front of the fireplace.

There was an ancient rocking chair beside the fire, and in it sat a lanky, round-backed, gray-faced, gray-haired woman who was obviously Ma. When she saw the girl she asked her coldly where she had been. The girl did not seem to notice the remark.

"I brought you a new lodger, Ma," she said.

The woman looked unsmilingly at Bill, though she appeared to have forgotten her annoyance. "Picked him yourself, did you?" she asked the girl.

"No. He asked me if I knew any lodgings."

"So you showed him the top room, next to yours?"

"I showed him one of the big rooms first. He wouldn't have that. He wants privacy."

"Let's hope that's all he does want," the woman retorted. And to Bill: "I got two young girls sleeping up there. Are you married?"'

"No," said Bill. "And I'll tell you what you can do with your room, and your two young girls as well. You can—"

"Keep your hair on. I have to keep this place decent, you know, or else I'll have the bloody police nosing around. I want twenty-five shilling a week for that room, payable in advance."

Bill thought that he had better not seem too prosperous.

"I can't spare it," he said. "I'll give you ten bob in advance."

The woman nodded. "Happen that'll do. You don't seem a bad sort. What's your name?"

He told her. "What about meals?" he asked.

"Look after yourself," she said. "There's a stove in the dining room. We don't do no cooking for lodgers."

He thought about that. The midday meal he would have at the works canteen. Breakfast could be a few sandwiches. Supper could be fish-and-chips, or black pudding and peas. There remained the early evening meal.

"That won't do for me," he said. "I like to have a good tea waiting when I come home from work. And I like to have something packed for my breakfast."

The woman was coolly amused, but the girl said: "I'll make his tea, Ma. He can have it in here. And I can get his breakfast ready the night before."

"Keen, aren't we?" Ma sneered. And to Bill: "All right, that'll cost you another ten bob a week. But that don't include Sunday meals."

"I won't be here on Sundays. I'll go home to Sheffield for the day."

"And the night?"

"No. I'll be back here at night."

"I fancy you must be single, lad. All right, you're fixed up. Here, we'll have a drink on it."

Without rising from her chair, Ma reached to a cupboard, from which she produced a bottle and a half-pint glass. Without bidding, the girl went for another glass. From the shape of the bottle, Bill thought that it contained whiskey, Vat 69.

Ma poured two generous measures. Bill saw the label on the bottle. It was Vat 69, all right.

She handed him his glass. "Cheers," she said. "Our Junie'll bring you some water if you want it. I take mine straight."

Bill decided that if she could, he could. "Cheers," he said.

The kitchen door opened, and a young man entered. He was an ill-dressed young man, of about Bill's own age. Of medium height, he was sturdy and compact in build, and brisk in movement. He was dark, and not ill-favored, with snapping brown eyes. When he saw the whiskey he grinned, and showed his one disfigurement: his teeth were brown and uneven.

"I'm just in time," he said. "I'll have a drop of that, Ma."

"You will hell as like," said Ma, without asperity. "How's it gone on?"

He shrugged, and threw an early evening newspaper on the table. "It'll win next time out," he said.

She assailed him in that sudden way of hers. "You and your rotten tips. You couldn't pick a winner if it trod on you. Next time out! Next time out you'll be tipping summat else."

The newcomer might not have heard her. He was looking at Bill. As he looked, his gaze became peculiarly intent. Bill met the glance levelly. He knew the cause of that intentness. It was an attempt to assess physical prowess. As a man with a noticeable physique, he had seen it often enough on the faces of bullies, bouncers, tearaways and would-be fighting men.

"Who's this?" the young man asked. "He looks like a copper."

Ma looked at Bill with new interest. Very carefully, Bill spat in the fire.

"You've got imagination, kid," he said. "You'll get on, you will. If you live that long."

The effect of his remark upon the two women was not what he would have expected. Ma was grinning, a rather bitter grin. Junie was regarding him with pleasure: her lips were slightly parted.

"That's fighting talk, copper," the young man said.

Bill shook his head rather wearily. "No, kid; it isn't. You're out of your class. But if you keep on calling me 'copper' I might push you over and walk on you."

"You'll have to do it when I'm not looking."

"All right. I'll do it when you're not looking. A nice thought for you: it can happen at any time."

The young man looked at Ma. "Who *is* this wonder of the world?" he wanted to know.

"I'm the new lodger, and my name's Knight," said Bill. "*Mister* Knight to you."

"Where you from?"

"Are you the boss here?"

"Is he hell as the boss," said Ma.

"In that case I've told him all he needs to know. Who is he, anyway?"

"He's my son," said Ma, without pride. "Gunner Byles, they call him."

"Gunner Byles!"

"Yeah! Anything funny about it?" snarled the subject of the conversation.

Bill ignored the interruption, giving his attention to Ma.

"It's his real name," she explained. "His Dad was a bit crackers, you see. He'd been a artilleryman, and he thought nobody else had ever been a soldier only him. When the lad was born he went and registered his name as Gunner. A proper silly ass, he was."

"Well, happen it's as good a name as any other," said Bill. "H'm, I suppose I'd better go and collect my luggage."

"Where is it?" Gunner asked. "Central Station?"

"No. City Square."

"Gimme a florin and I'll fetch it for you."

"Don't let him!" Junie cried. "He'll sell your best suit."

27

Gunner moved quickly. He slapped Junie hard across the face. She staggered back with a cry. Bill was horrified. He hit Gunner under the ear with enough force to send him reeling right across the room. It seemed that he was about to crack his skull on the wall, but fortunately there was a chair in the way. It tripped him and brought him down.

Gunner lay crumpled on the floor. Junie stood with a hand to her face, gazing wide-eyed, not at her brother but at Bill. Mrs. Byles, who had not moved from her chair, also stared at Bill. "Christ," she said in awe. "You've killed him."

"I'm sorry," said Bill. He went over to Gunner, and stooped to raise one of his eyelids. "Got any smelling salts?" he asked.

Both women shook their heads.

"Ah well," said Bill. "He'll wake up in a minute."

"He'll wake up in the morning, happen," said Ma. "If he's still alive. Coo, what a clout!"

But her son was tougher than she thought. He opened his eyes, and then with a grunt of effort he sat up. Bill offered him the remains of his whiskey, though he was watchful in case it should be thrown in his face.

Gunner took the whiskey and drank it, and handed the glass back to Bill. Then he remembered. He felt his jaw tenderly, and glared.

"What did you do that for?" he demanded.

Bill had apologized to Mrs. Byles, but he had no intention of apologizing to Gunner: never, at any time, for anything: not to a man like Gunner.

"Never hit a woman while I'm around," he said firmly.

"She's my sister, not yours."

"It doesn't matter. I can't stand it. It makes me mad."

Gunner rose slowly to his feet. He did not seem to be seriously hurt. "Are you going to let this fellow come in here and run the place?" he complained to his mother.

"It might be a change," she replied. "You been trying to run it long enough. Happen he'll keep you in order."

Bill thought that he had better try to restore harmony.

"Here, kid," he said, taking a half-crown from his pocket and spinning it in the air. "Go get my stuff. Here's the ticket."

"Don't, he'll—" Junie began, moving to put Bill between herself and her brother "—he'll pinch summat."

Gunner snarled at her. "Shut up, you! I'll bring his luggage. I won't touch a thing."

"If you do," said Bill, "I'll wring your neck."

chapter

three

Bill Knight slipped easily into the routine of his simple job at the Champion Foundry. He was a laborer. He was not asked to do anything that was beyond his capacity or understanding. For his part he worked as hard as his mates, but no harder. He did not want to draw attention to himself, either favorably or unfavorably. To be a nonentity was his aim: the man who wasn't there.

He settled down less easily, but as unostentatiously, into the household of Mrs. Byles. Junie was more than faithful to her undertaking. The meals she provided for him were generous in quantity and nourishing in quality, and often his "tea" was something special which she had prepared for him. The girl's mother watched with cynical but not unfriendly eyes. He was the accepted favorite lodger. When he returned from work each day, grimy and just a little tired, even Gunner ceased to suspect—if ever he had suspected—that Bill was a policeman.

After their first encounter, Gunner's attitude to Bill was normal, for him. He was an unfriendly soul except when he was in drink, and there were occasions when he could not refrain from the utterance of malice; but Bill sometimes lent him small sums of money, and Bill could and would give him a thick ear when angered, and usually he took care not to give offense.

The only common interest of the two men was horse racing. Bill had to dabble in that, to further the designs of Inspector

Smithson. And since he had to back horses, he thought that he might as well try to back winners. Gunner lived to gamble. He always thought he had a winner, and sometimes he was right. He was prepared to talk racing with Bill at any time of day, and far into the night if Bill would listen so long.

It was an unnatural existence for Bill. He liked a glass of beer, but not this life where public houses seemed to be the only places to go, and where betting was the chief excitement. Occasionally he went to the pictures simply for a change, irrespective of what film he would see.

He came to be on casual speaking terms with the landlords, barmaids and customers of the Woolpack, the Call to Arms, the Dog and Gun, the Friar Tuck, the Flying Dutchman, the Starving Rascal, the Trumpeter, the Greyhound, the Standard of Liberty, the Ring o' Bells, the Ship Inn, and several other licensed houses. During the midday break at the foundry, when he went alone or with some of his workmates for a drink of satisfying beer, he saw plenty of illegal betting. Sometimes the money and the betting slips were handed over with the landlord's knowledge, sometimes furtively because he forbade the traffic. Bill resolved not to make any reports about the places where betting occurred contrary to the wishes and instructions of the licensee.

One inn of the latter type was the Starving Rascal. Sam Gilmour owned his own place, and he was not tied to any brewery. He did not allow any betting and he served no drinks during non-permitted hours because, he said, he just couldn't afford to lose his license. Bill liked to go to the Starving Rascal because he was strongly attracted to the girl who served behind the bar. She was a lovely girl, he thought. The more he studied her, the more beautiful she seemed to be. He learned that her name was Gay, and that she was Gilmour's daughter.

In such a district it was to be expected that a young girl serving behind her father's bar would maintain a barrier of reserve between herself and the majority of the customers. Though the business of the Starving Rascal was conducted in a respectable way, its customers were far from respectable. Prostitutes frequented the place, and they were permitted to do so because they were known to be off duty: when they "worked" they found their prey in more opulent surroundings. Small-time bookmakers and their hangers-on were also to be seen there, and they were the financial giants among the customers. For the rest, bookies' runners, tatters, layabouts, professional scroungers, sluttish housewives, laboring types—English, Irish, and East European—and neighborhood youths and girls made up the bulk of the company. Some of them were bad characters with bad records. Some of them were bad characters without records. Some of them were not bad characters. Gay Gilmour served them civilly, and gave them the time of day, but offered no opportunity for familiarity. Her father, a laconic man, was also watchful to repel undue advances. The customers understood, and were not resentful. Gay was treated with respect. She sometimes heard an obscene remark, but invariably it was uttered unintentionally, in the heat of altercation. Altercations were frequent, and ejections commonplace. Sam Gilmour and his waiter, Abe Farley, were competent bouncers.

Upon his visits to the Starving Rascal, Bill usually sat on the stool at the rounded end of the bar, so that he could see Gay from head to foot as she went about her work. He liked to watch her, but he did not forget his manners; he did not obviously stare. Nevertheless, the girl became conscious of his interest, as girls usually do. She was accustomed to being looked over by male customers, but this time she took notice. Bill was an exceptionally fine-looking young man.

Sam Gilmour also took notice. The taciturn landlord was interested to the extent, one evening, of engaging Bill in conversation. He began with a brief remark about the weather, then he said: "You seem to have started coming in here middling regular."

"Yes," Bill admitted. "I work at Champion Foundries."

"Skilled man?"

"Not at that sort of work. I'm from Sheffield."

"H'm. What brought you to Airechester?"

"To see how the other half lives," said Bill, giving a civil answer to the pointed question because Sam was Gay's father.

The non-committal reply did not satisfy Sam, but he nodded as if it did.

"I notice you don't drink a lot," he said, glancing at Bill's half-pint of beer. "What makes you come into a place like this?"

"Somewhere to go," Bill replied. Then he said: "The place is all right."

"But the customers aren't, eh? Not your sort. That's what made me ask you, like."

It was Bill's turn to nod. "No need for me to mix with 'em," he said.

"You can't help it, lad."

Bill shrugged.

"Where you lodging?" was the next question.

"Ma Byles's place."

Sam did not try to hide his surprise. "What, with all the Paddies and the Poles?"

"No. I don't see much of them. I have my own room."

"M-mmm. They tell me it's fairly clean."

"It's rough, but there's no livestock. It'll do till I get something better."

"How's Clara going on? I haven't seen her in a dog's age."

"Clara?"

"Mrs. Byles."

"Oh, she's all right. She sits by the fire and knocks the whiskey back."

"You wouldn't think, would you, that she's less than fifty years old?"

"Go on! More like sixty!"

"No. That's whiskey and the trouble she's seen. She'll be forty-seven or eight, will Clara. And her oldest daughter will be nearly thirty. She started young."

"Is it right, she has a couple of daughters working day and night?"

"Yes. Alice and Amy, the two oldest. They each have their own little establishment. They reckon to work at the See-Saw biscuit place, but I reckon they'll make more in their spare time. I won't be a bit surprised if the other lasses go the same way."

When Sam uttered the last remark, he looked straight at Bill. The young man met his glance squarely, and grinned. "Not guilty, me lord," he said. "I don't mix there, either."

"You're wise," said Sam. "I wouldn't stay there so long, if I were you."

"You seem to know a lot about the Byles family."

"I'm related, in a way. Do you see much of Gunner?"

"As little as possible."

"He's no good, that lad. I don't like to see him come in here, but I never had occasion to bar him."

"Speak of the devil," said Bill.

Gunner Byles had entered the room. He saw Bill, and came grinning up to him. Sam turned away to serve a customer.

Gunner looked at Bill's half-pint glass. "Mine's a pint," he said, and Bill perceived that he was tipsy.

"You're drunk," he said.

"What of it? I can do another pint."

Bill looked at his watch. It was fifteen minutes from closing time. He would not have to endure Gunner's company for long. He ordered a pint of beer for him.

Gay served the beer. Gunner leered at her, and said: "Hello, Tulip." Gay ignored him, and he grinned at her uncompromising back. Then he picked up the beer and said "Cheers," and drank half of it in a long swig.

Bill wanted to shake him until he was sick. He restrained the impulse, and drank the remainder of his half-pint. "I'm going round to the Woolpack for the last one," he said, and rose from his stool.

Gunner drank off his own beer before he replied, then he said: "I'll come with you. I don't care much for the ale here."

Bill called a good night to Sam and his daughter, and walked out. Gunner followed him, without saying good night to anybody. They walked down Timberhall Lane together, and took the side street which led to the Woolpack. Bill was silent while Gunner gleefully told him about a ready-money bet which he had failed to place for a crony. The horse had not won. Gunner had told his friend that he had placed the bet.

They each had a pint of beer at the Woolpack. Gunner paid, and swallowed his pint as fast as he could so that Bill could buy him another just on closing time. Bill refused.

"I don't know where you put it," he said. "Two pints in ten minutes."

Gunner grinned, belched, and ordered the beer himself. "Oy," he said. "I'm as tight as a drum."

They quitted the Woolpack at ten minutes past ten.

"Let's go into town and see if we can pick up a bit of spare," Gunner suggested.

"Not me," said Bill. "I'm going home to bed. I've got to work in the morning."

"Happen you don't need any spare. Have you had our Junie in bed yet?

"Shut up. You make me sick."

"You ought to meet our Amy. She's a proper bit of crumpet. You'd be all right with her. I'll fix it up for you."

"Oh," said Bill wearily. "Give over, will you?"

They were making their way through alleys and narrow streets in the direction of Champion Road. On a corner, in the shadowed doorway of an empty shop, a dark figure stood. Bill peered into the shadow, and discerned a policeman.

"It's only a cop," said Gunner. "Peeping round corners, as usual."

"That'll do from you," said the policeman.

Gunner spat. "That to you," he said.

"You'd better go home," said the P.C., "before you're sorry you came out."

Gunner laughed. "You going to make me sorry?"

"It's just possible," said the P.C. quietly. He stepped out of the doorway. He was tall, a good six feet, but not heavily built. A fit man, perhaps, but not an extraordinarily strong one.

"Go on home, like I tell you," he said.

Gunner's reply was to the effect that he would go home when he liked. It was embroidered by some very filthy language.

"I won't tell you again," said the policeman.

Gunner, like all his kind, mistook forbearance for irresolution. He raised his voice, and embroidered his embroidery.

"Obscene and insulting language," said the policeman, moving forward. "You're under arrest."

Gunner turned to run, but the P.C. caught him, swung him round, and applied a wrist lock. They began to move away, walking close together with arms linked like two people who were very fond of each other. Gunner had to go. His wrist was bent like a hairpin, and the slightest extra pressure was painful. Escape unaided was out of the question. A sudden move to get away would have resulted in a bad sprain or a fracture.

"Let me go, you bastard!" he yelled.

"Go on, keep talking," said the P.C. ominously, and Gunner realized that all such insults would add up to so many cuffs on the head when they reached the jail.

"Help! Help! Rescue!" he bawled, turning his head and trying to look back at Bill.

Bill was in a quandary. He did not want Gunner to be locked up, though Gunner had certainly asked for it. Afterward Gunner would blame anybody but himself, therefore he would blame Bill for failing to help him. That might mean a return to his early suspicions. On the other hand, if Bill did rescue him, henceforth he would be safe from suspicion.

Bill was extremely reluctant to attack the policeman. His natural dislike of an unfair fight, his upbringing, and a certain *esprit de corps* were all against such an action. And he knew that the policeman, having made the arrest, would hold on to his prisoner until his strength was done. It was futile for Bill to plead with the man. Nevertheless, he pleaded.

"Let him go," he begged, overtaking and facing the pair. "He's drunk. He doesn't know what he's talking about."

The P.C. was wary. His right hand was free to deal with interference, and it hung suggestively near to the long pocket where he kept his baton. But Bill's air of entreaty disarmed him.

"I can't let him go," he said. "Not now."

"Let me take him home," Bill persisted. "I'll see he makes no more trouble."

"Sorry," said the policeman. "It can't be done."

Bill suddenly perceived that circumstances put him unalterably at cross purposes with his fellow officer. And it seemed to him that as an undercover man it was his duty to protect and consolidate his assumed identity. Crouching, he moved in quickly and knocked the defensive right arm aside, and struck hard at the body.

Air was driven out of the constable's lungs with a noise like the death rattle. He doubled up and fell. Gunner, released, was excited and triumphant. "Kick his bloody face in," he urged hoarsely, and made to do so. His swinging foot passed over the prone policeman's head as Bill caught him by the collar and pulled him off-balance.

"Come away, you bloodthirsty fool," said Bill, and he dragged Gunner off toward home. He was about to apply the same wrist lock which the P.C. had used when he remembered, just in time, that he was not supposed to know it. He bullied Gunner along by strength alone, and Gunner had to go.

Gunner soon ceased to struggle. "We showed him," he chortled as they walked toward home. "We put him in his place. By God, we put one over on the cops."

"They'll put one over on us if they catch us," Bill said soberly.

"They will that," said Gunner, still gleeful. "They'll get us in a cell and knock the stuffing out of us."

"Is that what they do?"

"Yeh, boy. Anybody who bashes a bobby, they bash him when they get him."

"Well, the whistles'll be blowing as soon as yond fellow gets his wind. Any of the bobbies round here know you?"

"Some of 'em do."

"Well, do you want to be picked up and get walloped?"

It was a sobering thought. Gunner began to hurry. "They'll happen come round to our place making inquiries," he said. "We've got some rough lads there. The best thing for us to do is to get indoors and straight to bed. Come on, let's run."

"No. Walk."

"Right, we'll walk as if nothing were. You're all right, Bill, you are. You bashed that bogey a treat. You're fit to travel."

"Don't talk so loud," said Bill.

The following evening, which was Thursday, Gunner wanted to go out with Bill. He was almost affectionate, referring to his new friend, fondly, as "Basher." Bill did not want the nickname, and he did not want the friendship of Gunner. Besides, at eight-thirty he had to telephone Inspector Smithson and report progress.

"Cut that out," he said. "Don't call me any such name."

"Okay, Bill, if that's the way you feel. Where shall we go?"

"Nowhere, together. That bobby will still be looking for two men. It's no use us asking for trouble. If I go out, I go out alone, and I keep away from the Woolpack."

"Oh, we'll be safe enough tonight. It'll be dark by nine o'clock."

"We won't be safe till that copper's forgotten what we look like, and he won't do that in a hurry. I'm going out on my own, I tell you."

"I think I'll go to the pictures," said Gunner.

"Now you're talking sense," said Bill with a measure of approval. "You'll be safe at the pictures."

He went to a cinema himself, but came out at half-past eight and made his call to Smithson. The inspector was pleased with what he had to report, and remarked that the time seemed ripe to take action against the landlord and habitués of the Dog and Gun.

"You might have to give evidence as to what you've seen," he said. "But we'll proceed by summons and the case won't come up until you've finished your plainclothes job. Have you made a few notes, like I told you?"

"Yes, I've made notes," said Bill.

"Good. We'll do several of those pubs before we put you into uniform. We'll quiet 'em for a bit."

"Yes, sir," said Bill, with no enthusiasm at all.

"Oh, I know you don't like it, but you're doing a good job. Stick to it, it won't go on much longer. And be careful. We don't want to find your body in one of those empty buildings."

"I'll be careful."

The inspector rang off with a final word of encouragement. Bill decided to go to the Starving Rascal, hoping fervently that Gunner would not be there.

Gunner was not there. Relieved, Bill took his usual seat at the curved end of the bar. Sam Gilmour nodded and spoke cordially. The daughter, Gay, smiled at him in more friendly fashion than hitherto. It appeared that his talk with Sam the night before had somehow broken the ice.

Bill stayed until closing time, drinking moderately as he usually did. The bar was not busy and, rather timidly at first, he was able to engage Gay in conversation. The talk did not attain a very high level. They asked and answered polite questions about each other: they discussed the film Bill had seen that evening, and other films; they mentioned holidays; they talked about the cricket season which had just ended, and the football season which had just begun.

Eventually Bill asked Gay if she would have a drink with him. She said that she did not drink, but would have a tonic-with-lemon, thank you.

"I might have a drink tomorrow night," she said. "Just one."

"Why tomorrow night?"

"It's the Licensed Victualers' dance. I'm going, after ten o'clock. There'll be a bar till midnight."

"A bit early in the season, isn't it? September."

She said that it was the first dance of the season. Bill wanted to know more about it. She was pleased to tell him. The tickets were twelve shillings and sixpence each. The dance went on until one o'clock. Evening dress was optional. There would be plenty of men in ordinary lounge suits.

"Is your young man taking you?" he asked.

"I haven't got a young man," she replied with just a hint of tartness in her voice. "I'm going in a taxi."

Bill remembered that he had to work on Saturday morning. Overtime. Nevertheless, he decided that he would go to the dance if he could get a ticket.

chapter
four

It was apparent that the murderer of Sam Gilmour had emerged from the cellar to commit the crime, and Belcher and Fairbrother badly wanted to know how he had got down there unseen and unheard. The two windows of the cellar had quite obviously not been opened for a long time, and they were protected at ground level by gratings whose fastenings were immovable in rust. The coal grating was secured on the inside by a chain and padlock, and so was the double-leaf trapdoor which could be opened to allow barrels of beer to be delivered. The padlocks showed no signs of tampering, and the keys for both of them were among those which had been in Gilmour's pocket.

So it was clear that the murderer had gone into the cellar from the bar itself, at some time during the day or evening. Questioning of Gay Gilmour brought the information that no beer had been delivered to the inn on the day of the murder. She also told the police that the two doors of the inn had remained locked until the lunchtime opening at 11:30 A.M., and that they had been locked again soon after the three o'clock closing hour. They had not been opened again until 5:30 P.M., when the evening session began. Therefore in all probability the murderer had entered the premises as a customer, and somehow he had managed to get into the cellar without being seen, while the landlord or his daughter was actually in or near the bar.

"He was sharp, if he did that," said Abe Farley to Inspector Fairbrother. "Sam wasn't exactly daft, you know."

Fairbrother had been questioning the part-time waiter about people who had been in the Starving Rascal on the previous evening. Abe himself was not above suspicion, though the idea that he might be suspected had clearly not entered his head. Apart from the murderer, he was the last person to have seen Sam alive. According to his statement he had quitted the inn at twenty minutes to eleven, calling good night to Sam and latching the door as he went out. Gay had already gone to the dance and, seemingly, the last customer had gone home. Abe had left Sam apparently alone, standing at the till and beginning a count of the day's takings.

Assuming—until there was some evidence to the contrary—that Abe was telling the truth, it seemed as if the murder had taken place before ten minutes to eleven, because "cashing up" was not a long operation, and Sam had still been standing near the open till when he was struck down. The murderer had not wasted any time. Fairbrother guessed that the man had listened behind the cellar door until he heard the waiter leave. Then he had quietly opened the door and struck hard with the hammer.

At the same time he had grasped Sam by the shoulder or the collar of his house jacket, and, as he fell, had pulled him so that he tumbled down the cellar steps. He had chased the body down the cellar steps, and found that he had no need to strike another blow. He had dropped the hammer and started to search his victim's pockets. He had taken money and keys. He had returned to the bar and closed the cellar door. He had pocketed all the money from the till, which was probably still neatly piled on the bar. Then—whether he knew that Gay was out, or whether he guessed that she was out because there was no light on the stairs —he went upstairs and looted the study. That would take him ten minutes or so. After that he went out, latching the door as Abe Farley had done. Quite probably, if he lived in the neighborhood, he was safely home by a quarter past eleven.

Fairbrother had also discovered that Sam had been a little hard of hearing, though he had been clever enough to conceal his defect in ordinary conversation. That, in all likelihood, was the reason why he had not heard the cellar door opening so close behind him. Had the murderer been aware of his deafness? Had that given him the confidence to open the door and strike?

"But it still beats me how he got into the cellar without being seen," said Fairbrother. "He'd have to be standing at this end of the counter, near the bar flap. If the bar flap was down—and it would be with customers at that end of the bar—he'd have to duck under it and then open the cellar door. Somebody should have seen him."

"You'd think so," Abe agreed.

"There could have been a diversion. Planned or accidental."

Abe stared woodenly. "What yer mean, diversion?"

"Some sort of a noise or disturbance to distract everybody's attention, so that the murderer could slip into the cellar when everybody was looking the other way."

"Well," said Abe. "There was a bit of a barney started at about ten past ten, but it didn't come to anything. It was an Irishman and one o' them Poles. They was shaping for a scrap, or at least the Paddy was. He picked a bottle up. Sam and me went and ushered 'em off the premises, like."

"You mean Sam lifted the bar flap and came from behind the bar?"

"That's right."

"That's it, then. That's when our man nipped into the cellar. Ten past ten. He couldn't have done it earlier because the daughter was in the bar until ten. Who were the two men involved in the disturbance?"

"The Irish lad is called Tom Casey. The Pole goes by the name of Tim, or Timmy. I don't know his proper name."

"Do you know their addresses, by any chance?"

"They're both at Mrs. Byles's, I think."

"Oho! She gets the talent, does Mrs. Byles. I'll be looking in at Hudson House. Can you remember who was at that end of the bar when Sam came out?"

Abe set his lips and frowned in painful cogitation, and finally confessed that he could not remember. Fairbrother read the list of customers out to him, slowly, in the hope that recollection would come.

"It was Friday," said the waiter. "I was too busy to take a lot of notice of folk. But I can't seem to think as there was anybody at that end of the bar just after closing time."

"What about this client, Gunner Byles?" asked Fairbrother, looking at his list.

Abe shook his head. "I can't be sure, but I think he'd gone when the bother started."

Fairbrother looked at the further end of the bar, where the flap was up. It was two strides from the opening in the bar to the cellar door. Beyond the end of the bar there was a passage which led to the men's room and the "back" door, which was actually at the side of the building.

"Which way would he go out?" he asked. "The back way?"

"He could go any way, back or front, whichever was handiest."

"I see," said Fairbrother, temporarily dismissing Gunner Byles from his thoughts. He also told Abe that he had finished with him for the time being. There was the matter of the stolen coins. It was time that the police knew their descriptions, and their value.

The photographers and the fingerprint men had ceased their flashing and puffing in the study, the relief constable was on guard there, and the place was ready for Fairbrother to take an inventory. He consulted Gay.

"Oh yes, Sam had everything listed," she said. "His catalogue, he called it. I'll show you."

The catalogue was a big loose-leaf book, handsomely backed in black leather. The collection was listed in beautifully clear copperplate writing. Fairbrother sought the descriptions of the coins which had been in the drawers emptied by the murderer. As he had expected, only gold coins had been taken.

When he had made it, the list of stolen coins was like a tally of the treasure of all time. Sam Gilmour had not specialized in the coinage of one period or one country. He had collected all the worth-while coins which came his way, probably buying many of them for far less than their collector's value. The list of gold coins ranged from the time of Socrates to the time of Abraham Lincoln, and from Mongolia to Morocco. There were louis d'or, gold mohurs, moidores, ducats, guineas, sovereigns, pistoles, eagles and double-eagles, ryals, angels and bezants. There was a gold stater of ancient Thrace, a solidus of Caesar Augustus, and a stater of ancient Britain of the time of King Cunobelin, whom Fairbrother took to be none other than Shakespeare's Cymbeline. It had been no exaggeration to say that Sam Gilmour's collection was worth thousands of pounds.

In all, seventy-four coins had been stolen. The collector's value of the coins was not given in the catalogue, but the inspector guessed that their intrinsic gold value would be something like three hundred pounds.

"I shall have to get an expert to value this lot," he told Gay. "It'll be a sin and a shame if the thief melts it down before we can lay hands on him."

"Oh!" said Gay. "Those lovely gold coins!"

"Too bad, isn't it?" Fairbrother agreed. "But he'll know we're on the lookout for them, you see."

He was watching her closely. That was his way. He did not regard her as a suspect, but until he had got his man he would suspect everybody to some extent. Her reaction to his hint that the police would be alert for the reappearance of the coins was normal and natural. He discerned no secret caution or nervousness behind her eyes. He thought once again that she was extremely good-looking in a taut, high-strung way.

Their talk was interrupted by the sounds of a mild dispute

outside the study. Fairbrother went to the door. The P.C. outside was gently restraining an old man who wished to pass him.

"No, sir," he was saying. "You can't go in there till I've asked the inspector."

"I want to see my daughter," the old man was saying, and even in protest his voice was calm.

"All right, Constable," Fairbrother said, and then Gay pushed past him. With tears in her eyes she embraced the old man. "Oh, Daddy!" she cried. "You're the only Daddy I've got now!" Her genuine emotion deprived the words of banality.

"I've just heard about it, my dear," the old man said. "I came straight away. Are you all right?"

She told him that she was, and that he must not worry, and that it was awful, and that the police had charge of everything.

Fairbrother studied him. The common and respectful English term "old gentleman" fitted him exactly. He was small, spare, and erect. His sober clothes were far from new, but they were neat and clean. His thin, bold-featured face was calm and kind, and lined by life's unfairness and trouble. He wore no spectacles, but he carried the white walking stick of the blind and purblind. His glance was dull and blank. That deadness of the eyes reminded Fairbrother of a sculptured Roman head.

"The old boy is just like Julius Caesar," he thought.

So this was John Harper, one-time prosperous lawyer, the putative father of Gay Gilmour.

"I shall come and stay here until other arrangements are made," Harper was telling the girl. "The place will have to be kept open in order to preserve the license. And you will have to have some help. You can't tap barrels and clean pumps. From whom do you buy most of your beer?"

She mentioned the name of a famous Yorkshire brewery.

"Very well," said Harper. "I shall get in touch with Sam's solicitor and suggest that he ask the brewers to send a competent man to act as cellarman for a few days. His expenses and wages will have to come out of the estate."

As he listened, Fairbrother reflected that although the old man was afflicted by feebleness of vision, there was nothing feeble about his mental equipment. His practical suggestions were clearing away the girl's worries and difficulties, and turning her thoughts from the recent tragedy to the near workaday future. He was doing her good. She could be safely left in his hands.

The inspector coughed to draw attention to himself. Gay introduced him. There was a brief talk about the necessary business of keeping the Starving Rascal open to the public, then he excused himself. He did not wish to question John Harper. Even he did not suspect an old man who could not see a barn door on a bright day.

"I must go now," he said. "I'll lock the study and take the keys. Do you mind?"

Gay said that she did not mind. It would have been all the same if she had minded. Fairbrother sent the uniformed constable on his beat, and departed himself. He wanted to interview an Irishman and a Pole. Under the same roof there was also Gunner Byles, and there was William Knight, policeman on confidential plainclothes duty.

Fairbrother took Adkin with him, and a search warrant. The time, now, was ten minutes past five. It was Saturday. Drunk or sober, most of Mrs. Byles's lodgers would be in their dining room. To fortify themselves against the ordeal of spending their wages they would be partaking of fish-and-chips, or large steaks, or bread and cold bacon, or bread and cheese, or bread and the queer sausages which the Poles liked. Now was the time to find them at home. In an hour they would be dispersed.

The two policemen walked into Hudson House, and into the big dining room. They stood just inside the doorway, looking round, and the murmur of talk immediately died. There were about a dozen men in there, some of them quite young, and they were variously engaged in preparing or eating the early-evening meal. Though it was Saturday, a number of them still wore overalls or rough corduroys. They were men who worked by the strength of their arms and hands. Some were big and brawny, and the smallest of them was sturdy.

"Look at that fellow, cuttin' bread," said Adkin, nodding toward a young Irishman. "You'd think he was cuttin' a tree down."

Fairbrother nodded, though he had not listened. He was studying movements and expressions, looking for signs of uneasiness, though he was aware that the uneasiness might have no connection with the murder he was investigating.

"Which of you is Tom Casey?" he demanded at last. The bread cutter's ginger head came up. His very blue eyes stared levelly at the inspector. "I'm Casey," he said.

"Will you step out into the passage? I'd like a word with you."

Casey put down his knife. "Oh, sure," he said. And when they were in the hallway: "You'll be asking me if I was in the Rascal last night. It's a bad do. I'm sorry for Sam. And for the poor young lady."

"You were there till what time?"

"Oh, a quarter past ten, it would be. Then I came home. I start work early, you see. Ah, I'm forgetting. I had some supper in a fish shop, before I come in here."

"What time did you go into the pub?"

"Nine o'clock, or about that time."

"Who were you with?"

"I was by meself. But I got talking to an auld woman who was in there. Then one or two of the boys from here came in, and sat by me."

"Who were they?"

"There was Jim Sloan and Peter Farrell, then there was a couple of Poles, Timothy and Johnnie. I don't know what other names they have. We don't talk to them so much: they're hard to make sense of. But they're not bad boys."

"Which one did you have trouble with?"

Casey showed his surprise. "Trouble? There was no trouble at all."

"I'm told that on one occasion you were on your feet, with a bottle in your hand."

The Irishman remembered, and laughed. "Oh, that. It was an impulse of the moment. Timothy drunk my beer. I coulda throttled him. It was too late to get any more. After time, you see. But it was all a mistake. He said he was sorry. Sure I wouldn't have hurt the little man, anyway."

"And then you were asked to leave the premises?"

"Well, Sam came and said: 'Do your fighting outside, Tom.' And the big waiter, Farley, looked as he was ready to bounce somebody. He's a bit too ready. Somebody might bounce him before he's much older."

"So you went out immediately?"

"We went because we was ready," said Casey, his voice hardening a little.

Fairbrother nodded. Casey seemed to be an honest sort. Besides, he had not made the first move in the trouble which was no trouble at all. The man called Timothy had created the diversion, when he drank Casey's beer. If he had drunk the beer on purpose, he would know that the Irishman would protest violently enough to draw attention to himself.

"Was Timothy's friend sitting with him at the time he drank your beer?" the inspector wanted to know.

"Yes, he was there."

"Did he go out with him?"

"As far as I can recollect, he did."

"Did your friends stay with you?"

"Yes, all the time."

"Did you see Gunner Byles in there?"

"I believe I did. He was at the bar."

"Whereabouts at the bar?"

"Well now, where was he? About the middle, happen. I couldn't be sure. Me recollection is hazy."

"Was he still there when you left?"

"I couldn't tell you that for the life in me. I don't have much truck with the boy."

"All right, thanks," said Fairbrother. "Is Timothy in there?"

"Yes, he's there."

"Very well, I won't keep you any longer. You can go and get your tea."

But when Casey returned to the dining room, Fairbrother followed him. Again his appearance was the cause of silence.

"Timothy," he said clearly.

A short, swart, slant-eyed man looked up sharply. To the policeman he was obviously a Pole, since to him as to the rest of Airechester all Poles, Esthonians, White Russians, Czechs, Hungarians, Ukrainians and East Europeans generally were Poles.

He beckoned, and the man followed him out into the hallway. "What's your real name, Timothy?" he asked.

The slant eyes were inscrutable, probably masking considerable alarm. "Name Timoshei Zaidulla."

"Where are you from?"

"From Taganrog."

"Where's that?"

"On water of Taganrog, on water of Azov."

"The Sea of Azov! That's a long way from here. You're a Russian, then?"

Timoshei shook his head. "I Tatar," he said, not without pride.

"A Tartar! Well, well! You were with Tom Casey last night, in the Starving Rascal."

The Tartar inclined his head affirmatively.

"Who told you to drink his beer?"

The dark face was suddenly indignant. "He tell pliss on me? I steal beer?" Then his tone changed. "Plissman, it—it acciden'. I not steal. I see beer mine. It mistake."

Adkin chuckled. "He thinks we're goin' to charge him with misappropriatin' half a pint of mild-and-bitter," he said.

Fairbrother was smiling too, but he said: "I wonder."

To the Tartar he said: "I don't care whose beer you drank. I only want to know why you drank it. Did somebody dare you to do it?"

"Dare? What dare?"

"Did somebody say: 'I bet you don't drink Tom's beer'?"

"No, no. It mistake. I sorry."

"You'll have a job to get anythin' else out of him," Adkin murmured.

"I'm afraid so," Fairbrother admitted.

He asked Timoshei if he remembered noticing any person near the end of the bar. He asked him about Gunner Byles. He asked about the other Hudson House residents who had been present. He interviewed those men, with negative results. He allowed them to resume their normal activities.

"Well," he said to Adkin. "It looks as if we'll never know whether or not that little disturbance was a put-up job. We'll just have to bear it in mind."

"Are you goin' to search?"

"Oh, certainly. Everywhere. You stay here till I get some personnel. I won't be a minute. Don't let any of these fellows out without searching them."

There was a public telephone box on the corner. Fairbrother spoke to Superintendent Belcher and made his request for more men, and returned to Hudson House.

"There's nobody stirrin' yet," said Adkin. "Ma Byles has been screechin' in the kitchen."

They waited, making up their diaries. Then Detective Sergeant Nolan arrived with five men and a policewoman. Three of the men were in uniform; some indication of the pressure of work on the C.I.D. at that moment.

Fairbrother gave his instructions. There was to be a man at each outer door. The other men were to be a search team under Nolan's efficient guidance. The policewoman was to remain where she was at the foot of the stairs, to observe and control movement within the house, and to be on hand in case she was required to search a female.

"If you want me," he said to Nolan, "I'll be in the kitchen with Adkin. I'm going to interrogate the old hen and her brood."

The party broke up. Fairbrother led the way into the kitchen, without knocking. He usually left his manners at home when he visited places where they would be taken as a sign of weakness.

Mrs. Byles was in her chair. She was about to consume a tot of her favorite beverage. Her eyes widened over the rim of the glass. She lowered the glass and said: "Who the hell invited you in here?"

"Nobody," said Fairbrother. He advanced into the room and slapped the edge of the table with his folded warrant.

"Oh," said Mrs. Byles. "What's up now?"

"General inquiries," the policeman replied. He looked around. Gunner Byles, with an evening paper in his hands, was sitting opposite his mother at the fireplace. Bill Knight was at the other side of the table, eating baked beans. Junie stood beside him, with her hand on the back of his chair. The other daughter, Rosemary, was sitting on an old sofa under the window.

Fairbrother neither nodded nor spoke to Bill, but not to ignore him he gave him an unfriendly glance. Then, with fierce geniality, he turned to Gunner. "Look who's at home," he said. "Just the man I want to see."

Gunner was not roused by the detective's manner. He looked up in a surly way, then returned his glance to his paper. Fairbrother thought that he had a worn, sick look, like a man who has not slept well. Too much liquor at lunchtime, probably, he conjectured. It could not possibly be Gunner's conscience which was bothering him. He had never shown the slightest indication of having a conscience.

"Ah, we're 'aughty like," said the inspector. "Were you in the Starving Rascal last night?"

"No," said Gunner, without raising his glance from the paper.

"Where were you?"

"Minding my own business."

"H'm. We are haughty. Where were you?"

"Happen you know already where I was."

"I do. You were in the Rascal."

"Well, why did you ask me, when you knew?"

"To see what you'd say. Why did you lie about it?"

"To see what you'd say. I can lie if I want. I'm not under oath."

"Oh, legal expert as well! Better be careful, Gunner, or you'll be arousing my suspicion."

"So what?"

"Reasonable suspicion. I can take you in and cool you off."

Gunner thought about that. Fairbrother gave him time to do so, then he asked: "What time did you go into the Rascal last night?"

"Nine o'clock, happen."

"Who did you talk to in there?"

"Nobody. I was on me own."

"Were you sitting down?"

"No. I were standing at the bar."

"Whereabouts?"

"Oh, about the middle."

"Who was near you?"

"I don't remember."

"Who was near you?"

Gunner sighed and raised his eyes to the ceiling in mock supplication, but the question was repeated. He named two people, and described others.

"All right. What time did you leave the place?"

"Just after ten. Five past."

"Are you sure?"

"Sure I'm sure. I was fed up of having nobody to talk to. I drunk my beer and cleared off just after they called time."

"If you were so fed up, why did you stay there until after closing time? Why didn't you go somewhere else for a drink?"

Gunner did not immediately answer, then he said: "I kept thinking Bill might come in."

"Bill who?"

"Bill Knight. Him over there."

"I see. Did you come straight home from the Rascal?"

Gunner's glance slid to his mother. She was watching him with cool interest. At last he said: "I didn't come straight home. I went for a stroll around Stag Lane and York Street."

"Dirty little pig," said his mother.

"Did you pick up a girl?" Fairbrother asked.

"No, I didn't. I talked to one or two. They wanted money."

"*Dirty* little pig," said Mrs. Byles.

"Didn't you have any money?" Fairbrother wanted to know.

"I'd none to spare for that lark."

"Did you speak to any girls you knew?"

"No. They were all strangers."

"M-mmm. What time did you get home?"

"Just about eleven."

"He's a liar," said Mrs. Byles. "He came in at half-past eleven and went straight up to bed."

"Shut up, you old bitch!" Gunner shouted.

"I won't shut up," she retorted. "Don't expect me to back you in your lies. I'm keeping right in the clear. I got a very good reason for keeping in the clear."

"Why did you lie about the time you came home?" Fairbrother demanded of Gunner.

"I didn't lie. I weren't noticing the time."

"I'm thinking you'd know the difference between eleven and half-past."

"I weren't bothering about the time, I tell you."

"I'm not satisfied with that," said Fairbrother. Actually, he was very well satisfied. He had uncovered a suspect.

50

"Before you left the Rascal, did you see that bit of a barney between Tom Casey and Timothy the Pole?" he asked.

Gunner's eyes flickered. "I didn't see no barney."

"I think you did. That was when you dodged into the cellar."

Gunner turned pale. "Me? No, Mr. Fairbrother. I never went into the cellar."

"Possibly we shall be able to prove that you did," said the inspector, and as he spoke his glance strayed to Gunner's shoddy, uncleaned shoes. Perhaps there would be coal dust embedded in the shoe soles: small particles of coal which could be identified as coming from the same seam as Sam Gilmour's.

It also occurred to Fairbrother that the interrogation was rather public. It was quite contrary to normal police procedure. But with Mrs. Byles ready to denounce her son when he lied, her presence was an advantage. He wondered why she did that. It was unnatural. But then, in his opinion nobody in his right senses would consider Ma Byles to be either normal or natural. She could be roughly described as inhuman.

"A very interesting situation, Gunner," he commented. "We find that you can't account to our satisfaction for nearly an hour and a half of your time. And at what a time! What clothes were you wearing last night?"

"Same as he has on now," said Mrs. Byles.

"The same shoes?"

"Aye, the same shoes, and just as mucky."

"Was he wearing a raincoat or anything?"

"No, he was just as he is now."

Fairbrother addressed Gunner: "You'd better go and change your clothes. I want your suit and shoes for examination. Your shirt, too."

"You can't make me get changed!"

"No. But I can take you with me, and then we'll see what I can make you do when I get you inside. Go and get changed!"

Grumbling, and obviously apprehensive, Gunner threw down his paper and rose from his chair.

"You'll find nothing," he predicted. "Victimization, that's what it is. You won't find a thing against me, and then I shall sue for wrongful arrest."

Fairbrother grinned at him, and said to Adkin: "Go with him, and see that he doesn't try to hide anything."

When the two men had left the room, the inspector turned his attention to Bill Knight. His expression was unfriendly. In the presence of Mrs. Byles he dared not risk even the faintest flicker of an eyelid to inform the young man that he understood his position.

"You're still with us, I see," he said. "I've had my eye on you, in case you thought you'd like to emigrate to Philadelphia, or someplace."

"I won't run away," said Bill, meeting his sardonic gaze. "I've nothing to be afraid of."

"I'm not so sure. You don't say much when you speak, do you?"

"I told you all I know this morning."

"That wasn't much, was it? Happen I shall want to talk to you again before the night is out."

Bill shrugged. "You're wasting your time."

Fairbrother carried the act a little further. "I never waste my time," he said. "I have a feeling I shall find things out about you, lad, before I've done."

"He's got nothing to do with a murder, anyway," said Mrs. Byles scornfully.

"How do you know?" the policeman demanded. "You haven't known him five minutes."

"That's five minutes longer than you've known him," she retorted.

The talk was interrupted by the arrival of a sergeant and a constable in uniform.

"We were sent on here to see if we could be of help, sir," the sergeant said.

Fairbrother nodded. "Search this room," he said. "You know what to look for."

"Very good, sir," the sergeant said.

"You, what's your name, Knight," said Fairbrother. "Stay right here. I'll be back."

Bill did not reply. Junie said indignantly: "It's a shame. You're just picking on him."

Fairbrother was pleased. It seemed that he had established Bill as one who had no reason to love the police. He grinned wickedly, and went out to see how Nolan and his men were doing.

chapter
five

The search of Hudson House and its occupants produced three books of Irish Sweepstake tickets, four bottles of home-made vodka, one collection of disgraceful "art studies" found in a Ukrainian's pocket, and Henry Thompson, who was wanted for wife desertion at Cambridge. It yielded nothing which could be regarded as direct evidence for Fairbrother's case, but he was not disappointed. He was too experienced an officer to have high expectations so early in a murder job. Nevertheless, he did have hopes that Gunner's coat would provide evidence. It was of a brown tweedy mixture with some red in it, and dirty at that. He thought that it might have tiny specks of blood on shoulder or lapel which a laboratory test would reveal. The suit, shoes and shirt were sent to Police Headquarters, and Gunner was sent along with them.

Before he also went back to Headquarters, Fairbrother had another talk with Bill Knight. The talk was brief. "Come on, you," he said with menace. "You'd better come with me. I would have a few more words with you."

"Now you're wasting my time as well," said Bill, but he went along without further objection.

In the C.I.D. office the two "suspects" were kept apart. Bill sat in the main office, while Adkin stood at a desk close by. Since he had not yet been informed that Bill was a fellow officer, the detective was watchful as he typed out his shorthand notes. Gunner was taken into Fairbrother's small office, where he was seated near the desk so that the desk lamp could be adjusted to shine on his face. This was not any form of torture or third degree, because the light was not strong enough to worry him unduly. It merely allowed Fairbrother to perceive his every change of expression.

A C.I.D. clerk sat at a small table in a corner, in order to take notes. Fairbrother decided to begin by lulling Gunner. He gave him a cigarette, and had one himself. But before he could begin the interrogation Nolan came and called him out of the office.

"Here," the sergeant said with an air of suppressed excitement. "I've something to show you."

Under a strong light, with a strong glass, Nolan showed Fairbrother a number of very, very small spots on the right shoulder and lapel of Gunner's coat. They looked like blood. They looked like blood which might have flown in a fine spray from Sam Gilmour's head when he was hit with the coal hammer.

"Lock those clothes away," said Fairbrother. "Get them off to the laboratory the first thing in the morning."

He returned to Gunner, and gave him a light for his cigarette. "Now we'll just go over last night again, to get it right," he said comfortably, and he began again to ask questions about Gunner's visit to the Starving Rascal, and his movements later. Gunner answered with apparent willingness. He was not deceived by Fairbrother's manner, but now that he was in the enemy's hands he saw no profit in making things difficult for himself.

When that was over, the inspector stretched himself, and said lazily: "My word, I never thought I'd put my finger on the right man first bang off. I'm wondering how much you got, and where you put it."

Gunner was not slow in getting the meaning of the casually spoken words. This was what he had expected. This was it, the hard word spoken softly.

"I didn't do it," he said.

His inquisitor smiled. "I think we'll find something on your clothes," he said. "It'll be strange if there aren't traces. Blood, you know. You'd be surprised how it gets splashed about."

His voice was confident. He was almost certain that the spots on Gunner's coat were dried blood. But he did not tell Gunner, yet, that he knew of them. He merely attempted to terrify him with the threat of scientific investigation.

"At the laboratory they'll go over every square inch of your clothes," he said. "They'll find everything there is to be found. They'll put them under ultra-violet, and under infra-red. Every little stain will show up like luminous paint. Then they'll run a special little vacuum cleaner over them, and collect every speck of dust and every fleck of metal. Everything will go under the microscope, and it'll all be identified by spectral analysis."

"They'll find nothing on my suit," said Gunner nervously. "If there's blood, it'll be my own. It'll be what got there when Bill Knight hit me."

"He hit you? When was that?"

"When he came to our house at first."

Fairbrother pretended to be hopefully interested in Bill. "He's violent, is he?"

"He's violent all right. He's a proper tearaway."

"What made him hit you?"

"I were having an argument with my sister, our Junie. He interfered."

"Did he make your nose bleed, or something?"

"He hit me on my ear. When I blew my nose after, there was blood on my hanky. I might have blown a drop or two on my coat."

"But suppose it isn't your type of blood?"

"How can it be aught else?"

"It can be someone else's blood, of a different type. That's the whole point of the thing, isn't it?"

Gunner thought about that. He did not like this talk about blood. It worried him. He was getting altogether too much police attention.

"Bill Knight, he's real violent," he said. "He hit a policeman."

Fairbrother sat up, astonished. "He did?"

"Yers. Knocked him flat."

"Whatever for?"

"The policeman was locking him up."

"What had he been doing?"

"Obscene language. I heard the bobby say so. Shocking, it was."

Fairbrother pondered. Obscene language? That was certainly out of character. The man did not even speak unnecessarily.

"Was he drunk?" he asked.

"Pie-eyed. I was trying to get him home. He called the bobby all sorts of names."

"Did you interfere?"

"I stopped him from kicking the bobby when he was down. I pulled him away, and he turned on me. I told him to come away and not be a fool. I got him away evencherlly."

"Didn't you want to see a policeman's head kicked in?"

"No fear. They might a-dragged me into the job as well."

"Well, well," said Fairbrother, extremely skeptical. "He sounds like a terribly bloodthirsty man. But he has an alibi for the Gilmour job."

"It might be made up."

The inspector nodded thoughtfully. "I'd better hear Knight's side of the tale," he said. "You can wait out there."

Gunner was placed in Adkin's care, and Bill entered the office. "Leave us for a little while," Fairbrother said to the C.I.D. clerk.

When the two men were alone, the inspector brought out his cigarettes again. "Sit down, Knight, and we'll have a chat," he said. "I must say that you're behaving extremely well. I've tried your patience, with a purpose of course. Nobody suspects that you're one of us. It's up to you to see that nobody ever does."

"Yes, sir," Bill said.

"Hanging around pubs and getting evidence for betting jobs isn't very interesting, is it?"

"It's not my idea of being a policeman."

"Nor mine. I guess you'd sooner be working on a real crime."

"Yes."

"Very well, you can forget the betting lark. We've got a murder on our hands, and you're my secret agent. You're Johnny-on-the-spot. From now on you concentrate on the murder. So how does the job look to you now?"

"It looks all right. It's something worth while."

"Good. Have you anything to tell me?"

"I told you everything I knew."

"Possibly you did, but let us consider Gunner Byles. He could have done it. He was in the pub, he can't account for his time, and he's a bad egg. He lied to me tonight, but that doesn't mean a lot, because he's a born liar. Have you noticed anything, anything at all, which might seem to involve him a little more?"

"There was one little thing," said Bill. "Gunner told you he stayed at the Rascal till closing time because he thought I might join him there. That was a lie. He knew I'd gone to a dance. He saw me leaving Hudson House with my best suit on. He asked me where I was going, and I told him."

"Therefore he must have stayed on at the Rascal for some other reason. That's a help. Anything else?"

Bill shook his head.

"Take your time about it," said Fairbrother patiently. "Think about the Byles family. Did any of them say anything about the crime? Or has any little thing happened?"

"Well, naturally they talked about it a bit. I mean, the girls did. Gunner and his mother didn't say anything at all."

"That might mean something."

"Yes," said Bill. "There was something else. It could be connected. And yet I don't know."

"What was it?"

"Junie was asking Rosemary if she had seen her new gloves. She more or less accused her of having them hidden somewhere. Anyway, she can't find 'em."

"I get your meaning. Gunner might have taken them to do a job at the Starving Rascal. Could he have worn them?"

"Junie is a big girl. I daresay he could have squeezed his hands into them. If he split 'em, he wouldn't worry."

"What were the gloves like?"

"I don't know. I don't remember ever seeing them."

"Well, if Junie mentions the gloves again, get a description."

"I'll do that, sir. Do you really think Gunner's the murderer?"

"He's as likely a client as I've seen, so far. By the way, strictly in confidence, he tried to set the hounds on your trail. He says you're violent. Did you once hit him?"

"Yes. He hit Junie. A proper crack it was. I can't stand that sort of thing. I banjoed him before I thought, like."

"Did you bring blood?"

"I never saw any blood. I caught him fair and square under the ear."

"He says you banjoed a policeman, too. Is that true?"

Bill looked at the inspector. "I'm learning about people," he said. "I didn't think they could come as low as that."

"Did you hit a policeman?"

Bill did not immediately reply. He considered the advisability of denial, but only for a moment. He was working as a spy, and temporarily his whole life was a lie. One more untruth, in self-defense, would not matter. But he did not like to tell lies. They were acts of cowardice, and liabilities in the memory. Unlike the truth, they led to mental confusion. Moreover, he did not want to start a career with a lie. He told himself that he was not so bothered about being a policeman. They could sack him if they liked, he wouldn't worry.

"Yes, I hit a policeman," he said.

Fairbrother was not as shocked as he might have been. This young man was so cool and sensible; and honest apparently. He wouldn't strike a fellow officer without having a very good reason for doing so.

"What made you do a thing like that?" was the half-smiling query.

"I sort of had to. I did it to keep from being suspected myself."

He gave Fairbrother the details of the incident. "I had to get Gunner away," he concluded.

"Why? Couldn't you have left him to take his medicine? He'd certainly asked for it."

Bill could not put into words what he knew of Gunner's character: the opinions arrived at through tortuous emotional processes, the cynical disbelief in everything except his own welfare, the accurate intuitive guesses arising from wrong suppositions, the right answers from the wrong figures.

"I had to make myself solid with him," he said. "He suspected me a bit. I'm sorry about hitting one of my mates. I didn't hit him as hard as I might have done; just winded him."

As a senior C.I.D. officer, Fairbrother knew little of the minor affairs of the uniform department. He had heard nothing of the incident which Bill had described. Probably it had never been reported. It would do the unlucky P.C. no good to report that he had lost a prisoner and come off second-best in a brawl. He would perhaps think that it was better to wait, to bide the time until he saw Gunner, or Bill, or both of them again. When that happened, he would administer justice in the way which seemed most expedient. One thing was certain, violence would be done. There would be sore bones for somebody.

Looking at Bill, Fairbrother reflected that the vengeful P.C. would need assistance in coping with him. He also decided that he had better forget the matter. Justice for a murderer was more important than disciplinary action for a police recruit. After all, this man Knight had apparently thought that he was acting in the best interests of the force.

"Gunner says you tried to kick the policeman's face in," he said.

Bill grinned ruefully. "No, that was Gunner. I dragged him off."

Fairbrother nodded. That was in character, for Gunner. Kick a man when he was down. Mark him for life.

"You see the sort of fellow you're dealing with," he said.

"Sure. A proper poisonous little beast."

"All right. I'm going to let you go home now. Keep your eyes open and report everything which might have the slightest connection with the job. You can phone me here at any time. If I'm out you can leave a message. We'd better have a code name for you. What's your lucky number?"

"Thirteen will do. It's never been unlucky for me."

"Very well, call yourself Number Thirteen. Remember, only myself, Superintendent Belcher, and Inspector Smithson know who you are and what you're doing. And you won't report to Smithson any more. You're under my orders now."

"Yes, sir," said Police Constable Knight.

"If anybody asks you about this interview, tell them I tried to get you to talk yourself into trouble. Call me as many hard names as you like, it'll all be part of the act. I shall tell Gunner that you have denied ever touching a policeman. He'll expect you to deny it, anyway."

"Are you keeping Gunner here, under arrest?"

"No, unless he confesses, which is not very likely. I haven't enough evidence."

"I shall have to reckon to be mad at him, for shopping me. I might have to give him a bit of a shaking."

"Well, don't shake him too hard. We might want his neck for the hangman. Now, you know what you're looking for?"

"The stuff he stole."

"Yes. We have no exact figures in cash. We estimate about thirty pounds in notes, silver and copper from the till, and about fifty pounds in notes which Gilmour kept in a wad in his fob pocket. There were also seventy-four foreign coins, every one gold, collector's value not yet known, gold value about three hundred pounds. I'll see that you get a descriptive list of the coins."

"He was a fool to take those. They might hang him."

"So we hope," said Fairbrother. He looked at Bill thoughtfully. "You're pretty well established at Ma Byles's now. I think you'd be able to do your work better if you lost your job at Champion Foundries."

"They'll want me to work a week's notice."

"Couldn't you get yourself sacked on the spot?"

"I'll see what I can do. There's just one foreman I don't like. He thinks he's a wit, and he laughs like a drain when he can make somebody mad. But he can't take it. It should be easy. I'll enjoy it. I'll get mad at him and give him a bit of a shaking."

Fairbrother was amused. "You'll be a rum sort of policeman, you will," he said. "You'll be giving fellows a shaking when you should be locking 'em up."

"I'll be a good policeman, when I get the chance," said Bill.

Fairbrother let him go then, and sent for Gunner again. That young man had regained some of his normal truculence, and he was scowling with impatience.

"How long are you going to keep me here, Saturday night?" he demanded.

"Just a little while longer. I want to talk to you some more."

"But I don't want to talk to you."

"That I can readily understand. There might be a slip of the tongue. Incidentally, your pal Knight has given you the lie. He says you're a poisonous little beast."

"You didn't expect him to admit hitting a copper, did you?" asked Gunner with scorn. "Don't be so daft!"

Fairbrother was pensive. He sighed. "I'd like to pummel some respect into you, my lad," he said, "but in the circumstances I don't think it would be wise."

"You daren't touch me!"

"All right, I daren't touch you. Now, let's get things straight. You say you did not go into Sam Gilmour's cellar last night. Have you been in there at all, recently?"

"I've never been in there in my life."

"Ah well, we might find traces. We have your fingerprints on the file."

"You won't find my fingerprints, 'cos I weren't there."

"You could have been there, and worn gloves."

"I haven't any gloves. Never did have any. Anybody'll tell you that."

Fairbrother did not move a muscle, but excitement warmed him inwardly. Gunner *knew* that there would be no fingerprints on the hammer. He *had* worn his sister's gloves. He *wanted* the police to know that he did not have any gloves of his own.

"All right," the inspector said. "You can go home now. You know your way out."

He went and opened the door, to show himself so that the men in the outer office would know that Gunner was being *allowed* to go. A young detective entered the big office and slung his hat expertly on to a hook near the door. He called to the inspector: "The scribes are gathering, sir."

"Where? Out front?"

"Yessir. Photographers too. London men, by the sound of 'em. We've hit the front page, we have. It must be all quiet off the China coast."

"All right," said Fairbrother. "Take this young man and let him out at the bottom door. He doesn't want to meet the gentlemen of the Press."

Then he added: "But the Press might be seeing a lot of him before he's much older."

chapter

■
SIX

Superintendent Belcher's highly organized part of the Starving Rascal investigation went on as if Gunner Byles did not exist, and would continue to go on until Gunner or some other person had been charged with the murder. A charge so serious, in Belcher's department, meant a reasonable certainty in the minds of the superintendent and his staff that they had got both the murderer and the evidence to convict him. If there was any likelihood of acquittal, they would hold their hands, and wait, and watch, and continue to seek evidence. A man can only be tried once for a murder.

Meanwhile, at the Starving Rascal, after the police had made their comprehensive search and gone away, there was a hunt for evidence of another sort. The instigator of this was old John Harper, using the keen young eyes of Gay Gilmour.

"There must be a will somewhere," he said distressfully, on Sunday afternoon when the inn had been searched from attic to cellar for the second time. "Surely Sam made some provision for you, my dear."

"I think he did, in his own way," said Gay, frowning thoughtfully. "Ever since I was sixteen he's given me money—five pounds, ten pounds—at different times and told me to put it in the bank. I have nearly nine hundred pounds in the Airechester Building Society."

"That's something, at any rate," Harper said. "But there's Sam's money, and his insurances. And they won't be anything compared to the value of this business, and the value of the coin collection."

"Sam was never poorly, except for a bit of sciatica sometimes. He didn't expect to die. I don't believe he ever made a will."

"Oh dear! I hope he did. I sincerely hope he did. You were never legally adopted, Gay. You have no claim, no claim at all."

"I have as much claim as anybody else. I don't think he had any relations. He never mentioned anybody."

There was a queer, secretive look in Harper's dull eyes. "Sam had an elder brother who died fairly young," he said. "That was many years ago. The widow will be dead too, I suppose. But there was a daughter."

"And is she still alive? Who is she?"

Harper coughed. "You're quite sure that the will isn't somewhere in the study?" he asked.

"The police said they'd searched thoroughly. Inspector Fairbrother mentioned a will, too."

"He knows you're not Sam's heir?"

"Yes. I had to explain, when I gave him my real name."

"Yes of course. He won't gossip. The police are very discreet. I'll ask for the study keys, and we'll see for ourselves. The will might be in one of those shallow drawers."

"Mr. Fairbrother said they'd looked in every drawer, and under the lining of every drawer."

Harper sighed. "The police are very good at that kind of thing," he said. "They don't miss much. Tell me, did Sam ever employ any other solicitor besides Wigram?"

"Not that I know of."

"And Wigram says there never was a will. But there might have been. I'll write to every solicitor in town, just in case. And where there's a will there's a witness. We'll find out if any of his friends know anything about it."

"Yes, we'll do that," Gay said rather absently.

The old man looked at her with something like irritation. For many years of his life he had practiced as a solicitor, and he still had a lawyer's outlook upon matters of property. No will! It was all very untidy. There would be heavy legal expenses upon the estate before it was finally disposed of. And it might go to some quite undeserving person, some relation who had scarcely known Sam Gilmour. There certainly did not seem to be much chance of its going to Sam's blood daughter, whose name was Harper.

"There must be a will somewhere," the old man repeated. "I can't think that Sam . . . We *must* find a will."

"I'll go and get the tea ready," said Gay. Will or no will, the work about the house and the inn had to go on.

At Police Headquarters, though it was Sunday afternoon, Inspector Fairbrother was in communication by telephone with the forensic laboratory. The great Dr. Lang's senior assistant answered the phone.

"Culver here," he announced laconically.

"Fairbrother at this end," said the D.I. "Is the Doc available?"

"No, he's busy. What do you want?"

"What do I want? He asks me what I want! Evidence, my boy, evidence."

"I don't think we're ready to give you any, yet. Can't you wait? It's bad enough having to work Saturday night and Sunday, without being rushed by a crowd of coppers. We'll give you the goods as soon as we can."

"Sometime next week, or next month maybe? Look, alchemist, I've got a murder suspect at liberty. And he knows he's suspect. He might go and shove his head in the gas oven, or something, and then what good will your report be? I want enough evidence to lock him up, and then you can have all the time in the world. What about the blood on his coat? It is blood, isn't it?"

"Yes, it's blood. There's precious little of it, though. Doc is working on it right now."

"What group?"

"Almost certainly 'O.' But that's unofficial. Doc hasn't said so, yet."

"And what is the blood group of the *corpus delicti?*"

"Group 'O,' " said Culver. "A very common type."

Fairbrother was pleased. "Common or not, it's a start," he said.

"It might be a help if we knew your suspect's blood group."

"Yes. I'll see what I can do. I can't get a sample of his blood without his permission. Unless I accidentally or intentionally bust his nose and lend him my handkerchief."

"Tut tut," said Culver. "The ribald constabulary."

"What about the shoes?"

"Coal on the soles. I can't tell you anything more than that, yet. There's nothing in the pockets except the usual fluff and grit and tobacco dust."

"Never mind, the job is moving," said Fairbrother, and that ended his talk with Culver. He went along to Belcher's office with his news.

When he had listened, the superintendent sniffed non-committally. "Young Byles *could* be our man," he admitted.

"Is he good enough for locking up?" Fairbrother wanted to know.

Belcher shook his head. "If we keep him locked up, we've got to charge him," he said. "We can't do that, because we haven't the evidence and we're not even sure he's our client."

"But suppose he gets worried, and does something crazy?"

"Let's hope he does get worried. Then he might make a move. He might want to start spending the money he's got. To get it he'll have to go to the place where he's hidden it. The gold coins will be in the same place. If we get him with them, we've got him right."

"Oh. Have you got some men sitting on his tail?"

"Not yet, but I soon will have. I anticipated you. I've been on the phone to old Morris Greenbaum. His tailor shop is just across the yard from Ma Byles's place. From his side window a man can see her side door, and he can also see who goes in and out by the front door."

"Didn't Greenbaum object?"

"Not at all. He guessed what job we were on, and he's known Sam Gilmour for thirty years. He's going to call round here with a key. As soon as it's dark I'm going to put an observer in there with a wireless. He'll report to a car waiting down the road, round a corner."

"Two men in the car?"

"Three. We'll do the job right. Two men can tail young Byles and ring the changes on him. The car can tail them."

"That should work. And then we've got this man Knight working on the inside."

"Yes. He's a good physical type for a policeman. Like one of the old sort."

"I think he'll turn out to be a good man, sir. Though inclined to be rather rough."

"Rough? How?"

"Oh, just an impression he gives me. He's gone home to Sheffield today. That's his Sunday habit. He thought it might look suspicious if he didn't go."

"Quite right. If Byles is our man, he'll be suspicious of every-body."

"He won't be sleeping so peaceful at night, either. But if we're going to leave him at liberty, I think I'll call it a day. I haven't had a minute to myself since this job started."

"Yes," said Belcher. "Go home and get some rest, Inspector. Then we'll see what tomorrow brings."

Gunner Byles went out early, in daylight, that fine September evening. He returned home in darkness, shortly after nine o' clock. By that time the police observer had been installed in Morris Greenbaum's workshop, but he did not observe Gunner's arrival. Neither would he have observed his departure, if he had been there earlier. Nobody saw Gunner go out, and nobody saw him come back. But when he went out by the front door at ten minutes past nine, the fact was duly reported. Superintendent Belcher's "tailing" plan went into operation.

Unfortunately, Belcher had made a mistake in his choice of personnel. Gunner, like all his kind, had always been deeply interested in the police. As a result, he knew nearly every one of the members of the Airechester C.I.D. by sight. Moreover, he was nervous and wary. At half-past nine, as he walked the short distance from the Dog and Gun to the Trumpeter, he perceived that he was being followed by a detective. The sudden knowl-edge was a great shock to him. He stopped, and his hands trem-bled as he lit a cigarette. He looked back. The man who followed him had turned away down a side street, but further back, on the other side of the road, there was another tall figure of an appearance which was familiar and unmistakable to him.

Two of them! Gunner began to perspire. He wondered, with feelings far deeper than mere concern, how long the police had been following him. When he thought about that, some of his confidence returned. Of course they had only been on his trail since he came out of Hudson House a few minutes ago. They could not have been watching his movements earlier in the evening. He chuckled nervously. No, they certainly hadn't been watching him then. If they had been, they'd have picked him up and wheeled him in so quick his feet wouldn't have touched the floor. They would that!

He chuckled again. He sniggered. They'd given him an alibi. The bloody police had given him an alibi! According to their reports, he had not left the house until fifteen minutes past nine. Well, well, and well! He began to feel that he was a very smart fellow.

He saw that the situation could be of great advantage to him in the near future. The longer the police maintained their watch on him, the longer he would have an alibi. He could give them the slip at any time, and they would be there to swear that he was at home. It was a doddle. It was a gift. It was a piece of cake.

He went into the Trumpeter and ordered a pint of beer. He was tempted to drink the beer quickly and hurry out of the place by the back door, simply to fool the police. But, he realized, that would be a mistake. It was better to let them follow him around under the belief that he had not noticed them. Yes, that was better. Never a backward look would he give.

He decided to stay at the Trumpeter until closing time, playing darts in the taproom if he could get a game. He was a good dart-thrower, and there was a chance that he might win some money. He could even afford to lose a pound or two. He had five one-pound notes and some silver in his pocket. It was far more than he was likely to need that evening, and yet not a suspiciously large amount. If the police stopped him and searched him that was all they would find. Gunner drank up and ordered another pint. Let the unmentionable police wait outside and die of thirst!

That evening, Bill Knight got back from Sheffield in time to call for a drink in the Starving Rascal. Gay Gilmour was serving behind the bar, and Abe Farley was sweating in his efforts to keep pace with the orders from taproom and snug. The bar-lounge was crowded. Many of the regular customers were keeping away from the place because the police might still be interested in it, but strangers from other parts of the city were there out of curiosity. Bill went to his favorite end of the room and, eventually, to his favorite place at the bar. Gay smiled a

welcome when she served him, but she was too busy to talk.
For that, he would have to wait until after closing time.

At twenty minutes to ten he was surprised to see Mrs. Byles
enter the room, accompanied by Junie. Ma Byles looked just the
same as she did at home, except that she had slipped on an old
gray-green coat to go out of doors. Junie also was casually dressed,
but in a new camel's-hair coat. She wore fine stockings too, and
her flat-heeled shoes were neat. Bill thought that she looked quite
attractive.

The older woman looked round the crowded bar with an oddly
satisfied smile. Then she saw Bill, and she began to make her
way toward him. Junie, who had seen him immediately, followed
willingly.

Bill was not pleased, but he smiled politely as they came up
to him.

"Thought you'd drink in a pub for a change, did you?" he
asked. "What will you have?"

"I just wanted to look the place over," Mrs. Byles replied. "I
haven't been in here for years." She cackled suddenly. "Not doing so bad, is it? Coining money!"

She agreed to have a whiskey. "A big 'un," she said. "John
Haig if they have it." Junie said that she would like a cocktail,
though she did not say what kind she wanted.

"You'll have nothing of the sort!" her mother snapped. "They
haven't time to mix cocktails for you. You'll have a half of beer."

Bill ordered the drinks, with another half-pint of beer for himself, and reached into his pocket for money. Mrs. Byles stayed
his hand. She extracted a folded ten-shilling note from the pocket
of her coat, and threw it on the bar. "This round is on the
house," she said. "The lawyer says they haven't found a will yet.
They won't, either."

"What will?" Bill asked, unable to understand what she was
talking about.

"Sam Gilmour's will," said Mrs. Byles. Her glance was fixed
on Gay, whose shapely young arms were flexed as she busily
pumped beer. "So that's the girl you're after, is it?"

Bill heard a gasp of surprise from Junie. He turned his head,
and saw the girl looking at Gay in hostile appraisal.

"She looks a bit precise, like," the older woman went on. "But happen she'll do better for you than one of my brood. Don't expect her to bring a fortune with her, though. She won't inherit. There's no will."

"She's Gilmour's daughter, isn't she?" Bill queried.

Mrs. Byles cackled again: a sudden, brief explosion of mirthless sound. "You'd better ask her. Happen she'll tell you all about it."

Her cryptic remarks were beginning to nettle Bill. "Well, whether she is or not, it's got nothing to do with you," he said bluntly.

The woman was amused. "Whether it has or not," she mocked, "that girl won't get this pub." She looked around. "I wonder what a brewer 'ud offer for it. Five or six thousand quid, I bet. Then there's them coins."

"What's left of 'em," said Bill, and then he could have bitten his tongue.

"Has some been stole?"

Bill did not hesitate, because hesitation betrays liars. "Whatsisname, Fairbrother said so, when he had me in."

She mused about that. "The gold 'uns?" she asked.

"I couldn't say."

"It would be. I bet our Gunner knew about that, and he never said a word to me. Just like him!"

"Well, you're not exactly on his side, are you?"

"I'm not exactly against him, either. He's my lad. But there's other considerations. I got to keep myself in the clear with this job. Right in the clear!"

"I don't suppose anybody's thought of accusing you," said Bill dryly.

"That isn't it. There's aiding and abetting, and accessory and that. I mean *right* in the clear."

"Well, naturally. But you don't want your son to be accused, just to keep your nose clean."

She looked at him shrewdly. "I don't mean to perjure meself for naught. If our Gunner has done it, he'll swing for it, whatever I say. You don't think a jury is going to take any notice of a lad's mother, do you?"

Bill had to admit that the unsupported evidence of a mother was not a very convincing alibi. A jury would sympathize with her efforts to save her son, but they would also shake their heads and say: "Yes, but she's his mother."

He wanted to ask her if she really thought that Gunner had murdered Sam Gilmour. If he did ask her, it was just possible that she might mention something which would be news to the police. But he was still only a recruit, and not a hardened policeman. He could not bring himself to ask her. Murder or no murder, he would not be the cause of a mother unwittingly providing evidence against her son.

"Well, good health," he said, raising his glass of beer.

The two women responded automatically to the toast. Junie took a small sip of her beer. Mrs. Byles tasted her whiskey, and nodded approval. Then she resumed the conversation on the same topic.

"There's no telling what our Gunner has done," she said. "He's a bad 'un. Always has been. And in some ways he's as barmy as his father."

"You keep saying that about his father. Why did you marry him?"

"He was a soldier. A very smart-looking artilleryman. Riding britches, spurs, shiny bandolier. I went and let him put me in the family way."

Bill was shocked, and he showed it. But the woman went on calmly: "I was too young to know any better. I went and married him."

"When did he die?"

"Fourteen year ago, when our Junie and Rosem'ry were little. When he come out of the Army he got a job with a steeplejack. After that, with him, it was only a matter of time. He fell off a mill chimley. I started me lodging house with the compensation money."

Bill was thoughtful. He looked back along the years, visualizing the Byles family when the male parent climbed around chimney stacks and church steeples for a living. Had Mrs. Byles always been like this, so indecently outspoken, so seemingly heartless? It was no wonder that the children were amoral. Bill could not feel sorry for Gunner: he did not feel sorry for a fox because it was born a fox. But he was sorry for Junie there, who had been listening with an expressionless face. What was she thinking? Was it in her mind that she had small chance of marrying a good man from a home like hers? Or was she too much the simple product of her environment to look more than a day or a week into the future?

Such matters did not appear to worry Mrs. Byles. She had been thinking of something else. "Anyway, I'm not too bothered about the coins," she said. "To keep right in the clear, that's the thing."

On the other side of the bar, Gay drew near to serve a customer. Mrs. Byles leaned forward and spoke to her. "Are you managing all right, love?" she asked kindly.

"Yes, thank you," Gay replied.

"That's right, love. The place'll have to be kept open, won't it?"

"I suppose so," Gay replied, and moved away.

Mrs. Byles watched her benevolently, and commented: "The lass is a worker, anyway." Then she turned to her daughter and asked: "How would you like to serve-on in a place like this?"

"It would be all right, I daresay," Junie replied. Then as certain possibilities dawned upon her, she said with more enthusiasm: "I'd like it fine."

Her mother nodded. "I've got my own barmaid ready and willing," she said. "I'll have to make up my mind."

"Have you had the offer of the pub, or something?" Bill was curious enough to ask. "Are you thinking of buying it?"

"No, I'm not thinking of buying it," the woman said. "But I might sell it. Or I might keep it. I haven't decided."

Then she said to her daughter: "Come on, Junie. It's cheaper drinking at home."

"I'll stay here a little while longer, Ma," said Junie, moving closer to Bill.

"You will hell as like. You're not old enough to be in pubs with fellers, even fellers like Bill. Drink your beer and we'll go."

Junie reluctantly followed her mother out of the room, and Bill blew a big breath of relief. He had been wondering what Gay would think if the girl stayed, with himself having to buy drinks for her. He also wondered if Mrs. Byles had perceived his dilemma, and if she had taken Junie away to save him embarrassment. An odd character, she was. A very odd character.

71

chapter

seven

When Gay had ceased to serve
drinks that night, she said as she took Bill's empty glass away:
"Don't go just yet. I'd like to talk to you."

Bill was more than willing to wait, and while glasses were
cleared, and washed, and dried, and polished, he watched her
brisk movements with pleasure. She knew that he was watching
her, and she dropped and broke a glass. It was a thing she rarely
did. She blushed furiously. She was annoyed because he had
witnessed her unusual clumsiness, and it was some time before
she returned his sympathetic smile. When she did, she thought
how nice he was. And so big and strong! She wondered if he was
a man who would make a good husband. Would he get on in the
world?

When she had finished with the glasses, all the other customers had gone. There was only Abe Farley, sweeping around
Bill with his broom.

"I want to thank you for being so helpful yesterday," she said.
"I haven't had the chance before."

"It was nothing," said Bill, slightly embarrassed. "It was only
what any man would have done."

"But not so capably, without any fuss."

"Well, is there anything else I can do? I'm only too willing,
you know."

"There isn't anything at the moment. This part of the business is going smoothly enough. I'm working for a salary now,
you know."

"A salary? Who'll pay it?"

"Sam's lawyer, out of the estate. The pub must be kept open,
you see. Mr. Wigram—that's the lawyer—says I've got to apply

for a temporary license at the next meeting of the licensing bench."

"I should think you'll be the youngest innkeeper in England. Will you stay on here?"

"I don't think so," said Gay. Then because she liked him she explained the unusual circumstances of her birth and upbringing to him. "So I'm not the heir, you see," she concluded.

"Unless a will is found."

"I don't think there is a will. We've looked everywhere. Nobody has heard even the faintest rumor of a will: nobody that Sam knew; none of the lawyers in town."

Bill was scandalized. "Surely they won't leave you destitute?"

She smiled. "Not quite. Sam used to give me money to put in the bank. It goes against the grain to lose the estate, but I won't be destitute."

"Who'll inherit, if there's no will?"

"Nobody seems to know. Or at least nobody wants to tell me. Daddy said something about a niece, the daughter of Sam's older brother. But he doesn't seem to know who she is."

Bill suddenly thought he knew who was the niece. And like everyone else, he did not want to impart the knowledge to Gay. He just stared at her and said: "It's a shame!"

"I think so too," she said. "But I can always earn my own living."

"Do you ever think of getting married?" Bill asked rashly.

She laughed. "Every girl thinks of getting married, silly," she said.

There was an interruption. Farley had put away his broom, and he was saying good night.

"Good night, Abe," said Gay.

The man went out. "Are you alone here, now?" Bill wanted to know.

She shook her head. "Daddy's upstairs. He's moved in, to keep me company. He'll be pottering around, getting supper ready. Would you like to stay to supper?"

Bill would have liked that very much. But he had promised Fairbrother that he would return to Hudson House in time to catch the family at supper, to get the gossip of the day.

"Thanks, no," he said. "Gosh, I'd like to, but I've got to get up early in the morning, and I've something to do before bed. Something to do with my job."

"You mean studying?"

"It's a sort of studying."

She smiled. She approved. He was trying to get on in the world.

"Will you ask me some other time?" was his rather breathless question.

"Yes," she said gravely. He seemed so much afraid that she would say "No."

"Soon?"

"Yes, soon."

"When's your evening off?"

"I don't know. There's no settled routine yet, since—since yesterday."

"Will you come with me to the pictures one night?"

"Yes. I'd love to."

There was a short silence: there seemed to be nothing else to say. But still he lingered, and she seemed to be content that he should stay.

"Who was that woman, and that girl?" she asked suddenly.

Bill realized that he had made a mistake. He had lingered just too long. "That was Mrs. Byles and her daughter," he said.

"Does she like you?"

"Who, Ma Byles? I've no idea."

"No, I mean the girl."

"Junie? Oh, she's just a kid. I don't take any notice of her. In any case, I can only be interested in one girl at a time."

"And who's the one girl?"

"Why, you are."

Gay was only half reassured. "Living in the same house, you could be interested in her when I'm not there."

"Oh, no, I couldn't. She's not a bad kid, I suppose, but she isn't in the same class as you."

"I saw the way she looked at you, and the way she looked at me. She's jealous."

"Well, I can't help that. I don't make up to her. She has nothing to complain about."

Gay laughed nervously. "We're talking like a courting couple, and we hardly know each other."

"I wish we were courting," said Bill with some eagerness. "I wish we were engaged."

"I wouldn't have you living at Mrs. Byles's place if you were engaged to me," she said, but she was smiling. Then she went on: "You'd better go, or Daddy will be coming downstairs to see what's the matter."

"Would he disapprove?"

"He'd disapprove of my supper going cold, while I stand talking to you," she said lightly.

That ended the conversation; the naïve, bantering, earnest conversation which was not greatly different from hundreds more, between young men and women, which were being whispered or spoken up and down the city at that time of night. Gay went to the door with him, to bar it behind him. He shook hands awkwardly, not daring to kiss her. He thought that she was not the sort of girl to give her kisses lightly. He had never been afraid to kiss a girl before, but Gay was different. She wasn't that sort. She had character. She had class.

He walked home in a cloud of happiness which was tinted gray at the edges by a doubt about Gay's reaction when she learned that he was a police agent. What would she say? He was afraid of what she would say.

On his way home he saw a black car waiting, and he was reminded of what he had to do. As he entered Hudson House he glanced briefly at Greenbaum's side window, but the watcher behind it did not betray himself by movement.

When Bill entered the kitchen, Junie did not greet him with her usual smile. She was sulky when she gave him his supper, and as he began to eat she asked abruptly: "Is that your girl?"

Bill played for time. "Which one?"

"You know which one. Her in the pub. Gay Gilmour."

Bill thought that this was getting a bit thick. This was persecution. Still, he had a curious reluctance to hurt Junie. She wasn't a bad kid. "No," he said.

"You like her, don't you?"

"Yes."

"Are you after her?"

"Lay off," he said mildly. "You're worse than Fairbrother."

"You are after her. She's your girl."

From her chair by the fireplace Mrs. Byles spoke up. "Junie, has Bill been making a pass at you?"

"No, Ma," the girl answered promptly, quick to defend Bill.

"Well, shut up then. He's a right to go after anybody he likes, without you wittering at him. Because you make his tea you don't own him."

Tears came into Junie's eyes. Without a word she flounced off to bed. Mrs. Byles grinned broadly at Bill, showing large yellow teeth. "That's your breakfast gone for a burton," she said. "If you want to be able to pick it up in the morning, you'll have to get it ready yourself. I think there's some boiled ham in the larder."

Bill nodded, and went on eating his supper. Before he had finished it, Gunner came in. A certain carefulness in his movements suggested that he was under the influence of drink to some degree.

"Drunk again," his mother accused. "You must have a lot of generous friends."

Gunner scowled at her.

"Where do you get your liquor?" she persisted. "Have you come into money?"

"No," said Gunner fiercely, "I haven't. I can win a bit of brass without telling you, can't I?"

Her smile was ironic. "Keeping your tips to yoursel', are you? I'm glad. It'll save me money."

"You've never lost any money through me."

"Only many a pound," the woman retorted. She turned to Bill. "Racing tipster, that's him," she said. "He doesn't know a hoss's withers from its brisket. Him back a winner!"

"I said I'd won some money!"

"You won it before it was lost, happen. What did you back?"

"Find out!"

"I didn't know a hoss called Starving Rascal were running yesterday."

Gunner glared wildly. "What the bloody hell do you mean?" he bawled.

"I mean what I said."

"Are you accusing your own son? How do you know there isn't a copper listening at the winder? You'd get me hung for murder, you would. Me as wouldn't dream of such a thing."

"You dreamed of it last night, anyway. Talked in your sleep, an' all. You talked so loud I came to listen."

Gunner stared in dismay. He groped for a chair, and sat down heavily. "Anybody 'ud talk in their sleep after a do with Fairbrother," he said. "A tricky bastard, he is. But he won't get me for it. I never did it."

"There was some gold coins stole," said Mrs. Byles. "They're mine by rights. I want 'em back."

"Have you gone batty? How are they yours?"

"Because my maiden name was Gilmour."

"How long ago was that, when you were a maiden?"

"Impident monkey! I'm Sam Gilmour's niece, and his only living relation. That's why I'm keeping in the clear, right out in the clear. They're not stopping my inheritance because I had summat to do with my uncle's murder."

Over by the table, Bill laid down his knife and fork very, very carefully. He hoped that he had been temporarily forgotten. He scarcely dared breathe for fear of drawing attention to himself.

He saw Gunner gazing at his mother in stupefaction. "You? You'll come into Gilmour's brass? What about the daughter?"

"She has no legal claim. She's only his chance-child, and there's no will."

"And that's why you turned against me, making me out a liar in front of the bogeys! You want shut of me, so's you can enjoy your money while I'm burning in quicklime."

"If you've done it, you'll swing for it. I can't help you, lad, one way or t'other. They never take notice of a man's mother."

Gunner was not listening. With unfocused eyes he was looking inward at his thoughts. "You tried to shop me for the sake of money," he breathed.

"I never did," the woman answered sharply. "I stopped you in a big silly lie, which they'd have showed up as a lie if I'd let you go on with it. And they'd happen have showed it up in front of a judge, where it mattered."

Still Gunner was not listening. He was biting his thumbnail in desperate cogitation. His eyes glittered with furious thought.

77

When at last he spoke, his expression was truly evil. "You tried to shop me," he said. "If they charge me wi' murder, I'll stop your caper. I'll make you laugh at the other side of your face. I'll tell 'em you egged me on to do it."

Mrs. Byles put a hand to her throat. She breathed as if she had been running. "Gunner! You did do it!" she whispered.

"I never did," he denied. "Don't you go telling anybody I said I'd done it. But if the worst comes to the worst I'll see you get nothing out of it. I'll tell 'em you put me up to it. They'll believe me, an' all."

Then Bill, the listener, realized that one person at least had not forgotten him. Mrs. Byles glanced sideways at him. She shook her head sadly, then she said: "You'll bear witness to what he's saying, Bill. He won't be able to stop me from getting my rightful inheritance."

Bill was silent, not wishing to intervene with so much as one word in this family quarrel. But he admitted to himself that Mrs. Byles had been both adroit and wise in having a witness present. She had seen from the start that her son could endanger her inheritance. That was why she had been so insistent upon staying "in the clear." So long as he had a spiteful tongue in his head, Gunner would have been a danger. Now, the danger had been eliminated.

Mrs. Byles rose from her chair. She seemed to have recovered some of her normal hard composure. "I'm off to bed," she said. "One of you see all lights out. I'm going to get our Rosem'ry to sleep with me tonight."

"Why? What for?" Gunner demanded.

"Because she's the loudest screamer between here and Pontefract," his mother replied. She took some keys from the pocket of her apron and locked up the cupboard where she kept her whiskey. Then she said, "Good night, all," and went out of the room.

When she had gone, Gunner turned to Bill. "Would you believe it?" he asked thickly. "She thinks I'd do her in. Me own mother! The owd hag!"

When Bill maintained a stony silence, Gunner sought to conciliate him. "Fancy her thinking I'd drag her into aught," he said with an uneasy laugh. "I were only kidding." Then with a change of tone he went on: "And her thinking I'd do a murder! There's a mother for you. I can't get over it. You don't think I murdered anybody, do you, Bill lad?"

"You'll have to excuse me, Gunner," was the reply. "I can't interfere in what goes on between you and your mother. It's not my place at all."

"Still, you don't think I'm a murderer, do you?"

Bill shook his head. It was a refusal to answer, but Gunner chose to interpret it otherwise. "I should think not," he said. "I couldn't do a thing like that. I'm no cold-blooded killer."

Bill got up, quite forgetting that he ought to prepare some sandwiches for tomorrow's breakfast. He thought that he had heard as much as he could remember and note, and he did not see how he would learn anything further by listening to Gunner. He had had enough of Gunner. The man's alternate whining and blustering was getting on his nerves.

"I'm off," he said. "Good night."

He went upstairs quietly, but not quietly enough. When he reached his bedroom door, the opposite door opened and Junie stood there in a pale blue silky nightgown. It was held up by narrow ribbons on the shoulders, and pulled in by a ribbon at the waist. On her splendid young figure it was more than merely attractive, and had Bill thought about it at all he would have realized that it was her very best nightgown, put on for the occasion.

As Junie came to him, he remembered that Rosemary had gone to her mother on the floor below. This, then, was an opportunity which many young men would have welcomed. Bill was enamored of another girl, but he also liked Junie. He did not rebuff her when she came and stood quite close to him.

"I'm sorry, Bill," she said, all contrition, letting him see her eyelashes. "I'd no right to pester you tonight. You're not mad at me, are you?"

"No," said Bill. "I'm not mad at you, Junie."

Junie came closer. The clean, warm smell of her was in his nostrils. Her hair brushed his chin.

"You never have made a pass at me, have you, Bill?" she murmured, peering closely at his tie as if she had not seen it before. "There's nobody but us two up here tonight."

Bill's virtue was assailed by his own imagination. He was aware of a weakening. He asked himself where was his will power, in which he had a certain pride. "It's you who're making a pass at me, Junie," he replied, feeling that it was a feeble thing to say.

"I can't help it, Bill," she answered simply. "I never knew a man like you before." Then she said quickly, "I'm a virgin. I haven't been knocked about."

He grinned at her. "I should think not, at your age."

"Oh, I don't know," she said. "Some of the girls round here . . . You'd be surprised."

Her confession of virginity had made her safe from Bill. "And so would you be surprised," he said. "Save yourself for the right man." He took her by the arms and turned her around, and gently pushed her into her room. "Go to bed," he said firmly. "I'm tired."

"Good night, big fellow," she replied, smiling at him. "Our Rosem'ry will stay down below after tonight. If she doesn't sleep in Ma's room, she'll sleep in the little room across from her."

"So what?"

"So there'll be other nights, won't there, when you're not tired?"

chapter

eight

Superintendent Belcher's city-wide "quiz program" delivered up no murder suspects, and his attention, with that of Fairbrother, became focused more and more upon Gunner Byles. But the widespread inquiries of the police, and the scope they allowed for headlines with words like dragnet, cordon, et cetera, did serve the purpose of drawing the attention of Press and public away from Gunner. Only the police knew that he was Suspect Number One. Only the members of his family and one or two of the more discerning lodgers knew that he was suspected at all.

With men watching the comings and goings at Hudson House, and with an agent inside the house itself, Belcher and Fairbrother could afford to wait, at least for a day or two. They knew their man. Gunner was a drinker and a gambler. He would want to make use of his ill-gotten assets. They hoped that his impatience would cause him to make some revealing move. If he made no move he could once more be brought to Headquarters and interrogated, and then released and watched again. This cat-and-mouse technique had been successful in the past, and it could be again. It would be a strain upon Gunner's nerves. It was just possible that he might pick up his loot and try to get out of the country with it. It was possible—such is the immeasurable stupidity of criminals of Gunner's type—that he would try to dispose of some gold coins. It was possible that he would in-advertently reveal the hiding place of the coins to Bill Knight.

From about eleven o'clock on Monday morning, Bill was ostensibly out of work and available to keep watch upon Gunner. To lose his job at the foundry he only needed to shake the fore-man very gently: just enough to make him drop his false teeth. The hilarity of Bill's mates incensed the foreman more than the fracture of his teeth. He rushed off to complain to Mr. Oates. Mr. Oates did not want to lose Bill, and he tried to make peace. But the foreman insisted upon something which he called justice, and Bill intimated that Champion Foundries was not big enough to hold the foreman and himself. Reluctantly, Mr. Oates told Bill to get his cards and go hence.

He walked into the kitchen of Hudson House at eleven-fifteen, to the surprise of Junie and her mother.

"What's up?" Junie wanted to know. "Are you poorly?"

"No," said Bill, registering a scowl. "I got sacked."

Junie's lips parted in dismay. "Will you—will you be leaving us?"

"I don't know," was the surly answer. "I'll have to see. I'm not leaving today, at any rate."

"You'll soon get another job," said Mrs. Byles in an unusually friendly tone. "There's no need for you to leave here if you run short of brass. Not for a day or two, anyway. What you been doing, hitting somebody?"

Bill shook his head. "A bit of a dispute," he replied.

"You're a good 'un at that. It don't always do, you know," the woman said mildly.

Bill shrugged, and stamped away upstairs to take off his overalls. Mother and daughter looked at each other. Junie looked unhappy, and Mrs. Byles smiled rather grimly. Bill's explanation was so much in the nature of human affairs—to their experience of human affairs—that they never dreamed of questioning it. Their lodgers, poor unlettered men but free spirits all, were frequently changing their jobs because of words or blows about this or that. Junie's dismay was not concerned with Bill's loss of a job, but with a fear that he would move on from there. As she looked at the girl, Mrs. Byles's shrewd eyes showed a glimmer of sympathy and affection.

"I wish our Gunner had been a lad like Bill," she said, and Junie stared at her. Then the mother said: "I don't want Bill to leave us yet. I want him around. He can handle Gunner."

She said no more, because Bill was returning. He seemed to be in a better frame of mind. "Where's Gunner?" he asked.

"He's out," said Mrs. Byles. "The pubs open at half-past eleven, and he has to be waiting on the doorstep. Didn't you know?"

"I think I'll go out for a drink myself," said Bill, but he picked up the morning paper.

Mrs. Byles noticed that Bill had turned to the racing page. "Shouldn't you be looking at the work adverts, instead of looking for winners?" she queried.

"Oh, to hell with work," Bill said. "I can afford a day or two's rest."

"You can't afford to bet on horses if you're not working," said Junie. "You'll have to look after your money."

He looked up from the paper, and smiled at her. "I can get a quid or two from home if I run short," he said.

"From the pater?" Mrs. Byles asked dryly.

He grinned at her. "From the mater," he said. He remembered that he need no longer take an interest in racing, except for purposes of small talk with Gunner. He remembered that now he was working on a murder job. Not without uneasiness he wondered what Junie and her mother would think of him if his evidence brought Gunner into the dock on a murder charge. Sometime they would have to learn that he was a policeman, and like the majority of people in Champion Road they regarded the police as natural enemies.

"I'll just go and have the odd one before dinner," he said, putting the paper down.

"Are you going to the Starving Rascal?" Junie wanted to know. The words came out reluctantly, as if she asked the question against her will.

"I might," Bill compromised. "I don't know yet."

"Will you have your dinner with us?"

"Well, thanks. What time?"

"No later than one o'clock."

"Right," he said. "You do look after me, Junie."

He took some folded one-pound notes from his pocket, and gave two to the girl. "I'll keep a little bit in reserve," he said. "Look after these for me. Don't go and spend 'em."

She colored with pleasure as she took the notes. "I won't spend 'em," she said earnestly, and when her mother laughed aloud she turned and said indignantly: "Well, I won't!"

"I never said you would, love," said Mrs. Byles, still laughing.

Bill went out to look for Gunner. There was hardly anybody whose company he liked less, but he had to keep in touch.

He failed to find Gunner, and he did go to the Starving Rascal. At noontime on a Monday the place was not busy, and Gay alone was able to cope quite easily with all the business there was.

When Bill went in there, she was behind the bar, leaning on it in conversation with a very neat, very handsome, quite tall and very slender young man who seemed to be saying it—whatever it was—with a smile. And as he smiled and spoke he looked deeply into her eyes. Quite a charmer, he was.

Bill's arrival had no effect upon the young man's smile. He gave the big steelworker one brief glance, and would thereafter have ignored him. But Gay could not ignore him. When she saw him she flushed and began to edge away in his direction, apparently waiting politely for the young man to finish what he was saying so that she could go and take the newcomer's order.

83

That was normal enough. Barmaids should not stand listening to charming customers when other customers are waiting to be served. The young man appeared to realize that. His smile was in no way diminished when Gay left him to attend to Bill.

Bill's need was quickly fulfilled. Gay said "Hello" to him before she served him, and as she gave him his half-pint of beer she said in a low voice: "You'll have to excuse me a minute. That's Mr. Draper, a brewer's representative. I'll come back to you as soon as I can."

"Okay, kid," said Bill with a smile. Business was business, he supposed. Gay had to talk to these people who called on her.

But as he watched the two talking, their talk interrupted now and again by Gay's attention to customers, it became obvious to him that Mr. Draper was not trying to sell his employer's decoctions to Gay, he was trying to sell Mr. Draper. And Gay's response to the effort was disturbing, though somewhat restrained because she knew that she was under observation. Bill began to see Mr. Draper as a possible rival for her affections.

Here was a fellow with a good job, for to be a brewer's traveler was to be well up in the world by Bill's measurement of personal economics. He thought that Draper must have had some sort of backing to get that job, at his age. He probably had good connections, and a good education. Bill could not hear what he was saying, but he could hear the accent, and it was what he called an Eton and Oxford accent. He knew the girls were impressed by that sort of thing: manners, dress, accent and station in life. They liked a bloke to have a good job. This fellow was certainly some competition for an out-of-work laborer who lived in a common lodging house. Jealousy burned in him. He began to see himself giving Mr. Draper a shaking. He also perceived that Gay would strongly disapprove of any such action. She was much too respectable to tolerate any sort of violence. So, it appeared, nothing could be done about Mr. Draper. Bill simply had not got the weapons with which to fight him.

But presently the brewer's traveler looked at his watch, and made a smiling departure. Gay served a new customer, then she came to Bill's end of the bar. She seemed to be slightly embarrassed, but she made no excuses. Bill thought that the embarrassment was due to her own knowledge that she had listened somewhat too enthusiastically to the traveler's pleasantries. It became very evident to him that this Draper business would have to be watched.

There was some rather flat small talk, then Gay suddenly frowned and said: "You're not in your working clothes. Why is that?"

"I got fired this morning," Bill said bluntly.

"Fired? Whatever for?"

"I fell out with the foreman."

Gay was distressed. "Oh, Bill! How ever will you make any progress if you keep changing your job?"

"I'm young enough. Every new job is new experience."

She shook her head. "Drifters don't get on. You've got to stay on at a place if you want promotion."

Bill could see her point of view. Security and settled routine. Women always sought those things. Nevertheless, he was nettled.

"Promotion?" he retorted rashly. "You talk as if I was in the police force, or something."

Gay looked at him. "Well, why not?" she said. "You're certainly big enough. The police is a good, steady job with plenty of prospects. And you'd look nice in a bobby's uniform."

"I'll have to think about it," he said, wishing to drop that subject quickly.

Gay suddenly remembered something. "Oh," she said, "I must tell you! We got the study keys back from Mr. Fairbrother this morning, so that we could look in there for the will. And we've found that something else has been stolen. The police don't know about it. Sam always kept a pistol in a drawer of his desk, and now it isn't there."

"What sort of a pistol?"

"I've only seen it once or twice. It was big and heavy, and it was loaded with six bullets."

"It sounds like a revolver. Were the bullets in a sort of round cylinder?"

"That's right. Sam once showed me how you could load it and unload it. He had two. The other is a different shape; a different sort of gun altogether."

"That sounds like an automatic. Where is it?"

Her glance shifted, but only for a moment. "I couldn't tell you," she said.

"Has that been pinched as well?"

"I don't think so. It wasn't kept in the study. I couldn't tell you where it is."

"Well, you searched everywhere for a will. Didn't you see the automatic then?"

"Yes, I did," she admitted. "There's a shallow bottom drawer in the till. It's a kind of secret drawer. You open it by pushing a button hidden at the side."

"And the automatic is in there? You're quite sure?"

"Yes. I looked this morning."

"It had better be surrendered to the police. You don't need a gun, and you haven't a license for it."

"I wish I'd never mentioned it," she said. "It slipped out. I don't want to give it to the police. It's the only protection I've got. Daddy couldn't protect me."

"But you can't use a gun."

"I can scare somebody away with it, can't I? Besides, I *can* use a gun. All you have to do is push up the safety catch and pull the trigger."

"You don't need a gun, Gay. Hand it in to the police."

"No," she said stubbornly. "It's for self-defense. I feel safer with it there."

"Does anyone else know about it?"

"No. Nobody in the world but you and I."

Bill sighed. The secret would have to be kept. If the police learned about the gun in the drawer, Gay would know who had told them. And anyway the gun was not doing any harm so long as it stayed in the drawer. It was extremely unlikely that Gay would every need it, and if she did need it she would not shoot anybody. Bill felt quite sure that she would never shoot anybody.

"You'd better tell Fairbrother about the gun that's been stolen, at any rate," he said.

"Yes, I'll do that," said Gay, in a tone which suggested that she would do it sometime.

"Do it now," said Bill firmly. "Get on the phone to Fairbrother. It won't take you a minute."

Rather reluctantly she went to the telephone. By now she

knew the Headquarters number from memory. She dialed, and was immediately answered. Presently she returned to Bill.

"Mr. Fairbrother is coming round here straight away," she said.

Bill realized that he had been questioning and instructing Gay almost in the manner of a policeman. He thought that it was time to get back into character. "If he's coming here, I'm off," he said. "The less I see of that fellow, the better I shall be. Cheerio."

"When will you be in again?" she asked.

"Tonight," he said. She smiled at him, and he went on his way feeling that perhaps Mr. Draper was not such a great menace, after all.

At eight o'clock that evening Bill made a telephone contact with Fairbrother. When he came on the line, the inspector was terse and peremptory. "Listen," he said. "We have reason to believe that a loaded revolver was stolen from Sam Gilmour's study."

"Yes, I know," Bill said.

"You know?"

"Yes," said Bill, seeing no reason why he should not let the inspector know that he was keeping in touch with affairs. "Miss Gilmour told me. I told her to phone you. Then I reckoned to make myself scarce because you were coming around to ask questions."

"Very good," said Fairbrother. "She didn't mention you. She thought you wanted to stay out of it. Well, it's something else to look for."

"You think Gunner has the revolver?"

"I think the murderer has it. Gunner is our only suspect, and he's a good 'un. Find that gun if you can, Knight."

"I'll do my best, sir. Do I hand it over to you when I get hold of it?"

"I've been thinking about that. It depends whether or not you find the gold coins at the same time. Miss Gilmour can't positively identify the gun, because she's only seen it about twice in her life. So the coins are still the most important. But we've got to disarm Gunner. If you find the gun and not the coins, bring it in and we'll tamper with the ammo. It sounds as if it's either a forty-five or a thirty-eight on a forty-five frame. I'll have half-a-dozen rounds of each prepared, just in case. Then when we've fixed it up you'll have to try and put the gun back in its hiding place before Gunner misses it."

"I understand, sir."

"It may not be as easy as it sounds. You'll just have to do the best you can. Have you seen much of Gunner today?"

"Only at teatime. I don't want to hang around him too much. I want to get him to hang around me, if I can."

"Yes, that'll be best if you can do it. You seem to be quite an intelligent man, Knight."

"Yes, sir," Bill agreed. "Where is Gunner now?"

"Ten minutes ago he was seen to enter the Running Stag. I expect he'll still be in there."

"And where is the Running Stag?"

"Haven't you found that one yet? It's in Stag Lane, just above Crown Row. A bit off your beat."

"I'll find it, sir," said Bill. He told Fairbrother about the scene in Mrs. Byles's kitchen on the previous night. The inspector was pleased. "My word," he said. "Now it really does begin to look as if Gunner is our client. Good work, Knight!"

That was the end of the talk. Bill left the call box and went to look for the Running Stag. He found it easily enough. Being on a main thoroughfare of the city it had a clientele which was different and more varied in type from a Champion Road tavern. It was also different in appearance. It was, in fact, a gin palace: all red leather, black bakelite, plate glass, chromium plate and neon lights. It was a place where the manager was not acquainted with his customers, and did not want to be.

Bill entered the main lounge bar. The time was eight-fifteen, and the place was not as crowded as it would be in an hour's time. He saw Gunner, with a girl. They were seated on tall stools at the bar. Gunner was staring morosely into a pint glass half-filled with beer, and the girl did not seem to be trying to cheer him up. She was looking around, and she saw Bill immediately. She gave him a glance of frank curiosity.

Bill looked at her and looked away. He observed that she was a well-shaped, medium-sized woman of twenty-six or seven. She was medium, too, in coloring, but handsome in a bold sort of way. The eyes, he decided: the boldness was in the eyes. She was smartly dressed, but she had not succeeded in losing a touch of commonness. No class there, he thought. She reminded him of somebody. He wondered where Gunner had picked her up.

He went and stood at the bar a few feet away from the pair. He ordered his usual half-pint of beer. While he was waiting for his change he glanced at Gunner, letting the girl see the glance.

The move served its purpose. In the bar mirror he saw the girl dig Gunner quite sharply in the ribs. She directed his attention to Bill, and asked a question. Gunner saw Bill, and his gloom seemed to lift. He smiled broadly.

"Oy there, Basher!" he called, beckoning energetically. "C'mere. Wanta intrajuice you."

Bill moved around a group of customers and joined them.

Gunner said: "Amy, this is Bill Knight, what I told you about. Bill, this is our Amy. Mrs. McGeen, if you want to know the worst."

Bill shook hands with the girl. "I didn't know Gunner had a married sister," he said.

"Parted, big fellah," Amy answered promptly. "Parted this many a long year. I'm as free as air."

Bill knew, then, of whom she reminded him. It was Rosemary. He said so.

"Yes, we were both baked in the same oven," Amy admitted. "Our Rosem'ry's a lively kid."

Gunner said something defamatory about Rosemary, then he said: "Our Junie is dead nuts on Bill. He can have her any time he wants."

Bill frowned. "She's only a child," he said curtly.

"Take no notice of our Gunner," said Amy. "He's a dirty little bastard."

"If I'm a bastard," said Gunner, "what does that make you?"

"Oh, shut up. I'm talking to the gentleman."

"Trying to take my pal away from me now. Is that it?"

"Take no notice," Amy repeated.

Bill took no notice. "Do you live around here?" he asked politely.

"She has a flat, not far away," said Gunner with a leer.

"Oh, go away," his sister said.

Gunner did go away, but only to the "Gents." In his absence,

Bill and Amy talked. The talk comprised mainly the civil questions and answers of people who have just met. Amy was not coy, forward, or inviting. She did not try to flirt. She did, however, openly appraise Bill with those bold eyes of hers.

Before Gunner returned, another man joined them. This was a very big man. He was as tall as Bill, and heavier, but about ten years older. He had the battered features and puffed eyes of a man with a record of fights—professional, amateur, or back-alley. His hair was short, and an ugly shade of ginger. His fine physique was beginning to run to fat, but, when he spoke, his utterance was in short, rapid rushes of words: a warning to students of rough-house psychology that he had a quick, fighter's brain.

"'Lo, Amy," the man said in his quick way. "You doing all right for yourself? This the young man?"

The man was smiling, but it was not a pleasant smile. Bill met his glance levelly, and without expression. Amy put her nose in the air, and looked straight at the back-bar mirror.

"You and I don't speak, Frank McGeen," she said. "Leave me alone, please."

"Don't be like that, Amy love." There was mockery in the voice.

"Don't 'Amy love' me! We're legally separated. I don't claim anything from you, and I expect you to keep your distance."

"Dearie me! Now we're impressing the new man, aren't we?" McGeen jeered.

Then Gunner returned, and perceived what was happening. "You leave my sister alone, McGeen," he said fiercely. "She wants naught to do with you."

"The head of the family in person! You helping in the family business now? A bit of pimping?"

"I'm no bloody pimp, McGeen!"

"No? You look like one. Come see my sister."

"You, talking about anybody being a pimp!" snarled Gunner, bitter because the man was obviously too strong for him to hit. "Worst there ever was! By hell, I wish I was as big as you! I'd show you!"

"Happen your pal's big enough," McGeen suggested, and Bill, the innocent bystander, was moved to quiet anger by the wanton challenge.

"Why bring him into it?" Amy demanded. "He's done nothing to you."

"He's with my wife, isn't he?"

"He isn't," said Amy. "He's with our Gunner."

"He could take you apart and grind you up for manure," said Gunner, whose thoughts had been dwelling pleasurably upon the possibility of his brother-in-law's downfall.

McGeen looked at Bill. "You're a likely lad, at that," he said. "You any good?"

Bill did not answer, and McGeen's lip curled. "Be off, yellow-belly," he said. "Beat it!"

"If I go," said Bill in quiet fury, "I'll take you with me."

"Don't," Amy pleaded. "Don't let him draw you. He's always looking for fights this way. He'll tup you and trip you and then lame you with his feet. That's the way he fights."

There was an interruption. McGeen's approach to the group at the bar had been observed. The last part of the altercation had been watched and overheard by the manager. Now he came and spoke to McGeen. He was a small, dapper, sharp-faced man.

"Outside," he said, looking up fearlessly at the big man's face. "Get out, pronto. And don't come back. I've had enough of you. From now on you're barred here."

McGeen looked down at the little man with naked hatred in his eyes. But he turned and went out without saying another word. The manager watched him to the door, then went about his business without speaking to the three who remained. His manner suggested that he did not approve of them, either, but they had been quiet enough before McGeen joined them. He had enough trouble getting customers *into* the place, without driving them out just because he did not quite approve of them.

"When you leave here," said Amy to Bill, "go out the back way. He might wait at the front with a couple of friends."

"He'll be at the back," said Gunner. "He'll expect Bill to go the back way."

"He hasn't so much sense," said Amy.

"He has. That's just about as much as he does have. I've always wondered whatever you saw in that clot."

"Ten years ago he was worth it. I knew he was no angel, but I didn't know he was going to turn out to be an absolute no-good."

"Sold his own wife," Gunner grumbled.

"Shut your trap!" said Amy sharply.

"Sold his wife for five pounds," Gunner affirmed.

Bill asked no questions, but he could not hide his curiosity. Raised eyebrows were enough for Gunner.

"Our Amy was a good lass," he said. "That dirty ponce offered her to a fellow for five pound. He was drunk and he was hard up. He said: 'Gimme a fiver and she's yours for the night.' So our Amy left him."

"I should damn well think so," said Bill, carefully not looking at Amy.

But Amy's eyes were not downcast, nor had she blushed. "That's all there was to it," she said.

"Ah, but it isn't," said Gunner.

Her glance was angry. "If you must tell the tale, tell it right," she snapped. Then she addressed Bill: "At that time McGeen and I lived in a house in Strasbourg Street. The fellow went home with us. Practically forced into it, he was, all because he'd smiled at me. He was scared to death of McGeen, and trembling like a leaf. But I was mad. I thought: 'Well, if a fiver is all I'm worth to that big ape, fair enough. I'll show him.' When we got home I let the fellow in at the front door, then I gave McGeen a good shove and tripped him the way he'd showed me how to do. I took him unawares. He fell over and I nipped inside and locked him out. He went wild, kicking and pounding at the door. The fellow inside with me was nearly paralyzed with fear. He didn't do nothing at all to me. He just gave me five quid and cleared off the back way, and glad to get out of it. Then I locked the back door as well."

Gunner laughed gleefully. "Tell Bill about the coppers," he said.

Amy herself smiled. "It served him right," she said. "He kept running round from front to back and back to front, punching at the doors. Then he broke a winder to get in, and along came two of the biggest cops I ever saw. McGeen told 'em I'd locked him out of his own house, and he said I had a man in bed with me. I leaned out of the bedroom winder and said it was a lie. The bobbies said I'd have to let a man into his own home. I said I daren't let him in, and I told 'em how he'd sold me for a lousy fiver. He said he hadn't intended selling me; it was a gag. It was just a shakedown, he said. Fancy the idiot saying that to two bobbies! They was disgusted with him, and they told him he'd better clear off to the Salvation Army till morning. He went scatty then, and broke another winder with his fist. So the bobbies kicked his backside all the way on the street and locked him up for being drunk and disorderly."

The last part of the story brought a grin to Bill's face. As a policeman, that was the sort of incident he would have enjoyed.

"And since then you've been parted?" he asked.

Amy nodded. "I went home to my mother, till I could get a little place of my own. I do all right." Then she added coolly: "My husband set the figure for me. Five pounds for the full night."

Again, Bill avoided looking at her. A woman who could talk like that was too much for him. But he was more embarrassed than shocked. He had enough worries of his own without agitating himself about other people's morals. In his opinion prostitution was simply a concern of the harpy and her foolish customer, and the customer was invariably a man who was old enough to know exactly what he was doing. Plying her trade and keeping strictly to her terms, Amy would do nothing to pollute the youth of the nation, because youth could not afford to pay her price.

Nevertheless, he realized that as a policeman he would have occasion to obstruct the activities of Amy and others like her. He, who had never talked to a prostitute in his life. He looked at Amy now, with some curiosity. Her eyes were clear, and so was her complexion. Apart from that bold look, her appearance was quite normal. In physical fitness she looked as if she were somewhat better than normal. It did not occur to him that she was not more sexually overworked than a respectable young wife with a healthy and uxorious husband.

Presently Gunner said to Bill: "Let's go somewhere else. I've had enough of this fellow's ale."

Amy said: "Yes, and I must be going. We'll all go out together, the back way."

"All right," Gunner agreed. "But it's a mistake."

It was a mistake. Gunner went first, warily. He paused just inside the doorway. Outside was twilight, but there was a neon sign over the door which illuminated the whole of the inn yard. Gunner suddenly leaped out into the yard, thus avoiding being hit from both sides by two men. He was immediately engaged in combat by a thickset man of about his own height. Amy rushed unwarily to his assistance, and received a back-handed slap on the face which sent her reeling against the doorpost. Bill followed to encounter McGeen, who had slapped Amy. He was ready for McGeen. The latter's attempt to seize his lapels was met by a hard body blow. McGeen belched stinking breath, but he managed to get the lapels. He pulled. His head came forward to butt, and his knee came up to cripple: a very old, elementary, but often successful trick. But Bill had been warned that McGeen would try to "tup" him, and he got his hands up in time. He caught the man's forehead on the heel of his left hand and, pulling back, he chopped down hard at the eyes and nose with his right. He blocked the rising knee with his own knee.

From this knee action, McGeen was the first to recover firm standing. He spun Bill round, tripped him, and threw him down; and followed closely, kicking. But Bill was rolling away even before he touched the ground, and he was covering in defense even as he bounced up onto his feet. Then there was an exchange of blows which ended when Bill landed a crushing right which sent McGeen staggering back. He was following up his advantage when he heard a scream of warning from Amy. Before he could turn his head to learn the cause of that, he was shocked by the impact of a lead-and-brass knuckleduster. It struck him high on the cheekbone, on the left side of his face. He realized dimly that Gunner must have been put out of action, so that now he had to fight two men. After that blow, he was hardly in a condition to fight at all.

Nevertheless, he managed to remain on his feet a little longer. He temporarily ignored McGeen and assailed the man with the knuckleduster, hitting him so hard that he went down. But it had been a mistake to turn away from McGeen. The next thing he knew was a firm grasp upon his collar and sleeve, and a shoe heel pressed against his ankle to make it the pivot of his balance. He was thrown down heavily onto the cobbles of the yard. He rolled, covering his face with his arms, for he sensed that soon he would have to protect himself from the feet of both his adversaries.

Meanwhile Amy was quite literally screaming bloody murder, and trying to hinder McGeen by beating him on the back of the head with her handbag. Her screams brought people from the inn and from the street.

The newcomers saw one injured man struggling to get to his feet, and two men kicking another who was down. There were growls of protest. But it takes a little time for honest, peaceable men to make up their minds to intervene in the affairs of hooligans, and there was no immediate move to stop the fight.

Then, from the street, a burly man in a dark suit and a bowler hat walked into the yard. He made no protest, and he did not hesitate. He went straight for McGeen, who was deeply absorbed in the infliction of grievous bodily harm, and turned him around and hit him. McGeen fell down, then looked up and recognized the man in the bowler hat. He sprang to his feet and fled. His companion also fled. Both men ran out of the yard and pattered away in the direction of Stag Lane.

By the time Bill realized that the fight was over, Bowler Hat was walking out of the yard. He did not see the man because when he rose to a sitting position he looked toward Gunner, who was standing on his feet and feeling gingerly in his mouth for loose teeth. Because Amy did not happen to know the name of the man who had intervened, Bill remained unaware that he had been rescued from serious harm by Detective Constable Adkin, whose tedious duty it was, this evening, to follow Gunner Byles about.

Bill rose to his feet and went over to Gunner. "You all right?" he asked.

"I think so," was the reply, "considering I've been walloped a couple of times with brass knuckles. I'll carve that sod like a Sunday joint when I see him. I'll carry a razor for him, that's what I'll do."

Bill also thought that a due vengeance would be sweet. "Who is he?" he wanted to know.

"Lew Frost, they call him. He's Frank McGeen's sidekick. They team up together in jobs of this sort. I'll slice him like bacon the next time I see him."

Amy came up, and assured Bill that she was unhurt except for a slightly swollen lip. "What about you?" she asked.

Bill had succeeded in protecting his face and genitals. His arms, ribs and back were sore, and he had a lump on his head like the top of an egg. The only visible injury was the welt on his face which the knuckleduster had made, but he knew that his face would be dirty like his hands and his clothes. That meant that he would not be able to present himself at the Starving Rascal before closing time. He could not let Gay see him looking as if he had been helping to put out a fire.

Amy saw the dissatisfaction in his face when he looked at his dusty trousers and scuffed shoes. "Come over to my place and have a wash and brush up," she said. Then she added quickly: "Both of you, I mean."

Amy lived not far away, in a street of battered Edwardian gentility where run-down property was let off in flats and furnished rooms. It was a little better than Champion Road, but it was well on the wrong side of Stag Lane and it was in the Champion Road area. She led the way through the open doorway of a tall house, climbed one flight of stairs covered in worn linoleum, and stopped at a door which was very noticeable because it had been newly painted. She produced a latchkey, and ushered the two men into what had once been a large front bedroom. There was an old marble fireplace which somebody had had the inspiration to paint glossy white, and the walls were done in a matt paint of a clean stone color. There was a modern suite in dark red velvet with a big deep settee which was placed in front of the fireplace, and the rest of the furniture, coffee tables, flower vases and such, reflected an ordinary, modern, but by no means deplorable taste.

Bill looked around with some curiosity. The next room, which had originally been much smaller than the living room, was divided up into a small bedroom, a smaller bathroom, and a tiny kitchen.

"Very nice," he said. "Everything you need."

"I painted it all myself," Amy said with pride. "And the furniture's all mine. And I've nobody to bother me as long as I pay my rent regular."

Bill looked at his hands.

"Here, let me have your coat," she said. "Then you can go and have a wash."

He peeled off his coat and rolled up the sleeves of his shirt. Amy's eyes sparkled when she looked at his massive arms. Gunner, watching her, grinned sardonically but refrained from comment.

While Bill had a wash, Amy brushed his coat. When Bill came out of the bathroom, Gunner went in. Amy did not brush Gunner's coat. She watched Bill while he stood before the mirror which was above the fireplace. He combed his hair, and while he was straightening his tie she came behind him and tried to grasp his thick moving biceps.

"Boy, aren't you strong!" she breathed. "I could tumble right over for you! I always did go for big men."

"It looks like it," was all Bill could find to say.

"You'd have exterminated Frank McGeen if it had been a fair fight," she said. "I could tell the way you were shaping."

Bill had his pride. He admitted that he thought he could have beaten McGeen. He said he thought that he was the fitter man of the two.

"I'll say you're fit," Amy responded with enthusiasm. "I'll bet you could give a girl a good time."

When she said that, with hot fingers on his arms, he was beset by a queer excitement. It was half a feeling of curiosity. He had heard men talk of women like Amy. If they liked a man they certainly knew how to make love to him. At that moment, the thought of Gay was not with him at all.

Amy slipped her arms round his waist and pressed herself against his back. Then she drew away as Gunner came out of the bathroom.

Bill picked up the clothes brush and flicked the dust from his trousers. Amy held his coat for him while he put it on. Then she looked at the small gold watch on her wrist, and Bill wondered if it was a gift from a gentleman friend.

"Twenty to ten," the girl said. "There's still time for a couple of drinks. Where shall we go?"

"The Con is the nearest," said Gunner. So they went to the Confederate Flag, a public house of a similar type to the Run-

97

ning Stag, in a street behind Stag Lane. Amy led the way into
the lounge bar, and Bill followed her. Gunner came last.

Among the people at the bar were Frank McGeen and Lew
Frost. McGeen was talking, and Frost, who half-faced the door,
was laughing at his remarks. Neither of them saw the three who
entered. Amy caught Bill's arm and said: "Hadn't we better go
out?" and Bill said: "No, certainly not." Gunner did not say anything. He looked quickly around. On a table near the door were
some glasses and an empty beer bottle, capacity one pint. Gunner
reached over and grabbed the bottle, and threw it at Frost. It
was a good shot from five yards' range. It caught the man full on
his grinning mouth. He reeled backward along the bar, sweeping
off several glasses with his arm as he fell.

Then Gunner was gone. Bill saw McGeen turn and look at
him, and at the door which was still swinging. Amy pulled at his
arm, to get him to the door, but he held his ground.

McGeen came toward him. The manager, a burly man, also
came from behind the bar.

"You threw that bottle," McGeen accused.

"No, he didn't," said a woman at the nearby table. "He had
nothing to do with it."

"It were a chap who came in and ran out again," said one of
the men with her.

"It was this man's pal, then," McGeen growled.

"I never saw the man before," said Bill, wanting to applaud
Gunner for what he had done. "He just followed us in."

"That's right. We don't know him from Adam," Amy corroborated.

"You'd better go and look after your mate. He's spitting
teeth," the manager said to McGeen.

The big man turned away reluctantly, still glaring ferociously.
The manager said to Bill: "Take no notice. It's some sort of a
mob do."

With that, Bill would have stayed for a drink, but Amy refused. "Do you want them to do you right?" she whispered
fiercely. "Let's get away!"

They went out, and across the road into a big fish-and-chips
shop. The shop ran straight through from street to street, the
front entrance being in Stag Lane. Two doors along Stag Lane

from there was the Boar Hotel, a place of some size and considerable tone. Amy led the way in, and into a snug bar which was all shaded lights and deep carpets and quiet voices.

"You can't get draught beer in here," she said. "Only bottled. But at least we can drink it in peace."

Bill ordered two bottles of light ale from a white-coated barman who was regarding Amy and himself with a certain amount of disapproval.

"I wonder where Gunner's got to," he remarked.

"Who cares?" Amy rejoined, smiling into his eyes.

chapter

nine

That Monday evening, Bill Knight's discretion was assailed by Amy McGeen's power of attraction. As they talked over their drinks, he did not see her as a promiscuous woman, something to be scorned; he saw her simply as a woman. She seemed to be a sensible and amusing woman, and a good sort.

But discretion won, or perhaps it was not discretion. A cool remark she made, about some man she had known, reminded him that last night, and the night before, she had been intimate with other men. He recoiled, with a revulsion which was both physical and mental. It was then that he thought of consequences. He was a policeman: he would be very unwise to become involved with a woman of her sort. Then there was Gunner, who would not keep someone else's secret. There might be trouble with Mrs. Byles, and there might be trouble with Junie. At any rate, Junie would be distressed. Bill did not want her to be distressed: she had been good to him.

Memory of Junie's artless confession of virginity came to him, and he grinned suddenly.

"Did I say something?" Amy wanted to know.

Bill shook his head. He finished his drink because the time was five minutes after ten, and the disapproving barman was frowning in his direction.

"I think that guy doesn't like me," he said. "I guess I look a bit too rough for this place, with a busted knuckle and a big bruise on the side of my head."

"Who cares what he likes, or who he likes?" Amy demanded quite loudly, looking at the barman with contempt. "Let's go. If you want another drink you can have one at my place. I've got plenty in."

"I'll see you to your door, Amy, but I won't come in. Gunner knows we're together. If I'm home very late—"

"What makes you think you might be home very late?" came the sharp query.

"Nothing," was the hasty disclaimer. Then, rather feebly: "You don't know me when I get my feet under somebody's table."

"Are you thinking it might cost you money?" Amy asked straightforwardly, without unfriendliness.

"Certainly not."

"Are you afraid the Gilmour girl might get to know? Gunner says you're keen on her."

Bill had not thought of Gay. There was indeed a possibility that she might hear of him consorting with Amy. And if she did, of course she would never speak to him again. He asked himself, what on earth had he been thinking about? Himself and a woman who was notorious! And all because she had made a few advances.

"I don't want Gunner shouting my affairs all over the place, that's all," he said. He looked at the clock again. "Come on, let's go. I'll see you home, at any rate."

"I'm no debutante. I don't need an escort," said Amy. "We'll go out of here together, but I'll take myself home."

Bill looked at her. There had been no rancor in her voice. She was neither hurt nor offended. The women of the Byles family, he thought, were certainly easygoing, or good-tempered, or tolerant, or something.

They left the hotel. Outside, Amy said: "Cheerio, Bill. Keep your eyes open in case you get ambushed." Then she stepped off briskly. Bill went in the opposite direction.

As he walked along, Bill thought about Amy's lightly-spoken warning. It was not likely that McGeen and Frost would be persistent enough to try to waylay Gunner or himself somewhere near Hudson House. But it was possible. Bill remembered Frost's knuckleduster. He began to sort out the larger coins among the change in his pocket. All the pennies, half-crowns, and florins he put apart in his hip pocket.

There were not many people about in Champion Road. Most of the inhabitants who were out for the evening were still lingering in bars or sitting in cinemas. The fish-and-chips shops and supper places were not yet busy. Bill was a few minutes too early. He hoped that he might even be too early for McGeen.

When he was about a hundred yards from home he heard a soft, clear whistle. It sounded to be behind him. He turned and saw a thickset figure emerge from an opening across the street, forty yards back. That was Frost, who had let him pass. McGeen came running from the direction of Hudson House.

Bill knew that he could not avoid conflict with both men. If Frost had been between himself and home he would have had a chance to brush the man aside and reach sanctuary. But he could not brush McGeen aside. McGeen could delay him until Frost came up. He moved five yards to the nearest street lamp and stood there in good light with his back to a six-foot wall.

McGeen was walking now, and so was Frost. There was no need for them to hurry. Or so they thought. But Bill was getting his change from his pocket. He had a good deal of change. He held most of it in his clenched right fist but thrust nine coins, in three groups of three, between the strong fingers. The edges of the coins protruded slightly.

Frost reached him first, but halted out of reach. He did not speak, but he grinned. Then McGeen came up, and said: "Now I've got you. My wife won't like your face when I've finished with you."

Bill did not reply. He was watching closely, looking for an opportunity to slip past McGeen and run home.

A voice hailed them. "Don't start without me. I'll make one in."

Bill recognized the voice of Tom Casey. McGeen did not. With a curse, he turned his head to look. Bill leaped forward and struck. It was a terrible blow. McGeen had instinctively moved in evasion, and the loaded fist caught him high on the side of the face, cutting flesh and biting into bone. He went down in the gutter like a smitten bullock.

Bill knew that now he had no need to run. He knew that McGeen was out of the fight. Apparently Frost knew it also. He fled as Bill turned on him. Bill did not pursue.

Casey came up, alcoholically lubricated in every joint. His gait was unsteady, his knees sagged, and his head rolled. "Holy Kerry, it's the cock lodger himself!" he said cheerfully. "Bless you, you've spoiled the fight."

Bill quietly dropped his coins into his pocket. "Thank you for being alive, Tom," he said. "You saved me from a hiding."

They stood looking down at McGeen. One side of the man's face was a bloody ruin. He was quite unconscious, and he snored a little as he breathed.

With wobbly head Casey pretended to look round for something. "Where did you put the poleaxe?" he asked, and then he said: "I saw you do that with one blow of your fist, man."

Bill nodded, and the Irishman said: "Don't ever hit me, man. Do me that favor, will you?"

"I'll never quarrel with you, Tom," said Bill. "I'm indebted to you." And then he said: "What are we going to do with this fellow?"

"You want to do something else to him?"

"Well, I can't leave him lying there, can I?"

"Why not? He's not dead."

"I'll ring for an ambulance."

"Do what you like," said Casey. He turned, and resumed his rubber-legged journey home. Bill went to the public telephone box, and dialed 999.

As is usual with a 999 call, the post-office operator asked for the caller's name and address. Bill said: "Tom Smith, twenty-two Tickle Street."

"Who are you kidding?" the operator wanted to know.

"I'm kidding you," Bill said. "But it's true there's a man lying injured in Champion Road, not far from Bagdad Street. You'd better send the ambulance."

After that, he waited in the shadow of the Hudson House doorway until he saw the ambulance arrive, then he went inside.

The family was in the kitchen. Bill was surprised to see Gunner already home, and Gunner was surprised to see Bill. He grinned, and said so. "Our Amy was making a dead set at you," he added.

Bill saw Junie's anguished face, and he observed Rosemary's look of amusement and curiosity. He also noticed that Mrs. Byles was watching enigmatically.

"Not she," he answered lightly. "You imagine things."

"Didn't you go back home with her?"

"I did not. After you ran away we had one drink at the Boar Hotel. I left her outside there, and she went home."

The pain went from Junie's eyes. She moved over to him as he sat down at the table. She squeezed his shoulder as she asked him what he would have for his supper.

"Oh, anything," he said.

She went into the pantry, and when she returned she was carrying a plate of cold roast beef and a plate of bread-and-butter.

Gunner glared when he saw the food. "Why didn't you tell me there was some beef?" he demanded.

"You never asked me."

"You put it where I couldn't find it, anyway. You had it hid. It's favoritism, that's what it is."

Mrs. Byles said "Oh, shut up." Then she said to Bill: "I'm putting your rent up when you get yourself another job, young fellow. You're getting more meals in this kitchen than I bargained for."

With his mouth full of beef Bill nodded his assent to the proposal. The woman looked at him with rare benevolence.

"Am I the son and heir in this house, or is he?" Gunner burst out.

"You're the son, but you won't be the heir."

"There'll be an heir, at any rate. That chap our Junie is feeding up will make sure of that. He'll be in bed with all your daughters before he's done."

Mrs. Byles did not deny the possibility. "Whatever he does,

he'll be straight about it," she said. "I'd like to see one of my daughters with a pup off him."

Rosemary giggled. Junie was laughing and blushing. Bill bent over his meal. He was not only embarrassed, he was ashamed. What would Mrs. Byles say when she learned that he was a policeman? She detested policemen. He had heard her say that she did.

"I'm not all that you think I am," he mumbled.

"Don't fret yourself about what I think," the woman said. "I know you're not an angel. No man is. But you've done very well so far, for all our Junie could do. And our Amy."

Gunner said, "Hell fire!" in absolute disgust, and went off to bed. A few minutes later Mrs. Byles sent the girls to bed. Then when she was alone with Bill she said quietly: "You do think our Gunner did that murder, don't you?"

He was taken by surprise. "What makes you say that?" he countered.

"Just the way you look at him sometimes. But you don't seem to mind being in his company. You even drink with him. Is that because of curiosity? Are you wanting to find out for yourself?"

Bill was astounded, and dismayed. He saw himself in danger of being unmasked by this strange woman. And he did not want to be unmasked. He did not want to be shown up as an impostor. It would be bad enough having to announce that when the time came, but it would not be so bad as being discovered to be a police spy.

"I don't want to find out for myself," he said.

"For somebody else then? The Gilmour girl?"

"No, I don't know that I want to find out for her, either."

"Why do you stop on here, after you've lost your job? Fellows don't, as a rule. Either they move on or go back where they came from."

"I've got to stay somewhere, haven't I?"

"It isn't because of Gay Gilmour, or whatever her real name is. I'm thinking she'd sooner have you living in another part of town."

"I don't know whether I shall stay here, anyway," said Bill. "Do you want me to go?"

She shook her head. "Stay as long as you like, lad. The place is big enough. Is it right our Gunner got Lew Frost in the teeth with a bottle?"

Bill grinned. "It's true enough. It was a right good shot."

"I know Frost. He's bad. Did the bother start with our Amy?"

Bill told her about that, and, because he did not know what Tom Casey would say, he also mentioned the ambush in Champion Road.

"You were middling lucky," she commented. "You got your own back. But I wouldn't get too thick with our Amy, if I were you. She got a bad bargain when she married McGeen, but it's no excuse for her being the shameless article she is. There's one good thing; they don't spoil two families."

"She doesn't seem to come here much."

"She doesn't come at all. We meet when I see her in the street, that's all. I wouldn't let her come here. There's too many men. I'm not going to give the coppers a chance to call this place a brothel. I'm keeping in the clear. Right in the clear."

"That seems to be your favorite motto."

"It is. Nobody looks after you if you don't look after yourself."

"You seem to take it well when your children don't turn out as they should. It doesn't break your heart."

"How do you know? You don't know whether it does or not, do you? But it's no use wittering. Take our Junie and Rosem'ry. I think our Junie's going to be the best of the bunch, but you never can tell. Those two know what day it is. They've known the facts of life since they were ten. They know what can happen to 'em if they don't behave. If they're going to turn out bad, they'll be bad, no matter what I say."

Bill was silent. He could not find tactful words to make the protest which was in his mind. But the woman seemed to understand.

"You didn't like it," she said, "when I made the crack about one of the girls having a pup off you. Don't worry. The girls know what they should do and what they shouldn't do, if that ever made any difference. They know I didn't mean it. That sort of talk passes for humor in this house. You notice how they laughed? We're coarse people, we are. We're not respectable. Respectable! There's a lot of shits as call theirselves respectable. Hiding their own sins and watching other folk so's they can speak badness about 'em, that's being respectable. Me and my girls don't owe nothing to nobody. Whatever else we do, we mind our own business and we don't *judge* people."

Bill refrained from comment. It had occurred to him that the change in the conversation had at least served to turn Mrs. Byles's attention from his affairs to her own. For the time being. In her reflective moments she would be thinking about him again. He would have to be careful. She was interested in him and she was alarmingly perceptive. Once again he heartily wished that this hole-and-corner business was finished, so that he could face the world squarely and let everybody know who he was and what he was.

Mrs. Byles was still dwelling upon herself and her children. "Anyway," she said thoughtfully, "my three oldest is a bad lot. Happen I failed somewhere, somehow."

"One never knows what to do for the best," Bill said sententiously, then he yawned and announced that he was going to bed.

He said good night to Mrs. Byles and went upstairs. He undressed slowly, thinking about the recent conversation. He was in no hurry. Nobody would tell him to get up in the morning. If he idled in bed till noon even his police bosses could not say anything to him, because he would be playing the part of an out-of-work foundry hand having a lazy day or two.

He had a bath, and lay in the warm water for a long time. Then he went to bed and lay smoking in the dark, in no hurry to get to sleep. His bedroom door was ajar. He always left it that way to strengthen his pose as a man with nothing to hide. The house was quiet, and so it was that he thought he heard someone move very quietly up the stairs and go past his door. The night walker went by with so little noise that only the faint creak of floorboards betrayed his presence.

Bill listened with suspended breath. He heard nothing more for a few seconds, and he was beginning to think that he had been mistaken when he heard a faint but definite metallic click. He listened, and he was unable to judge whether the sound had come from close at hand or from a little distance. He heard the click again, fainter this time, and then he heard nothing more.

He reached down and stubbed his cigarette on the floor. He

was now very comfortable in bed, and he did not want to get up. He was inclined to think that the noise he had heard was connected with something trivial, something which was no concern of his. He wondered about Junie, sleeping alone in the room across the passage. Perhaps she had been downstairs for something. Perhaps what he had heard had merely been Junie returning to her room.

Perhaps it was somebody, one of the lodgers maybe, creeping into Junie's room.

He was out of bed in an instant, groping for his slippers. He went to the door and listened. He looked out. A faint lightening in the otherwise complete darkness of the passage told him that Junie's door was open. He could hear her breathing evenly. There was no other sound.

He could not remember if Junie's door had been open when he came to bed, but he knew that she usually left it open. Everything seemed to be in order.

Still, he had heard a noise. He stepped across the passage and looked into Junie's room, but it was too dark for him to distinguish anything. He switched on the light. Junie was sound asleep. She looked very pretty and innocent in sleep. One arm and one soft shoulder were exposed. Her skin was faintly golden. One of these brown-skinned blondes, he noted.

He turned out the light and moved to the bathroom. There was nobody in the bathroom. So then, if there was an intruder on the top floor, he could only be in one place: lurking around the corner of the passage, where the locked door was.

Bill did not turn on the passage light, because that would have put him in silhouette at the corner. With his left hand outstretched, and his right fist ready, he groped his way forward in absolute darkness. He turned the corner and felt his way along to the door. The door was locked. It had the solid immovability of a strong door which has not been opened for a long time.

He felt rather foolish, and he was glad that no one could have witnessed his activities of the last minute or two. "This job is making you windy, Knight," he told himself. He returned to his room, and climbed into bed, and went to sleep.

chapter

ten

On the next day, Tuesday, Bill Knight was in the Starving Rascal only a few minutes after the midday opening time. He was Gay Gilmour's first customer of the day. She asked him if he had found a job, and his negative reply made her frown.

"You'll never do any good if you shilly-shally around like this," she said. "You won't live a thousand years, you know."

He understood that she was a serious-minded girl who was displeased with him for his own good. She wanted him to achieve something in life. That was reasonable and right. He had been brought up to think along the same lines.

"Don't you worry about me," he said. "I know what I'm doing. I've got my job picked out, but there's no hurry."

"What sort of job?"

"A job you'll be pleased about. But I don't want anybody to know till it's all fixed up."

"You can tell me. I won't spread it around."

"I know you won't," he said, smiling at her to remove all offense. "You can't if you don't know."

"Don't you trust me?"

"Sure I trust you. I'm just saving you the trouble of having to be careful what you say."

She pouted, and moved away to serve two women who had entered the bar. When she returned, he asked: "What's new? Have you found a will yet?"

She shook her head. "We've given up looking," she said. "Daddy is awfully worried. He's finally come round to the idea that there just isn't a will. I've thought all along that there wasn't."

"You don't sound worried. I don't think you realize what a few thousand pounds could mean to a girl like you."

"I certainly do realize, but you see I'd never thought about inheriting anything. I expected Sam to live for years and years. It isn't as if I'd been making plans about what I'd do with his money after he was dead."

"I see what you mean. It's a pity, all the same. It's a few thousand quid lost. Have you been told who is likely to get it?"

"No, I haven't. I think Daddy knows, but he pretends he doesn't. He doesn't want me to know."

Bill decided that if John Harper did not want to tell her about Mrs. Byles, neither did he.

"What's going to happen, then?" he asked. "They'll have to do something about this place. They're just using you, giving you the responsibility of looking after everything. And not a sausage will you get out of it."

"The estate is paying me," she said, smiling at the touch of indignation in his voice. "And it's a roof over my head. I might as well be working at this as working at something else."

"Oh, I suppose so," he growled, and then he made a mistake. He had been trying to keep one side of his face slightly turned away from her, but now he forgot. She noticed his bruised and swollen cheekbone.

"Have you been fighting?" she asked sharply.

"I did have a bit of trouble," he admitted. "I couldn't help it. It was forced on me."

Her lips were compressed in disapproval. "Where?" she asked. He told her.

"Who were you with?" she demanded.

Feeling that he was innocent of blame, he told her the entire story. And then he wished he had told her only part of it. The mention of Amy McGecn made her really angry. He would not have believed that she could be so scathing and contemptuous.

"Fighting in a pub yard!" she said with a curling lip. "And in what company? Gunner Byles and his sister! I've heard about her and I know what she is."

"I just happened to meet them," Bill explained.

"You're just like all the others who come in here," she said bitterly. "You're a low-lifer. It was plain from the start, and I don't know what made me think you were different. You came to Airechester and made straight for Champion Road, like a crow to the flock. Why didn't you go to a decent neighborhood? If you had anything about you, you wouldn't stop at the Byles place for two minutes. And you'd be out looking for a decent job, instead of sitting there drinking."

"I tell you the job's looked after," he said. "It's practically nailed on."

"I don't believe there is a job. You're just too bone idle to go and look for one."

"I tell you I've got a job."

"It's all the same to me whether you have or not," she said disdainfully. "It's no concern of mine."

Bill could only take so much of that sort of thing, even from Gay. "I was just going to point that out to you," he said with a glint in his eye.

She walked away from him and served a customer, and then she remained aloof at the other end of the bar. Watching her, Bill got the impression that she was expecting some particular person, and quite soon he knew that he had not been mistaken. The door swung open and the handsome Mr. Draper entered, with a breeze and a haw-haw and a big smile. He made straight for Gay, and her own smile was gay indeed. Bill could not bear to see it. He drank off his beer and stamped out of the inn.

"To hell with her," he swore as he went in the direction of the Friar Tuck Inn, and he glared so fiercely at a passer-by that the man shrank from him. The pain of intense jealousy was like a poison working in his vitals. The feeling was new to him, and he was in no state to diagnose it. The way he saw it, the sight of Gay making eyes at another man just made him sick.

He went into the Friar Tuck and ordered a double whiskey, and drank it neat. Then he bought a pint of beer to wash away the taste of the whiskey. The beer also cooled his temper. The pangs of jealousy abated. He dismissed the slender Mr. Draper from his thoughts, and considered Gay's point of view with regard to himself.

He had a mind which was conventional according to his upbringing and past environment. His ideas were the ideas of his class and country. He saw Gay's view of life, and he also perceived that it was a view almost suffocating in its righteous mediocrity. And yet he could not blame her for that. He told himself that she was a respectable girl and a girl of character. To remain unsmirched in her environment, she was compelled to keep to a rigid line of thought and conduct. When she married and moved away from Champion Road, he thought, she would grow more tolerant.

"Of course I look like a no-good to her," he reflected. "How can I look like anything else? It's a wonder she speaks to me at all. It's a wonder she ever even noticed me."

It occurred to him that the only way he could ever be right with Gay was by revealing who he was. He could not do that until the Gilmour murder was cleared. So get it cleared. Get it cleared and then tell Gay that he had been an undercover man. Only then could he satisfactorily explain his presence in Champion Road, his pub crawling and fighting, and his inferior lodgings.

Gay was one person in the district, perhaps the only one, who would applaud him and respect him for the part he had played. The others would have a hard name for him, because he was a policeman. But what did he care about any of them or all of them? Gay was the only one he cared about.

He took a long drink of his second pint. Get it cleared, he thought. How? Well, not by drinking pints of ale and waiting for something to turn up. He would have to wait a long time before Gunner Byles turned anything up. Gunner was as cunning as a whole family of foxes. He would not reveal anything. He would have to be forced in some way.

Gunner still had money, though he never showed a significant amount of it. The bulk of it was still hidden, probably with the coins, in a place where he could get at it. If the money and the coins were hidden in an accessible place, they could be found. They might even be in Hudson House. The police had searched the place, but they could have missed something. Bill decided that he would make a further search, when he had the chance.

He also decided that now was the time, or any day about noon. Gunner was invariably out at some pub, discussing the day's racing with anybody who was interested. Junie and her mother were in the kitchen, preparing the midday meal. Rosemary was

111

at Woolworth's store in City Street, where she was employed. The lodgers were all out at work, or in the pubs.

Now, Bill would have liked to leave the remaining half-a-pint of his beer, but he did not want to draw attention to himself by conduct which would be regarded as insanity in Champion Road. He drank the beer in two long swigs, and left the inn.

He was unperceived as he entered Hudson House, except by the police observer behind Greenbaum's window. The lodgers' common room was deserted. He listened at the kitchen door and he heard women's voices. He climbed the stairs, treading softly on the bare boards.

There were five doors on the first landing. Gunner's bedroom, his mother's, Rosemary's, a bathroom, and the lodgers' upstairs dormitory. To be sure that he was alone he looked into all the rooms except Gunner's. He did not look into Gunner's room because the door was locked.

The locked door excited him. It seemed to him that it would not be locked if there were not something worth the finding on the other side of it. He pondered how to get in. He knew that, if he asked, Fairbrother would provide him with an instrument to open Gunner's door, but he did not want to waste time in asking for help. He had a feeling of urgency about getting into the locked room.

He went into Rosemary's room, which was next door to Gunner's. Standing well back from the window he looked down into the yard. It was deserted. He opened the window and saw that Gunner's window was quite near, but it was closed. He stood on Rosemary's window sill and opened the window at the top, and leaned out. By craning he could see that Gunner's window was secured by an old-fashioned screw fastener. There was no way into the room by the window.

He returned to the landing and examined Gunner's door again. It had an ordinary mortise lock which appeared to have nothing special about it. He wondered if there would be another key which fitted it. He found a key on the inside of Mrs. Byles's door, but it was immovable in Gunner's lock. Then he tried the key from the inside of Rosemary's door. It turned smoothly in the lock.

He entered the room, and relocked the door. He gazed around.

The bed was untidy. It had that sunk-in-the-middle look of an old mattress which is seldom shaken up and never turned over. Apparently nobody ever made the bed unless Gunner did, and Gunner didn't. On a chair beside the bed there was a cup without a handle, with a small quantity of water in the bottom. There was also the lid of a shoe-polish tin which served as an ashtray. It was full of cigarette ends and ash. There was a careless scattering of ash, cigarette ends and spent matches on the floor near the chair.

Over the foot of the iron bedstead hung a pair of trousers and a soiled shirt. There were old shoes under the bed. The piece of carpet beside the bed was worn down to the jute. There was a chest of drawers with a tilted mirror on top. Over the mirror hung two creased ties and a crumpled collar. In the built-in wardrobe, clothes hung on hooks instead of on hangers.

Unlike the other bedrooms, which were clean and tidy, the room was fusty and dusty. Stale air lingered there. Bill sniffed it, and said "Pah!" The dust on the window sash, and on the thumb-piece of the screw fastener, showed that the window had not been opened for weeks.

There was dust everywhere, and especially on the floor. It showed that none of the furniture had been moved recently. Bill reflected that if any of the furniture was moved now, the dust would show Gunner that his room had been surreptitiously searched.

Obviously the dust had been a guide to the police in their search of the room. They had not found it necessary to move the furniture. Bill decided that neither would he move anything, unless he could lift it bodily and replace it exactly. But search he would. Thoroughly. More thoroughly than the police, he hoped.

He rummaged in the drawers, and lifted them out to make sure that none of them had a false back. He examined the built-in wardrobe, feeling the walls with his spread hand. He went through the pockets of all the clothes, and felt the linings and hems. He examined the bed, and the bedclothes, and the iron bedstead. He made sure that all floorboards were intact, and he went around the skirting boards as far as possible.

He straightened his back and stared around with a baffled air.

The walls and ceiling of the room had been distempered, a long time ago. The distemper had faded to an indeterminate blotchy gray color, but in no place did it show a crack, or a break of any kind.

There remained only the door and door frame, the walls and skirting behind the chest of drawers and under the bed, and the woodwork around the window. He examined the door and the window, and found nothing. He dared not move the chest of drawers. So he turned once more to the bed, which stood in a corner close to the wall.

He went down on hands and knees, and looked under the bed for the second time. For the second time he lifted up dusty shoes and felt inside, and carefully replaced them. The thick dust under there showed traces of recent disturbance. By the police when they searched, Bill supposed. He struck a match to see if the dust had been disturbed right up to the skirting boards.

The policeman who had searched under the bed had not crawled right under. Bill guessed that he had used a strong torch and seen a smooth, months-old layer of dust, and had reasoned that since nobody else had crawled under there neither need he. So the considerable length of skirting covered by the bed had not been examined.

Bill thought about that. Had the police lifted the bed away from the wall and then replaced it? That was unlikely, because they would then have tested the skirting and left footmarks beside it. Was there any other way of getting at the skirting? Of course! By moving the bed a foot or so away from the wall and then lying across it face down. In that way a man could reach the skirting and never leave a mark in the dust on the floor.

With some satisfaction because he had found a way to search in a place which had been missed by experienced police officers, but with no real hope of finding anything, he set to work to move the bed. He lifted it carefully and noiselessly, first by the head and then by the foot, setting it down gently so that it did not drag and make a mark in the dust. Then he stretched himself across the bed and looked down at the skirting, which was some seven inches deep. Right in the corner the board had warped and sprung a little away from the wall. He hooked a fingernail and then a finger behind the board, and pulled. He had to pull hard. He gasped with excitement when he saw a cavity behind the board. He pulled harder, and bent the board sufficiently to get a hand into the cavity. His fingers touched cool steel, and he pulled out a short jimmy with a one-inch spread at the business end.

One housebreaking tool. Good. What else? Next came a biscuit-colored leather glove, and there was something inside it: a small wad of folded notes. Bill counted them. There were twenty-five one-pound notes. He replaced them in the glove and thrust his hand into the cavity again.

This time he brought out a real prize. It was the second glove, and into it, as if it were a holster, a revolver had been thrust. The gun was an old Webley .45, and it was loaded in all six chambers. Bill put it aside. He groped around in the cavity again but found nothing else except an old-fashioned door key about five inches long. There was nothing else but fragments of brick, pieces of plaster, and dust. No coins. That was a disappointment.

In a hurry now, he replaced everything in the cavity except the gun and the key. He let the board go back into place. He moved the bed back into the corner, and then he picked up the gun and the key and pocketed them.

He listened at the door, then stepped out and locked it behind him. He replaced Rosemary's key, and he was just stepping away from the door when somebody came running up the stairs. There was no time for Bill to hide. He could only stand there, perfectly still.

Junie Byles came up the stairs and turned away from Bill, taking the further flight up to her own room. He held his breath as his glance followed her up the stairs.

Perhaps the intense anxiety in that following gaze conveyed some feeling to her, or perhaps his tall broad figure standing in the middle of the landing made some change in the light of a place which was as familiar to her as her own face in a mirror. She stopped on the stairs, and turned.

"What—" she began.

He stepped forward with a finger to his lips. "Quiet!" he ordered in a forceful whisper. "Go on up, as if you hadn't seen me. I'll explain later."

She stood looking down at him, more puzzled than suspicious.

"Go on," he urged, still speaking in a whisper. "And not a word to anybody. I'll tell you all about it tonight."

He smiled then, a rather taut, forced smile, and made a gesture indicating that she should go up to her room. Her own answering smile was doubtful, but she obeyed him.

When she had gone he made his way downstairs and out of the house. As he made his way toward Police Headquarters he wondered what he would tell Junie, when the time for an explanation came. He hoped that at least she would keep quiet until he had a good story ready.

chapter

eleven

Bill caught Fairbrother at Headquarters just as he was about to go to the canteen for some lunch. At first Bill was greeted with a frown, but when he said that he had found something lunch was forgotten. They returned to the inspector's office, and Bill produced the revolver and the key.

"Where did you find these?" was the inevitable question.

Bill described the cavity behind the skirting board, and he enumerated its contents.

"No coins?" Fairbrother asked.

"No coins."

"You're quite sure?"

"I'm quite sure."

"A pity," said the inspector. Nevertheless, he was pleased. He was also worried by a feeling that a man with as little experience as Bill would be sure to have made some mistake.

"Did you leave everything as you found it?" he queried. "Are you sure Gunner won't know you've been in his room?"

"He won't unless he finds that the pistol is missing, before I can put it back."

"But you must have disturbed the dust under the bed."

Bill told him about that. Fairbrother was impressed.

"Congratulations," he said. "It's a simple thing when you think of it, but it has to be thought of. You're good, you are."

"I'm not as good as all that," said Bill. He mentioned that Junie had seen him on the landing.

Fairbrother's anxiety returned. "Oh hell," he said. "She's bound to talk. You've had it."

"I told her I'd explain. I daresay she'll keep quiet."

"An eighteen-year-old girl? You've got a hope! What will you tell her?"

"I'm blessed if I know yet. I'll have to think of something."

"There's one thing. She may not connect your presence on the landing with Gunner's affairs. If she's got no idea you're a police agent, she'll think you were snooping around with the idea of pinching something out of Ma Byles's room."

"Well, in case she does spill the beans, the best thing for me to do is to replace the gun and the key in Gunner's room as soon as possible."

"How right you are!" Fairbrother snatched up the telephone, and soon he was talking in that tone of friendly urgency which policemen often reserve for those who assist them without fee.

"Hello, Bert. Those little items I asked you about. Are they ready? . . . The forty-fives are? Well, those are just what we want. Listen, Bert. Can you nip round with 'em right away? . . . Yes, we've got the gun, and we're in such a hurry to put it back. . . . You'll bring 'em round? Well, thanks, Bert. Thanks a lot."

"He's coming here with the bullets," he said, putting down the receiver. "Now then, what about this key? Any idea which lock it fits?"

Bill did have an idea, but he preferred not to say so. "If you can make me a copy I'll try it around," he said.

The inspector nodded. "It might lead you to the coins, you know. But we haven't time to take it to a locksmith. I'll have to take an impression. Wait here. I'll see if I can scrounge a bar of soap."

He went out, and returned with a long bar of crude soap of the kind used for scrubbing in municipal buildings. He cut the soap lengthwise and put the key between the two halves. He then put the soap on the desk and pressed down upon it with all his weight, until he had made a mold.

"There," he said, handing the key back to Bill. "We'll manage to make a copy, somehow. You'll have to call for it this evening, if you haven't been turned out of Hudson House."

They waited then for the man Bert. Fairbrother commented about the bruise on Bill's face. "How did the fight start?" he asked.

Bill told him.

The inspector was amused. "You'd have got a pasting if it hadn't been for one of your mates. Detective Officer Adkin dashed in there and chased 'em off."

"Convey my thanks, will you?" said Bill.

Fairbrother looked at him. "I'm told that McGeen was picked up in Champion Road later on. Not far from Hudson House. They say he looked as if he'd been hit by a cannon ball."

"Is that so? I hope he wasn't badly hurt."

"Not fatally, at any rate. They patched him up at the Dispensary and sent him home. He didn't say who'd clocked him. Did you do it?"

"If I did," said Bill, "it was in self-defense."

"I daresay it was. You're a rum lad. You can find trouble, all right. Incidentally those two, McGeen and Frost, are on my list. They were in the Starving Rascal on the night of the murder. I'm just telling you as a matter of interest. There's nothing to connect 'em with the job."

"I'd say they're good enough for it," said Bill.

"I agree with you," Fairbrother replied. "But I think Gunner Byles is our man."

Then Bert was shown into the office. He was a stout, red-faced young man who wore a sporty suit and large spectacles. He carried a small Gladstone bag.

He went straight to the desk, put down his bag, and picked up the gun. With the casual ease of long practice he "broke" the gun and ejected the six rounds onto the desk, talking as he did so. "You don't half rush a man, when you give him a bit of a job to do."

"Now then, Bert," said Fairbrother. "You know how we depend on you in these gun jobs."

"I notice you never give me anything for it. Not a sausage."

"Just send your bill in, Bert lad."

Bert grinned, and squinted through the gun barrel. "It'll do," he said. "This old gun hasn't seen a lot of active service. The rifling is in tip-top condition."

He took a small vise from his bag and began to fasten it to the edge of the desk. "I'll ruin your woodwork," he said with friendly malice.

"Carry on, Bert," said Fairbrother. "Who cares about a bit of an old desk?"

Bert padded the vise, and then with padded pliers he detached the leaden bullets from each of the six rounds. He put the bullets in his pocket, and he emptied the propellant from each beheaded copper cartridge into an envelope. Then from his bag he brought out some powder of his own, and poured a carefully measured quantity into each cartridge.

"Plenty of flash and bang about this stuff," he said. "But not too much drive."

"Clever, these Chinese," said Fairbrother.

Bert nodded, and then he took what appeared to be a handful of cotton wool from his bag. He unrolled the cotton wool, and disclosed six bullets. They looked exactly the same as the bullets he had put in his pocket. "I blackleaded 'em to make 'em look old," he said.

"And are these guaranteed not to hurt anybody?" the inspector asked.

"They wouldn't knock a pimple off your nose," said Bert. "They're heavy, but they're hollow."

He explained how he had made an oversize mold and a core, so that he could manufacture a slightly oversize, hollow bullet. He had made a number of bullets, and filled each one with a compound of heavy powders, mainly powdered graphite. "When the gun is fired," he went on patiently, "the bullet will naturally be driven through the barrel. But because it's oversize the lands in the barrel—the projecting ridges of the rifling—will cut that thin lead into bits and pieces. The whole thing will disintegrate."

"Have you tried firing one of these bullets?" Fairbrother wanted to know.

"Of course. I've fired several. There's an old kettledrum in my cellar. I stood it up on a bench and fired at it from two yards range. The drumskin wasn't even punctured."

"Well, that sounds safe enough," was the relieved comment. "And does it have the sound and appearance of an ordinary discharge?"

"It throws a bit of dust out," Bert admitted. "But it looks pretty much like gunsmoke. It won't hurt anybody, because people have a tendency to shut their eyes for a second when a gun flashes in their face."

While he talked, Bert had been assembling the doctored rounds of ammunition with careful dexterity. Bill, himself a man of his hands, watched him with great interest.

Very soon Bert loaded the treated shells into the revolver and pulled down the safety catch. "There you are," he said, handing the weapon to Fairbrother.

"And there you are," said the inspector, passing the gun to Bill. "Off you go. You may not have a minute to spare."

Bill departed, leaving the others talking. As he went he heard Fairbrother say: "I hope your freak bullets are never put to the test. I don't like firearms."

"I love 'em," was Bert's reply.

The time was twenty minutes past one when Bill left Police Headquarters. He was a good half-hour late for lunch when he arrived at Hudson House. He thought he had better have his meal first and go upstairs afterward.

He went into the kitchen. Gunner was at the table, eating. Junie was perched on the end of the sofa, smoking a cigarette. Mrs. Byles was saying: "You don't want to start with them things. They'll make your teeth brown."

Bill sat down at the table. Junie put out her cigarette and went to get his dinner from the oven. "Where you been?" Gunner asked, speaking with his mouth full.

"Out," said Bill.

"Huh. Starving Rascal, I bet."

"I was in there for ten minutes," said Bill.

"I notice you still keep away from there," Mrs. Byles said to Gunner.

He snarled an insult. She looked at him with cool speculation.

Bill gave Junie's hand a friendly squeeze when she put his dinner before him. She said, "Ooh, that hurt!" and looked pleased about it. As she smiled at him she seemed to be no longer doubtful about him. She was content to wait for his explanation, or else she had invented one for her own reassurance. He reflected that she was a good kid, a damn decent kid.

"I think we'll get you a job as a barmaid, Junie," said Mrs. Byles, as if the notion had just entered her mind for the first time. "It'll give you a chance to meet the lads."

"I don't want to meet any lads," said Junie.

"Only Mr. Knight," Gunner observed. "She only wants to meet Mr. Knight. He's a lad, all right. He's a lad and a half."

Bill grinned as he ate his dinner. Junie said to her brother: "Don't you wish you were?"

"I'm as good as he is, any time," Gunner said shortly. He pushed his empty plate away and took a final swig at his mug of strong tea. He stood up, pushing his chair back as he did so. "I'm off," he said, picking up his cap on the way to the door. "I got business." The door slammed behind him.

"Where's he going?" Bill asked, as if he did not really care whether or not he was answered.

"He's off to the billiard hall," said Junie. "He's going to play somebody at snooker for a pound."

"That's where he's getting his money, playing snooker," said Mrs. Byles. Then she added: "So he says."

Bill nodded, thinking about Gunner. He would undoubtedly play more than one game of snooker. He would talk about racing with the layabouts and unemployables who frequented the billiard hall. Racing results would be coming in half-hourly. Gunner would probably not be home until teatime.

Bill finished his meal and lit a cigarette. He talked for a while with the woman and the girl, about nothing much. Then he threw away his cigarette end and yawned. Watching carefully with sleepy eyes, he said: "I think I'll go and have a lie down. There's nothing else to do."

"You might as well," said Mrs. Byles, so blandly that he wondered if she knew, or suspected, that sleep was not in his mind. Junie said nothing, and her face was without expression. There was no way of telling what she thought.

Bill went upstairs to his own room, and put the revolver and the key under his pillow. Junie's bedroom door was open. He looked in. The bed was neatly made. He folded back the sheets and made an apple-pie bed. No sooner had he finished than Junie appeared in the doorway. Though he had been alert for an interruption, he had not heard her come up the stairs.

"What are you doing in my room?" she demanded.

"Why, nothing," he said with exaggerated innocence. "I was just looking round. You keep it nice and tidy."

"People don't go into other folks' rooms for nothing. What are you after?"

"Nothing, I tell you. What is there in your room that could possibly interest me?"

"I don't know, but it's funny. Had you been in Ma's room when I saw you this morning?"

"Crumbs, no!" he said. "I was going to go into Rosem'ry's room, but I changed my mind when you spotted me."

"What did you want in there?"

He grinned. "I was going to tell you, but now I won't."

She looked hurt, and worried. "We get all sorts here," she said. "We get thieves, sometimes. And we haven't known you for long."

His grin faded. "So you think I'm a thief," he said coldly.

"Oh, Bill," she cried. "I don't really. I don't want to think that. It would be so awful if you were trying to steal from us."

He stood looking at her. She met his glance with troubled eyes. "Come here," he said, stepping toward the bed.

She came into the room. "Take your shoes off," he said, turning the bed down a little.

Her eyes were wide. Vivid color came into her cheeks. "Wha —what are you going to do?" she breathed.

Looking down at her, he realized that her faintly-golden skin was very clear and fine, something special. He realized that she was a right bonny girl.

"Go on, take your shoes off," he ordered.

She kicked off her shoes.

"Now get into bed," he said. "Go on, I'm not going to touch you."

"What have I to get into bed for?"

"Go on! Do as I tell you!"

Never moving her wide-eyed, perplexed glance from his face, Junie got onto the bed. She sat in the middle of it, near the pillow. Her knees were up beneath her chin and her skirt tucked around them, and her legs were close together, hugged in her arms. He had to smile. He had guessed, somehow, that she would get into bed that way.

"Well, go on," he said, smiling broadly now.

She pushed her feet down into the bed, then she tried to slide into a recumbent position. She did not get very far. An expression of panicky amazement came into her face as the folded sheets stopped her.

"I can't get in," she wailed, and then she began to laugh. "Oh, Bill, you silly beggar! You've done something to the bed."

"Do you mean to tell me you've never seen an apple-pie bed before?"

"No, I never," she said, and he had a pang of pity for her. He perceived that a girl reared in the Byles family must have missed a great deal of innocent childish fun. He remembered Mrs. Byles's words. "They've known the facts of life since they were ten." Poor kid, he thought.

She got out of the bed. "How did you do it? Show me," she demanded.

He showed her. Her eyes sparkled. "Shall we go and do our Rosem'ry's bed?" she suggested.

"Well, not just now. I'm ready for a nap. Some other time, happen."

"We'll do Ma's as well."

"No fear! Not me. I'm leaving your mother's bed alone."

She put her arms round his neck and pressed her strong young body against him. Holding her lightly, he smiled down into her face.

"I am glad," she said. "It was just a joke, and I was thinking all sorts."

"I told you I'd explain, didn't I?"

She nodded contritely, and then she kissed him. "I wish you'd hold me forever," she said.

The warm sweetness of her aroused considerable feeling in him. It also brought his conscience into full operation. Deception in the interests of duty was necessary, but this was something else entirely. It wasn't fair to indulge in even a little dalliance with a girl when at the same time he was trying to find evidence which would convict her brother of murder. Besides, there was important work to be done. And furthermore her mother probably knew that she was upstairs with him. Her mother might come upstairs at any moment.

He gave Junie a gentle squeeze and pushed her away. "You're far too forward for your own good," he said. "You'll get yourself into trouble."

"I'd love it," she replied, seizing his arm and giving it a sudden fierce hug.

"That's what you think. Now go downstairs and let a man get some sleep. And don't go telling your mother I've been in your room. She might not like it."

She released his arm with reluctance, and put on her shoes. He listened to the brisk, happy patter of her footsteps as she went downstairs. He went and lay fully clothed on his bed, and lit a cigarette. When he had smoked the cigarette, he decided, he would go downstairs and replace the gun and the key in Gunner's room. And this evening he would receive a copy of the key. He thought that he could walk straight to the door which it would open. And through the door might be the way to the stolen coins, the all-important coins.

twelve

On Wednesday morning the Starving Rascal case suddenly came to life. It came to life in the ancient city of York, some twenty-five miles from Airechester. A very big man with a spectacular wound on one side of his face entered the small shabby shop of a jeweler whom the local police had suspected, at various times, of receiving stolen property. The jeweler looked at the man and his injury with interest. The latter was cut, abraded, contused and swollen, and it looked very sore. The jeweler decided that it was a beauty, and he wondered what instrument or part of a house had caused it.

But he ceased to think about that when the man put a roughly molded bar of gold on the counter. He picked up the bar, and weighed it lovingly in his hand. His eyes glittered with greed, but behind the greed was the shadow of regret. Because he was not honest he read the regular police circulars more closely than other jewelers, and he was thinking of seventy-four stolen coins which could have been melted down to make a bar similar to the one he held in his hand. Even so, he might have taken a chance and bought the gold for a fraction of its value, and got rid of it quickly through one of his available channels. But the theft he had in mind was connected with murder, and transactions with murderers or the accomplices of murderers were altogether too dangerous.

The big man was watching him steadily. The jeweler looked up at him, and felt afraid of him.

"You want to sell it?" he asked. "I'd better weigh it."

With the gold in his hand he turned to go to his back room.

"Hold on a minute," the man said suddenly, and the jeweler's nerves jumped. "Leave the gold and bring your scales here."

"As you wish," the jeweler said. He put down the gold and went for the scales.

Like nearly all fences, the jeweler had the heart of a stool pigeon. Now he saw a chance to get into the good graces of the police. If he put a murderer into their hands, perhaps they would be less suspicious of him for a while. It would be easy enough to do, if his nerves could stand the strain of waiting and delaying the dangerous-looking stranger.

As he went into the back room, which was a small workroom, his apprentice looked up. The jeweler put a finger to his lips, for silence. Then he drew the finger across his forehead, which the apprentice knew to be the "copper" signal. Then he made the action of dialing and listening to a telephone, and then he drew three nines in the air.

The apprentice nodded. The jeweler picked up his scales and returned to the shop with them, without having been appreciably delayed. He casually closed the door of the workroom behind him. The apprentice slipped out the back way to the shop next door, where there was a telephone.

York is a notably ancient city, but there is nothing antiquated about its constabulary. The police responded to an emergency call from a jeweler as quickly as they would have done in London or Liverpool or anywhere, and in three minutes' time a car came sliding at speed round the corner and into the street where the jeweler had his shop.

As soon as the car appeared there was movement near the jeweler's. A sturdily built man who had been standing at the curb strode to the shop window, and then began to walk away. A moment later a big man came out of the shop and saw the police car, which was now quite close to the shop. He also began to walk away.

In the car were two detectives and a police driver. "We'd better have both those fellows," said one of the detectives, who was a sergeant.

"Shall I take the lookout?" asked the driver. "Then you two can get the big bloke."

"Right," said the sergeant. "Let us out."

The car ran a few feet past the big man, and stopped. The

two detectives got out. "Hey, John!" called the sergeant. "Come here. I'd like a word with you."

The big man did not seem to hear him. He turned and walked into the nearest shop. Or at least he walked to the shop door. It was a pie-supper place, and at that time of day it was closed.

He turned in the shop doorway, and faced the two policemen. "Now, John," the sergeant chided. "Don't try to be awkward. I want you to go back to the jeweler's shop with me."

The big man nodded. He came out of the shop doorway and began to walk along between the two officers. As he walked he put his right hand into his coat pocket. Instantly the young detective on that side seized his forearm with both hands. "Whatever it is," the young man said. "Bring your hand out without it."

Again the big man nodded. His hand, still firmly held at the forearm, came from his pocket empty. The detective released him, then thrust a hand into the pocket and brought out the bar of gold. "My oh my, look at this," he said.

On the other side the sergeant craned to look. His head came forward and down. The big man immediately struck at the exposed jaw with his right fist. He knocked the sergeant flat.

He turned to deal with the other man, but as he turned he was met by a fist which was weighted with a bar of gold. He in his turn was knocked flat. He was not allowed to get up until he had been handcuffed.

When all three men were again on their feet, the sergeant said: "That was a dirty trick, John," but he did not threaten physical reprisals. They walked to the jeweler's shop and entered. The proprietor was leaning on the counter holding his head.

"What's the matter with you?" the sergeant asked.

The man looked up, and revealed that one of his eyes was already closing. "Somebody tapped on the window," he said, "and straightaway that fellow hit me in the eye and ran out of the shop."

"You're a wild man, John, but happen we can tame you," the sergeant said. And to the jeweler: "Why did you call the police?"

"He tried to sell me a home-made bar of gold."

"This one here?"

"Yes, that's the one."

"Right," said the sergeant. "I'll be back for a statement. Come along, John."

The big man spoke for the first time. "All right, nark," he said to the jeweler. "Remember me, will you? You'll see me again one day. And you'll be awful sorry when you do."

As the three men went out, the jeweler held his stomach tenderly and thought of his ulcer. Suppose that man wasn't a murderer, and suppose he didn't get hanged. He might come back someday. Or some of his pals might come. The jeweler wished now that he hadn't called the police. He could just have told the man to go away, and then said nothing to anybody. The ulcer was going to be very bad, he knew. And the eye was bad already.

Outside the shop, the two detectives and their prisoner were met by the police driver and the sturdy man. This man, it appeared, was making no trouble. Nevertheless the sergeant said: "Put the darbies on that john," and the man was handcuffed.

In the York City C.I.D. office the prisoners were searched. Two offensive weapons, namely a knuckleduster and a small sap of the type known as a life preserver, were found in the pockets of the smaller man. The men gave their names as Francis McGeen and Lewis Frost, of Airechester. They were put in separate rooms. Frost was interrogated first.

"Where did you get the gold?" the sergeant asked him.

"What gold?"

"The bar of gold your pal had."

"What pal?"

"McGeen. Are you going to tell me you don't know him?"

"Oh, I know him."

"You were dogging out for him while he sold the gold, weren't you?"

"I weren't. I were just walking along the street, on my lawful occasions, when this copper comes and drags me in. Han'cuffs, an' all, and me never done a thing."

"You were dogging out. You tapped on the window to warn McGeen."

"Did you see me?"

"Yes," said the sergeant, stretching a point.

Frost was silent. His expression of disgusted resignation intimated that here we were, in the hands of the lying police again.

"What were you doing in York, anyway?" the sergeant asked.

"I come for a day out. Must've been wrong in my head."

"Did you come with McGeen?"

"We met in the train."

"And you stayed together. And he asked you to be his lookout while he went into the jeweler's."

"I'll come clean," said Frost wearily. "I'll tell you the whole truth. He asked me to wait for him while he went into the shop. I know naught about any gold. I just waited. While I were waiting I just strolled a little way on the street, and got arrested."

"Didn't you know why he went into the shop?"

"No. And I didn't ask."

The sergeant grinned. "All right," he said. "We'll see what Airechester City knows about you."

He went to the telephone, and was soon in connection with Airechester C.I.D. When he mentioned a bar of gold he was put through to Fairbrother.

"Frost and McGeen?" said Fairbrother. "Am I interested? I'll be with you in half-an-hour."

The sergeant left the telephone and went to talk to McGeen.

"Where did you get the gold?" he asked.

"In Airechester."

"Whereabouts in Airechester?"

"Everywhere. Door to door."

"The old-gold caper? Diddling old maids and widows?"

"Diddling nobody. I paid a good price for everything."

"Why did you melt it down?"

"Better to handle that way."

"Can you prove you got it by going from door to door?"

"Can you prove I didn't?"

"Somebody might be able to. Why did you come all the way to York to sell it?"

"I was going to see how I could do in York, door to door. So I thought I'd see if I could get a price for my gold."

"Why did you choose that particular shop?"

"I picked it at random."

"Did you know the man?"

"No."

"Had you heard of him?"

"No."

"I'd have thought you'd go to a better shop than that."

"No. The big shops want too much bounce. It's the little fellows who'll give you a price."

"You mean the big shops won't touch stolen property, don't you?"

"I mean what I said."

"Where did you get the gold?"

"I've told you."

"Have you ever heard of a man called Samuel Gilmour?"

"Sure, everybody has. He was murdered."

"Did you know him?"

"I knew him by sight."

"Have you been in his pub lately?"

"No, not lately."

"Were you in his pub on the night he was murdered?"

"No, I wasn't. Hey, what is this? Are you trying to fasten a murder on me?"

"No," said the sergeant. "I'll leave that to someone who is better acquainted with you."

Nevertheless, he persisted with his questions for another twenty minutes. Then Fairbrother arrived, attended by Adkin and his bowler hat.

The inspector smiled when he saw McGeen, but the smile was only a matter of showing his teeth. His gray eyes were merciless.

"Well, Frank," he began breezily. "We meet again in the usual happy circumstances. What happened to your face?"

"I was playing with a kitten," McGeen growled.

"And it kicked you. Too bad. But to business. I know you can't wait to tell me how you got hold of Sam Gilmour's gold coins."

McGeen hinted that the inspector was suffering from hallucinations concerning gold coins. He told his story of door-to-door trading, trying to get unwary people to sell old-fashioned brooches, rings and watch chains for much less than their intrinsic value. He affirmed that he was an honest trader.

Fairbrother ruthlessly demolished the story. He proved conclusively that McGeen had neither the knowledge nor the equipment for even the simplest transaction in precious metal. He did not have a jeweler's glass or even a cheap magnifying glass to look at sterling marks. He did not even have the usual little triangular file. He did not know the price of gold per fine ounce, and he did not know the difference between a pennyweight and the weight of a penny.

McGeen had always rather fancied himself as a man who could stand up to police interrogation. He had had a lot of experience. He now perceived that he was beaten and stultified by Fairbrother's barrage of questions, and his vanity was hurt. He became angry.

"You've proved nothing!" he shouted. "And you never will!"

The inspector's grin was devilish. "I'm doing all right," he said with satisfaction. "And I shall do better. Your furnished room in Airechester is getting the once-over at this very minute. We might find something there."

"You might plant something there, you mean."

"Well," said Fairbrother, who had never planted evidence in his life, "if my men show me something they say they've found in your room, who am I to give them the lie? I've got to believe my own men, haven't I? I'm on a murder job, you know. I can't afford to waste any evidence at all. I've just got to clear the job. So long as somebody gets hanged for it, I'm not particular who it is. You'll do as well as anybody else."

McGeen, a hard and plucky man, looked into the other man's gray eyes and grew afraid. The police were enemies. He hated them. He also measured them by his own yardstick. If he was capable of perjury and treachery, so were they. He believed that they would manufacture evidence. He believed that they would get an innocent man hanged rather than have an unsolved murder on their books.

And Fairbrother, who maintained a high standard of police integrity, wanted him to believe it.

"You'd see an innocent man hanged?" There was just the slightest tremor in the man's voice.

"I'd see you hanged, anytime. You ought to have been dropped into the water butt the day you were born. You've never been anything but a menace to decent people and a burden on the community."

"You can't say that about me!"

"I can. It's the truth. You've never done an honest day's work in your life. If you can't beg, borrow, blackmail or steal the price of a pint, you go running to the Public Assistance, and they're daft enough to listen to you. But this time you've had it. You've been caught with gold in your possession, and you were in the Starving Rascal the night Sam Gilmour was murdered."

"He just told me he wasn't," said the sergeant who had made the arrest.

"He would," said Fairbrother. "But he was there all right, and I can prove it. And I'll be very surprised if he can alibi himself out of the job."

When he made the last remark, he was watching the prisoner closely. He thought he saw the expression of guarded perturbation deepen to dismay. Good! No alibi.

"I hope you won't try to hold on to this man," he said conversationally to the York City sergeant. "You see how it is. He's probably melted down all the gold coins. But Sam Gilmour also had some silver coins in his collection. If our men find a few of those in this fellow's room, as I'm hoping they will, we've got him right."

The York man did not know all that was in Fairbrother's mind, but he knew that deception was being practiced upon the prisoner. He knew that the Airechester man had no intention of manufacturing evidence. And he knew just what to say.

"Well, we don't want to obstruct a murder job," he said thoughtfully. "We have several charges lined up. There's the jeweler, assault and battery. There's assault on police. And there's the bullion offense if he hasn't a license. On the other man there should be a charge of carrying offensive weapons. But I daresay the superintendent will agree to proceed by summons. I think he'll let you take both men."

"I never did a murder," McGeen protested. "You can't fix it on me."

Fairbrother smiled at him. "A bird in the hand," he said.

"I—I bought those coins!"

"Who from?"

"Gunner Byles."

"When?"

The answer did not come immediately. McGeen was obviously

thinking hard, to get his story right. "Last Saturday morning," he said at last.

"What time?"

"Just after half-past eleven."

"Where?"

"Outside the back door of the Friar Tuck."

"And, at that time, did you know about Sam Gilmour's murder?"

"No. I didn't hear till later."

"I thought you wouldn't have heard. Did you ask Gunner where he got the coins?"

"Yes, of course I did. He said he'd had 'em a long time. He said he used to save 'em."

"And you believed him?"

"Yes. There was no reason why I shouldn't have believed him."

"Says you. Was there a third party present?"

"No. Just the two of us."

"How many coins were there?"

"Seventy-four. I counted 'em."

"How much did you pay Gunner for them?"

Again McGeen hesitated. There was, possibly, an offense here of receiving stolen property. A conviction for that, for a man with his record, would undoubtedly mean several years' imprisonment. And behind that, in his uninformed mind, was the fear of being convicted as an accessory after the fact of murder. Therefore he had to show that he had bought the coins thinking that they were honestly come by, and to do that he had to say that he had paid a reasonable price for them. He had no idea what was a reasonable price for seventy-four gold coins.

"A hundred quid," he hazarded.

"And you thought that was a fair price?"

"Well, I got 'em as cheap as I could. Gunner isn't too bright."

"He's only about ten times as bright as you. When did you ever have a hundred pounds?"

"Last Saturday morning. I had a lucky run last week, on the horses. And I had a good night Friday at the dogs. Greenhill Stadium."

"You were in the Starving Rascal on Friday night."

"That was after I'd been to the grey'ounds. I'd made a packet by the third race, so I come away so's I wouldn't lose it all."

"Very sensible of you. Was Lew Frost with you?"

"No. I was on my own."

"Is Frost in this at all?"

"No, he don't know a thing."

"Why did he give warning when the police arrived on the scene this morning?"

"Force of habit, happen. He don't know anything."

"All right. You bought the coins from Gunner, then you heard about Sam Gilmour. Why didn't you bring the coins to the police?"

"I didn't know they had anything to do with Gilmour. There was nothing in the paper about coins."

"But you knew about Gilmour's coin collection."

"I never did. I didn't know a thing about it."

"Oh, you liar! But a jury might believe you, at that."

McGeen was startled. "Are you going to put me in front of a jury?"

"I'm hoping to put somebody else in front of a jury, and you'll have to testify. You'd better make a right job of it, too. If you don't, I'll see that you get a lagging for receiving."

"You can't have it both ways."

"Neither can you. I feel like a criminal myself, having to use a specimen like you for a witness. I don't believe for one moment that you paid a hundred pounds for those coins. But it's your story, not mine. I'll just have to be satisfied if you can get it accepted as evidence. You'll have to think up a convincing reason for melting those coins."

"Well, after I bought the perishing things I started to get windy. I thought Gunner might've half-inched 'em somewhere. I couldn't do with 'em being traced to me, so I melted 'em down."

"And destroyed the best evidence of the lot!" Fairbrother shouted in sudden anger. "You ignorant, blundering fool!"

McGeen flushed, but he held his tongue. He knew that he was not yet out of the wood. The thought of a long prison sentence was still with him.

The inspector glared at him for a long moment. "I ought to

kick you for that," he said, but his voice was calmer. Then he said: "You and Frost reckoned to have a fight with Gunner and another fellow on Monday night, didn't you?"

McGeen's glance slid to Adkin, the man whose intervention had ended the fight. He said nothing.

"Was that a put-up job, to tell the world that you weren't on trading terms with Gunner?" the inspector wanted to know.

"It was just a fight. It wasn't Gunner. It was the other fellow who was shining up to my wife."

"But you've been parted from your wife for years."

"That don't matter. When I see her with another fellow I always want to bat his ears down."

"I see. All right. When we've got permission from the superintendent I'm taking you and Frost to Airechester. There are a few things I've got to do before I even pretend to believe this tale of yours. What suit were you wearing on Friday night?"

"This one."

"How can I be sure of that?"

"It's the only suit I have."

"Very well," said Fairbrother. "If that's your only suit you're going to wear a pair of bobby's trousers for an hour or two while it's examined. And don't worry, they'll be old trousers. No policeman would wear a pair of pants that you'd had your filthy legs in."

chapter

thirteen

In Airechester, while the statements of McGeen and Frost were being dictated and typed, and while their clothes and all their belongings were being examined, Fairbrother set to work to strengthen the case against Gunner Byles. In the tissue of lies which McGeen had told him, he perceived what he believed to be one basic truth. McGeen had got the coins from Gunner. And that was the one material thing in the man's evidence against Gunner. How much he had paid for them was not important, except to protect him from a charge of receiving property which he knew to have been stolen. Without that protection he would not give evidence, so it seemed that the police would have to accept his story as he told it. Whether a judge and jury would do the same was a matter of some doubt. Fairbrother frowned when he thought of that. On principle he disliked employing a witness whom he knew to be lying, even if the lies were quite immaterial to the case. Furthermore, he had seen what could happen to liars at the hands of shrewd old judges and ruthless opposing counsel. McGeen, as a witness, was a gamble. He might blunder, he might not. He might be believed, he might not be believed. There was one thing to be thankful for: the jury would not know him as the police knew him.

Fairbrother thought that it would be a good thing if there was some real evidence to support his belief that McGeen's bar of gold and Sam Gilmour's stolen coins were of the same metal. He went to the Starving Rascal and began to look through the correspondence in Gilmour's study. He found the notepaper of a local society of numismatists, with the address of its secretary. The man lived in Wakefield. But when the inspector telephoned he was informed that the secretary was away from home, on business. The woman to whom he spoke sounded like a sensible person, so he introduced himself and explained his need for some expert advice about coins.

"You want Mr. Sands, the president of the society," the woman said immediately. "He knows an awful lot about coins. He lives in Harrogate. He's retired from business, so he'll probably be at home this afternoon."

Fairbrother got the full name and telephone number from her, and thanked her. He rang up Mr. Sands, and gave his name and rank. Sands, with the beginnings of interest in his voice, courteously asked what he could do for the Airechester police.

Fairbrother spoke of Sam Gilmour's coins, and Sands was horrified, in a gentle sort of way, at their destruction. He said that he had known Mr. Gilmour well. He was very sorry about his death. He would help in any way he could.

"I have a list of the coins, giving the condition of each one," the inspector said. "Would it be possible to ascertain their total weight, by weighing similar coins which are in similar condition?"

"A long job," said Mr. Sands. "Would you like to read the list to me?"

Fairbrother read the list, giving the condition of each coin, mint or otherwise.

"A good non-specialist collection," Sands commented. "Some rare coins, but none which are unique. You'd be surprised at the number of ancient coins still in existence. Nobody ever willingly throws a coin away, you see."

"Can it be done?" Fairbrother wanted to know.

"I think so. I'll do it for you, if you like."

"That's extremely kind of you. Won't it involve a great deal of trouble for you?"

Sands said that he had a number of the listed coins in his own collection. He had friends who would have others of the listed coins. He thought he could get the weight of all the coins. He would be most careful and particular, weighing the coins in lots when that was possible. If the inspector would like to leave it to him . . .

"I'll do that gladly, Mr. Sands," said Fairbrother. "But it might mean that you would have to appear in court, possibly as an expert witness."

"I don't mind that," was the reply. "I have been an expert witness before. It will also mean that I shall have to do all the weighing myself, with my own hands."

"Exactly, sir. You've got the idea. Are you sure it won't be too much trouble?"

"Not at all. It will give me something to do. One gets bored sometimes, in retirement. Besides, I want to help you with the Gilmour case. Poor Mr. Gilmour!"

With that, Sands got pen and paper and wrote down the list of coins as Fairbrother slowly dictated it. That was the end of the interview. The inspector was delighted with the promised assistance.

When he had put down the telephone he sat in thought, gazing at the exhibits on his desk. They had been taken from Frank McGeen's furnished room. There was a lump of modeling clay, which had been used to make a mold, and a small metal crucible of the sort used for melting lead or solder. Part of the inside of the crucible was thinly coated with gold. Its new condition indicated that it had been bought or borrowed simply for the purpose of melting Sam Gilmour's gold coins. As evidence it was not important, but it was evidence.

There was a perfunctory knock on the office door, and a clerk entered with a report. It was from the forensic laboratory. A little more evidence against Gunner Byles. Microscopic fragments of coal found on the soles of his shoes were identical with samples taken from the coal cellar at the Starving Rascal. They were of the same quality, from the same coal field.

A minute later another clerk delivered the completed statements of McGeen and Frost. Fairbrother read them through. With the laboratory report, he took them along to Belcher's office.

The superintendent read the documents. He frowned over McGeen's statement.

"Do you think I ought to arrest Gunner Byles, now?" Fairbrother inquired.

The older man was doubtful. "I don't like this tale of a hundred pounds," he said. "If McGeen ever had so much, he wouldn't use it for any sort of deal. He'd get rid of it in his normal way; drinking, betting, and women."

"But, assuming for a moment that he did pay so much for the coins, he didn't use *all* his cash. When he was picked up in York today he had twenty-seven pounds and some silver in his pocket."

"And how much had Frost?"

"Thirty-eight shillings."

"H'm. Whatever it is, Frost hasn't got much stake in it. You'd better let him out, quick."

"I'm going to let them both out, when we get their clothes back. There's no point in holding them. But what about Gunner?"

The superintendent thought about Gunner. "Have him in and see what he has to say about this new stuff," he suggested.

"I thought I could risk charging him."

"How much did you say he had hidden behind the skirting board?"

"Twenty-five pounds, in one-pound notes."

"It's a funny amount. Approximately eighty pounds altogether was taken from the Starving Rascal."

"Gunner might have another hiding place."

"He might have, but we haven't found it. I feel that there's something queer about the whole thing. Something we don't know. I wouldn't advise charging young Byles yet. He can't run away. We have him under observation whenever he stirs out of the house."

"Very well, sir. No charge yet," said Fairbrother, somewhat disappointed. He left the superintendent, and went across to the police canteen for a light meal. It was teatime. Normally, he would have been getting ready to finish work for the day, and go home for his tea.

After tea he returned to the C.I.D. Adkin was there, with another communication from the laboratory. The clothes and shoes of McGeen and Frost had been examined. "Nothin' on 'em," said Adkin. "They're waitin' to be collected. Shall I go get 'em?"

"No, I want you," the inspector said. "Let Traffic do it."

On the internal-line telephone he arranged for the motor patrol, maid-of-all-work of the police, to collect the clothes and restore them to their owners. He left instructions for the two men to be released as soon as they were ready to go.

"Come on," he said to Adkin. "We'll go and see if they've been talking."

They went along to the detention room where the two men were confined. But first they looked into the room next to it, where a C.I.D. clerk and a policewoman sat. They were wearing earphones, and holding notebooks and pencils. Fairbrother raised his head and his eyebrows in a question, and they both shook their heads. So it appeared that McGeen and Frost, left together in a room which was wired for sound, had not said anything which was of value to the police. Perhaps they suspected that there was a dictaphone, perhaps they were just being careful, or perhaps McGeen was not confiding in Frost.

Fairbrother and Adkin entered the detention room and closed

the door. They stood looking down at the two prisoners. Both men were wearing old police trousers and policemen's blue shirts. Frost sat leaning forward on a hard wooden chair, with his elbows on his knees. McGeen was trying to sprawl on a similar chair, with his hands clasped behind his head. McGeen seemed to be bored, Frost was morose. Fairbrother threw Frost a cigarette, which was caught deftly. Immediately McGeen moved one hand from behind his head, to catch his cigarette when it came. The two men accepted lights for the cigarettes, giving thanks for neither. They smoked hungrily, inhaling deeply.

The tobacco mollified Frost. His voice was almost mild as he asked when the hell he was going to be allowed to go home.

"In less than half-an-hour," said Fairbrother. "Your clothes are on the way."

"It isn't right making us wear coppers' cast-offs," Frost went on.

"Of course it's right. They've been stoved since they were last worn. And they'll certainly be stoved again when you've had 'em on."

Frost let that pass, and brought out his next complaint. "Are you trying to starve us into submission, or what? Not a bite to eat or even a drink of water have I had since breakfuss time."

That was a legitimate complaint, and the one who complained could even allege that it was a mild form of torture. The inspector perceived that he had committed an error of omission. To prevent repetition of the complaint elsewhere, he decided that the two men must have a meal before they were released. He gave Adkin instructions about that, and sent him away.

"I'm sorry about that," he said. "You shall have something at once."

"I should think you ought to be sorry," Frost grumbled, enjoying the novelty of an apology from a policeman.

"It was an oversight. I am sorry, I assure you."

McGeen spoke up. "When do I get back my bar of gold?"

"Never" was the word which came to Fairbrother's tongue, but he did not utter it. He had yet to prove that the coins which had been melted by McGeen were the coins which had been stolen from Sam Gilmour.

"You can't have it yet, at any rate," he said. "It's being held as material evidence."

"But will I get it back, when everything is settled?"

"I can't tell you. It won't be for me to decide."

"Well, I'm glad of that."

The inspector grinned. "I'm sure you are," he said. He noticed that the cigarettes were nearly smoked, and he handed over two more.

A few minutes later Adkin arrived, with a tray containing baked beans, toast, and two pots of tea. Fairbrother waited until Frost and McGeen had begun to eat, then he said: "You can go home as soon as your clothes come, but don't either of you try to leave town. If you try to run away I'll whip you in so fast your feet won't touch the floor. And now I'll leave you."

"Good-by," said McGeen, with sarcasm.

"You could've gone long since," said Frost.

With Adkin in willing support—he could see promotion staring him in the face if this job worked out all right—Fairbrother got a car and drove to Hudson House.

When he walked into the kitchen the evening meal was over, but all the family was still at home. Bill Knight was there too, sitting in his usual place at the far side of the table. He was playing Patience with a well-worn pack of cards, and Junie sat beside him, watching his strong hands as he dealt the cards. Gunner also sat near the table, and he too was watching Bill's game. Mrs. Byles was in her own chair, and she had put on her glasses to read the paper. Rosemary was over by the window, looking at a catalogue of woolen sweaters for women.

"Good evening, all," said Fairbrother as he entered. And before anyone could answer: "All right, Gunner. Get your cap and come along with me."

Gunner changed color. "What's up now?" he scoffed. "What the hell am I supposed to have done now?"

"The same thing. Come along."

Reluctantly, grumbling, Gunner went out with the two policemen. They said "Good night" as they went. Gunner did not.

When they had gone, there was silence in the kitchen. Everyone looked at Mrs. Byles, who sat deep in thought. She seemed to make a decision.

"Well, they've taken him," she said. "Junie, slip your coat on and come wi' me to the telephone box. I'm going to speak to Mr. Wigram, the lawyer."

"Are you going to ask him to take on Gunner's defense?" asked Bill.

"No," said Gunner's mother. "This is private business. Gunner can arrange for his own defense. He reckons to know a lot about police court lawyers. Ha! He knows damn all, like his father."

Junie and her mother went out to the telephone just about the same time that Gunner arrived at Police Headquarters. As he reached the top of the steps with his escort, McGeen and Frost walked out of the C.I.D. When Frost saw Gunner he made a rush at him. But Adkin caught the man under the chin with the heel of his broad hand, and sent him reeling back.

"You can stop that lark," he growled.

"He hit me in the teeth with a bottle," Frost protested.

"It served you right," Fairbrother told him. "Go on! Get out of here, will you? Fade!"

"Huh! You're not talking so nice now, I notice."

"So what? Do you want me to kiss you good night, or something? Get out of my sight!"

McGeen laughed, and went out. Frost followed, grumbling. The two detectives took Gunner into Fairbrother's office, and a C.I.D. clerk, at a nod, followed them in and seated himself at a little table in the corner. Gunner looked at the clerk and growled: "Some more stuff for the record. Can that bloke write the truth down?"

"He can," said the inspector. "So be careful what you say."

"He won't put down what I say, 'cause I shall say naught."

"I think you will. We've got a little more, Gunner, a little more. What made you choose that shoddy tea-leaf to buy Sam Gilmour's coins from you?"

Gunner stared. "What tea-leaf?"

"Frank McGeen. He was caught with some gold. It was an ingot made from the coins you sold him."

"I sold him nothing!" Gunner bawled. "I never had any dealings with that bastard in me life!" He broke off and stared at the floor, distraught but deep in thought. "So it was McGeen did it," he said, not addressing anyone in particular. "Him and Frost, the two of 'em. They did it, and now the rotters are trying to get me hanged."

Fairbrother was unimpressed by what he regarded as an act, but he was willing to let Gunner talk. "Are you trying to tell me that McGeen and Frost murdered Sam Gilmour?" he asked.

Gunner did not reply. His unfocused gaze was still on the floor, and he was breathing hard. Then he looked up and asked: "What was that you said?"

The inspector repeated his question.

"Well," said Gunner. "They were in the Starving Rascal that night."

Fairbrother pretended to give consideration to the remark. Though McGeen and Frost had indeed been in the Starving Rascal on the night of the murder, they had been sitting at a table in the corner of the bar-lounge. They had had no opportunity to dodge behind the bar and sneak into the cellar. They had been in conversation with two women who, while not being quite respectable, were neither prostitutes nor criminals. They had left the inn with the two women at a time when the rest of the company were quitting the premises. Abe Farley had remembered seeing them leave, because they were the sort of men he liked to keep his eye on. They had walked a short distance along Timberhall Lane with the women, and had then parted from them. Fairbrother had no doubt that the evidence of the two women was true. They were only slightly acquainted with McGeen and Frost, and they had no reason to lie for them.

"They were in there," he admitted. "But I don't see how they could have got down into the cellar."

"They'd as much chance as anybody else, hadn't they?"

Fairbrother shook his head. "No," he said. "You were the one who had the chance, and you took it. Then you sold the coins to McGeen."

"I tell you I sold him nothing."

"How did he come to have them, then?"

"How the hell do I know? How much does he reckon to have paid me?"

"A hundred pounds, so he said."

Gunner threw back his head and howled with quite genuine mirth. Then he demanded with scorn: "When did that ape ever have a hundred nicker?"

"Last Saturday morning, by his account," said Fairbrother, a little out of countenance. Adkin and the C.I.D. clerk were grinning broadly. Belcher had been extremely doubtful. Anyone who knew Frank McGeen found it hard to swallow the tale of a hundred-pound deal in coins.

"Where does he say he got this famous hundred pound?" Gunner queried.

"He had a run on the horses, and a good night at the dogs."

"He never did. If he'd won that much money he'd have been drunk for a week. Besides, he'd have bragged all over the town, and I'd have heard of it."

"You did hear of it. That's why you offered him the coins."

"Look, Mr. Fairbrother," said Gunner earnestly. "I give you my word, I never made a deal with McGeen in my life, even though he is my brother-in-law. I never had any dealings with Frost, either. I hate the guts of those two fellows, and I'm not on speaking terms with 'em. I wouldn't trust either of 'em as far as I could throw the Town Hall. I was in a fight with 'em a-Monday night, and then I got Frost in the mouth with a bottle. Look how he rushed at me tonight."

"You could have quarreled since Saturday."

"If I murdered somebody and stole some coins, and sold 'em to a bloke, am I going to get into a fight with him and then knock his pal's teeth down his throat so's he'll get mad at me and shop me? Does that sound reasonable?"

"It could happen. Thieves do fall out, you know," Fairbrother said, but he had to admit—to himself—that Gunner had an argument. Moreover, he was remembering Belcher's disquiet about the amounts of money involved. Gunner was believed to have got about eighty pounds from the Starving Rascal, in addition to the money from the sale of the coins. But he had only twenty-five pounds hidden in his room. Where, then, was the rest of the money? It could be hidden elsewhere, but that was unlikely. And yet Gunner, closely watched, did not seem to have been gambling heavily. He could not bet on credit, because he was blacklisted

144

all over the place. He had to deal with the small ready-money bookies whose runners frequented the pubs of Champion Road. They would accept his money, in large amounts, but he would not dare to bet so heavily with them because he would not trust them to pay out the much larger amounts that he hoped to win. Besides, informers around the pubs had been on the lookout for people who were spending a lot or gambling with what passed for big money in that district. The only place where Gunner could have lost fifty or a hundred or a hundred-and-fifty pounds unnoticed was at the greyhound track. And he had not been to the greyhound track.

"Empty your pockets," the inspector said. "Put your stuff on the desk."

Gunner obeyed with apparent willingness. Then he held up his arms while Adkin searched him. He had in his possession two one-pound notes and some change, the key of his room, cigarettes and matches, a dirty handkerchief, a piece of billiard chalk, a pocket knife, and a tattered notebook from which many pages had been torn in order to write bets.

Fairbrother stared thoughtfully at the uninspiring collection. Gunner, watching him hopefully, began to press his argument. "Can't you see, Mr. Fairbrother, it was McGeen? Him and Frost, very likely. He must've stole them gold coins from Sam Gilmour, because he certainly never bought 'em. If he had a hundred quid he wouldn't buy gold for the price of copper. He'd be off to the dogs or the races, trying to turn his hundred into a thousand."

"Shut up," Fairbrother said. He paced about, pondering. There was undoubtedly something very, very wrong about Mc-Geen's story of how he had acquired Sam Gilmour's coins. Perhaps it had been a mistake to let the man get away so easily. Inquiries would have to be made with a view to finding out if he had in fact not been winning money on horses and dogs, but losing it.

"Stay with this man," the inspector said to the clerk, and he went out of the office with Adkin. When he was outside he said: "I wish I could get hold of Number Thirteen."

"Who's Number Thirteen?" Adkin asked.

Fairbrother realized that he had made a mistake. Now, Adkin

would be curious. And what Adkin wanted to know he would take steps to find out. It would be better if he were told, at once.

"It's that chap Knight; he's a policeman."

Adkin whistled. "How come?" he asked.

"He's a recruit who's never paced a beat. Inspector Smithson had him out on a pub-crawling job. Betting. Now he's working for me, on a murder."

"That's a sweet set-up, sir."

"It's a help. I'm hoping he'll have some news for me tonight."

"Pull him in," Adkin suggested. "Pretend you want to talk to him in a hostile sort of way."

"I don't want to do that too often. Ma Byles is awful sharp, you know. She might say 'Fee fo fi fum, I smell a stool pigeon.'"

"I smell a dove what coos," said the Echo.

"We've got an hour to wait. I don't want to talk to Gunner again until I've heard from Knight."

Adkin licked his lips. "An hour to kill," he said. "I wonder when I'm ever goin' to taste a pint of pig's ear again."

"That's an idea," said Fairbrother. "We'll leave Gunner biting his fingernails and we'll prop up a bar for an hour. We've earned it."

They went for a drink, but at five minutes to eight they were back in the C.I.D. When Bill Knight telephoned, Fairbrother took the call in the main office.

"What's new, Thirteen?" he asked. "Have you done anything about that key?"

"Yes, sir. This evening after you took Gunner away. The key opens a door in the passage beyond my bedroom. I thought I heard somebody creeping around there the other night."

"What night?"

"Monday. Getting on for midnight."

"H'm. Did you hear anything else? Later, I mean."

"No. I went to sleep. The noise was very faint, and when I looked around I couldn't find anybody. But what I did hear was commensurate with somebody quietly opening that door."

"Was what?"

"Commensurate, sir. I mean it sounded like somebody at that door."

"I see. Never use a word like that when you're writing a report.

The inspector won't know what it means. I'm not sure you're using it right, anyway. When you unlocked the door this evening, what did you find on the other side?"

"Empty rooms, all dusty and dirty. It was a sort of warehouse. All the outer doors were locked, but there was one ground-floor window which has been used quite a lot recently. It's a sash window. There are a lot of marks and fingermarks in the dust."

"Did you open the window?"

"Yes. It opened easily, without a lot of noise. It opens into a yard which brings you into a narrow street that runs parallel to Bagdad Street."

"Conduit Street, that is. So Gunner has been going to and fro unknown to our watchdogs. They've been giving him a perfect alibi, which now he has not got."

"Why did you come for him tonight?" Bill asked.

Fairbrother told him about McGeen and his adventure in York, and his subsequent statement. "How does that sound to you?" he asked.

Like everyone else, Bill was doubtful. "I can't see it, sir," he said. "It's out of character for Gunner, too. I don't think he'd risk marketing those coins so long as he had a shilling in his pocket. And he'd do as McGeen did, he'd melt them down first. And McGeen is the last man in the world he'd try to sell them to. He hates the very sound of his name."

"I'm beginning to believe he does," said Fairbrother thoughtfully. "All right, Thirteen. Keep in touch. Ring in at, let's see, half-past eleven in the morning, and we'll see what's doing then."

"Very good, sir," said Bill.

Fairbrother put down the receiver and stood stroking his chin. He was remembering some of the well-worn precepts which Belcher had dinned into him when he was a young detective. Explore every avenue. Leave no stone unturned. Take nothing for granted. All men are liars. Trust nobody.

All right. Axiom Number One. The inspector turned to Adkin. "I want a list of all the recent crimes in town. Break-ins, with a one-inch jimmy or a pocket knife."

"Yessir," said Adkin, and he went for the records. Fairbrother paced about, feeling slightly worried. He was wondering if he

147

had made a mistake, a mistake for which he would have to accept the responsibility himself.

"Well?" he demanded, when Adkin returned.

"One job and two attempts in Gladstone Street, Sunday," the detective said. "Discovered ten-thirty P.M. The job was an insurance office. Safe untouched. Only petty cash taken: five pounds, twelve shillings."

"Not enough. What else?"

"Parker Street, Monday night. Two small lock-up shops; a butcher's and a health food store. M.O. two-two, with a one-inch jimmy or case opener. There was no cash on the butcher's premises, and nothin' was stolen. From the till in the nuts-and-raisins place, twenty-eight one-pound notes, seven ten-shillin' notes, eighteen shillin's in mixed silver and six pennies."

"Thirty-two pounds odd," said Fairbrother. "That's about the right amount." And as the other man stared at him without comprehension he asked: "What time was the job done?"

"Between midnight and two ack emma, if the man on the beat is to be believed."

"The time is right, too. No dabs, I suppose?"

"The only fingerprints were those of the two women who keep the shop."

"What about light?"

"Both shops are fairly well lit through the front windows by a street lamp outside. But there were a few spent matches lyin' around."

"H'm. That sounds more like Gunner than ever. He never did have a flashlight on a job. I think young Master Byles has done it on us. While we watched the front door, he went out by his own special exit."

"I don't get it."

"You soon will," said Fairbrother. He told Adkin about the gun and the key, the jimmy, the gloves and the money in Gunner's bedroom. He also told him what Bill Knight had seen, heard and discovered. "So you see," he concluded.

"My word, yes," said Adkin excitedly. "Everythin' fits. The time, the tool, the M.O., the amount of money stolen. He's done it on us, all right. Are you goin' to put it up to him?"

"No. Not tonight, at any rate," the inspector said. "I'm going to let him go."

He thought about Gunner. That young man was first and foremost a gambler. He was like McGeen in that respect. With money in his possession he would always be hopeful of making more money by betting, and he would not turn to other activities until all his capital had gone into the pockets of bookmakers. Thus he could not be called a professional thief. He was a casual, an irregular. He would at any time purloin anything which he saw lying around unwatched, but he would not make the effort of breaking into a place unless he was short of money. Therefore he had been short of money at midnight on Monday. Therefore it appeared that he had not stolen Sam Gilmour's money, or Sam Gilmour's gold coins. He was not "good" enough for a charge of murder.

Then what about Frank McGeen? Was he good enough? He had some money, and he had had the gold. He also had a lying explanation as to how he came to have the gold. Fairbrother decided that McGeen was not yet good enough to be locked up.

But he was uneasy about McGeen. He had a feeling that he was lacking in perception somehow or other. He had missed something which was as obvious as the bruise on the man's face. After letting McGeen go free, Fairbrother hoped fervently that he hadn't made a mistake, a big mistake.

chapter

fourteen

At eleven-thirty on Thursday morning Bill Knight talked to Inspector Fairbrother on the telephone, and stated that he had nothing to report. Then he stepped out of the telephone box and stood in the sunshine—for it was yet another fine morning of that fine September—and debated with

himself as to how he could make up his quarrel with Gay Gilmour. And since he still could not tell her the truth about himself, he decided to trust his luck. He made his way to the Starving
Rascal.

He went to the inn with no feeling that he was neglecting his
duty. Gunner Byles had gone out by the front door at ten
o'clock, and he had been seen and followed by the watching
plainclothesmen. He was being looked after. There was nothing
for the undercover man to do.

When he entered the now familiar bar, Bill was surprised to
see Mrs. Byles and Junie there. They were seated at a table near
a window, in conference with Gay, John Harper, and a tall,
middle-aged man of distinguished appearance. This latter person
was dressed in an immaculate charcoal-gray suit, a dove-gray
waistcoat, a snowy-white shirt, a bow tie and shoes which shone.
He wore his clothes with the negligent air of one who has for
years spent all his waking hours in a state of being well-dressed.
His long hands were white and very clean, and he moved one of
them now, in a small persuasive gesture, as he talked.

The man had an unopened brief case on the seat beside him,
but there was no hat beside the brief case. Therefore, Bill concluded, he had come to the inn in the fine Humber car which
was now standing at the curb outside. He guessed that the man
was Wigram, the solicitor. He also guessed that the conference
had started before opening time, because none of the people at
the table had drinks in front of them.

He went to his usual place at the rounded end of the bar,
which was almost the furthest point in the room from the group
at the table. But, facing the bar, he faced in their general direction. He could watch them without seeming to be curious.

Gay, who was flushed with indignation about something, left
the group and came to serve Bill. Without her the discussion
went on, John Harper being the object of Wigram's calm per-
suasion. Whatever the lawyer was saying, it appeared to be un-
answerable. That was made clear by Mrs. Byles's flinty approval
as she listened, and by the old man's air of pained attention, as
if he hoped against hope to find a defect in Wigram's argument.
Junie was not listening. She had looked at Bill when he entered,

and she continued to look. He did not have to be a mind reader to see that she longed to leave the table and join him.

Gay did not return to the table. When she had served Bill, she went and took an order in the taproom. Then she returned to Bill. Facing him across the bar, with her back to the group in the corner by the window, she spoke to him with low-voiced vehemence. Her recent quarrel with him seemed to have been forgotten.

"Oh, now I wish Sam had made a will," she said. "What do you think? That woman is going to own this place. She says she's Sam's niece, and I'm sure she's as old as he was."

Bill played safe. "Well, just imagine!" he said.

"Yes. And now she wants that girl working here. She says she wants one of her family to know something about the business, in case anything happens to me."

"What could happen to you?"

"She says I might suddenly decide not to go on any longer, because I have no financial interest in it. She says I'm only young, and I might suddenly chuck the whole thing up. Well, I might at that. I don't want that girl here."

"Can they make you have her? You're in charge here, aren't you? You're running the place."

"Yes, but that woman is the prospective owner, and her wishes carry a lot of weight with Mr. Wigram. He says it would be safeguarding the estate if the girl learned the business."

"Well, there's no will, and there's no trustee. I don't see how Mrs. Byles or Wigram have any sort of say until the probate court has decided she can have the estate."

"Mr. Wigram has applied for some sort of a grant, a grant of letters of administration."

"And has he got it yet?"

"No."

"Well, there you are."

"But he says he soon will get it. And he's also been in contact with the brewers who sent a cellarman to help us out. Mr. Martin, they call him. He's downstairs now, doing something. The brewers think Mrs. Byles's request is reasonable. They don't see why that girl shouldn't come here, and work behind the bar."

Bill didn't see why, either. The request was reasonable. But he did not want to have another quarrel with Gay. "She might take a certain amount of work off your hands," he said cautiously.

"I don't want her. I don't like her. The brewers are only backing her mother because they want to go on selling their beer to this place when she gets it."

Bill smiled. "Don't be like that, Gay. You don't even know the kid. You've never spoken to her in your life."

"And I don't intend to. I never want anything to do with that Byles woman or any of her family."

Bill could not help but say it. "She's your cousin, by blood."

"Then I wish I'd never been told that Sam was my father," was the heated retort. "Whose side are you on, hers or mine?"

"Steady on, Gay," Bill protested. "You know very well whose side I'm on. Why don't you calm down and be reasonable? What is it you have against young Junie?"

"I just don't like her, that's all. Have you never disliked somebody on sight?"

"Many a time. And I generally found they were all right when I got to know 'em."

"Oh, you!" said Gay. She flounced away in response to the taproom bell.

Bill wondered if he ought to drink up his beer and depart, before he got into another quarrel with Gay. She certainly was in an unreasonable mood. Mind you, he reflected, it was a typically feminine sort of unreason. A man would have to dig a long way before he found the real cause of antipathy, but it would be there all right, and real enough.

Gay returned to draw some beer from the pump nearest to Bill. "I don't know why you stay at that low Byles place, anyway," she said with great feeling. "Why don't you find a decent place?"

Bill could give her no true reply. "I'm looking round for one," he fibbed. Then he said with a forced grin: "I'd better get out of here, before I'm in trouble again."

Gay did not answer. She went away with the beer she had drawn. He glanced at the group in the corner, of whom Wigram still seemed to be the chairman. He saw Junie whispering to her mother, and he saw Mrs. Byles look in his direction and nod. He had nearly half-a-pint of beer to drink, and for the sake of appearances he could not leave it. He drank it quickly, but when he put down the glass Junie was there beside him.

"Hello," he said gruffly. "I'm just going."

Her smile vanished. She looked disconsolate. In his irritation he felt a pang of pity, as if he had hastily smacked a small child and come to regret it.

"I thought you might like to buy me a drink," she said wistfully.

"I would, but not here," he compromised. "I'm going round to the Flying Dutchman."

"Take me with you," she suggested eagerly. Then as she looked into his face: "But you don't want me, do you?"

Poor little Junie, he thought. Nobody wants Junie. "Come along then," he said. "If your mother doesn't mind."

"She won't mind," said Junie with instant gaiety. She called to her mother: "I'm just going along the street with Bill."

Mrs. Byles looked surprised, then she grinned. Then she saw Gay return to the bar, and she saw the sheer shocked astonishment of her gaze as Bill went out with Junie. She was amused, in her grim way.

Bill had hoped to be out of the place before Gay reappeared in the bar. Though he dared not look at her, he also was aware of that outraged glance. He quailed inwardly, and he reflected ruefully that he had once more been maneuvered into the doghouse.

Within the unromantic precincts of the Flying Dutchman, Junie said that she would drink the same as Bill, and he ordered two glasses of beer.

"I shall soon be selling this stuff," she said, as she cautiously tasted the beer. "I'm going to work at the Starving Rascal." She shivered. "Ugh! That Gilmour girl doesn't want me. She hates the sight of me."

Bill did not reply, and Junie went on: "I wouldn't be like that. I'd fight it out fair and square, with no holds barred."

"Fight what out?" Bill asked. "Is there something between you two?"

Junie looked at him in surprise, then she laughed. "Is there?" she echoed. "Wow, you'd be amazed."

"All right, I'll be amazed then. What is it?"

"Don't reckon to be so daft. Of course you know. You're enjoying it."

"I'm enjoying nothing," said Bill, but he perceived Junie's meaning. And he certainly was amazed. That Junie liked him he knew. That she could be jealous of Gay he understood. But that Gay could be jealous of Junie, well, that was ridiculous. Gay wasn't chasing anybody, she was the one who was chased. She was the desired, not the desirous. In any case, how could she regard young Junie as a serious rival? The whole thing was absurd.

"I guess she's jealous of everybody," said Junie.

Bill could not see it. Gay couldn't be jealous of Junie. Annoyed because Junie sort of hung around, yes. Not wanting him to be seen with Junie or any of the Byles family, yes. But not jealous. The two girls weren't in the same class at all. Admitted, there was nothing much wrong with Junie. She was a fine girl. But she wasn't in Gay's class at all. She didn't have the character and, and, well, the class.

But Bill did not tell Junie that. He had had enough of arguing with women. Let the thing work itself out. If Junie had to go and work at the Starving Rascal contrary to Gay's wishes, all that Bill Knight had to do was to stay away from the place for a day or two. In a day or two, he hoped, the investigation of the Gilmour murder would have been satisfactorily ended, and charges made. Then he would be able to leave Hudson House, and he would also be able to go and tell Gay all about himself.

"What's on your mind?" Junie wanted to know.

"Oh, this and that," Bill replied.

"You're mysterious, aren't you? You never say anything about yourself. Ma says you're a deep 'un."

Once more Bill was aware of danger from Mrs. Byles.

"You shouldn't tell people what other folk say about 'em," he said severely. "When your mother said that, she didn't intend you to tell me."

"Oh, she wouldn't worry."

"That's not the point. I'm thinking about common tact and good sense."

Junie was contrite. "Oh, you're teaching me to be tactful."

"Well, you don't just go about saying everything that comes

into your head. What made your mother say I was deep? Doesn't she like me?"

Junie turned wide, innocent eyes upon him. "If she doesn't, I shouldn't tell you, should I?"

Bill laughed. "I'm not the deep one around here," he said. "Come on, drink your beer and we'll go back and face the music."

"I think Ma likes you, really," said Junie. But Bill said: "Go on, drink your beer. Let's get going."

When they got back to the Starving Rascal, Mr. Wigram had departed, and Mrs. Byles was ready to go home.

"Come along, Junie, it's all settled," she said. "You're coming here tonight, to work. Now I've got somebody of my own on my own property. Possession is nine points of the law. Good morning to you, Mr. Harper."

She also spoke to the stout, middle-aged man who now stood behind the bar, and when she was at the door she turned and looked at Bill. She did not say anything, but he felt that she wanted him to go along too. He gazed levelly at her, and stayed where he was. She smiled, shook her head very slightly, and went out. Junie followed obediently.

John Harper peered distressfully round the room and discerned Bill. Or at least he discerned the tall, broad shape of Bill. He was not sure of his man until he heard his voice: "Hello, Mr. Harper. Will you have something to drink?"

"Well, thank you, Bill—may I call you Bill? I believe I do need a drink. I'm rather upset this morning. I'll have just a small whiskey, please, with a drop of cold water."

"Where is Gay?" Bill asked, when drinks had been served.

"She's upstairs, preparing lunch. She can do that, now that Mr. Martin is here. Poor Gay. She's annoyed with us all."

"Well," said Bill honestly, knowing that he was speaking to a reasonable and intelligent man, "I don't see what there is to argue about. It looks as if the property will eventually pass to Mrs. Byles, and what she's asking for seems sensible enough to me. But Gay has no need to put up with it if she doesn't want. She can always leave. She could walk into the best hotel in Airechester and get a job. She has no need to stay in this crummy district."

"Yes, but I'm afraid she's still inclined to be proprietary about this place. It's still her home, you see. She hasn't fully realized that it will soon belong to somebody else."

"Happen Mrs. Byles has guessed that. Happen she's afraid that Gay will suddenly realize the exact position, and walk out. Mrs. Byles is trying to make sure that this place is kept open until she gets the full title to it. Until she is in a position to sell it."

"But the brewery have a man here. They'd see that the place was kept open."

"Mrs. Byles is making sure. She's having one of her own people here as well, just in case. I don't blame her."

"Nor do I. You appear to be an intelligent young man, Bill, considering that you have had no legal training. You also appear to have some sympathy for Mrs. Byles."

"I'm on Gay's side, Mr. Harper, you can be sure of that. But she's raising all hell about something that doesn't matter two hoots."

Harper nodded sadly. "She seems set. I'm afraid she won't stay here very long after that girl comes."

"She seems to hate the whole Byles family, for some reason."

"Well, they'll get the money and the property which should be hers, won't they?"

Bill stared. "What difference does that make?" he wanted to know. "Gay wouldn't inherit in any event. They aren't robbing her of anything."

"Women take a more personal view of these things than men. I don't think she looks at the matter precisely as you do."

"But she's never seemed to be greatly bothered about the inheritance."

"Would you be bothered about an estate which may be worth ten thousand pounds?"

"You bet your life I would."

"Well, there you are. Gay certainly is bothered. She tries to conceal her disappointment from you and from me. Then she shows it by an increased dislike of the Byles family."

Bill thought about that. He wanted to be in sympathy with Gay. He supposed that her attitude was logical, in an illogical sort of way. He much preferred to believe Harper's explanation of it, rather than accept Junie's ridiculous allegation of jealousy.

"If you'll pardon me for saying something," Harper continued. "Gay feels very strongly about you staying on at the Byles house. She simply can't understand that. Why do you stay there? It isn't your sort of place. You can't fool me. You're not the type to stay there. I wonder what your reason is, and so does Gay."

Bill was mortified. There it was again! The Byles place! Why wouldn't these people credit his story that it was cheap, clean, and moderately comfortable? Because they thought it wasn't respectable. Respectable respectable. What could he tell them to assure them that it was respectable in practice? He knew. Nothing. They would believe lies, but not the truth.

Then he had an idea. At least he could put them off with lies. His undercover duties would surely end within seven days. The Gilmour job would surely come to a head within a week. Then he would be free to speak.

"My rent is paid a week in advance," he said. "I've given my notice. I leave next week."

"Have you got another place?"

"Not yet."

"Well, you could always come here for a day or two, if you hadn't a place. I'm sure Gay would feel safer at night with a strong young man in the house. She can't get much comfort from the presence of a purblind old wreck such as I am."

"We'll have to see," said Bill. He wondered what Mrs. Byles would say if he left Hudson House and went to stay at the Starving Rascal.

Then Gay came downstairs. "Is lunch ready, my dear?" the old man asked.

"Nearly," she said distantly. She did not look at Bill.

"Bill is leaving Mrs. Byles," said Harper. "He's given his notice."

The information did not quite succeed in making the sun shine for Gay, but it did melt the ice a little. There was a subtle change in her attitude, a touch of satisfaction, as she said tartly: "Well, it's about time, isn't it?"

chapter
fifteen

That sunny Thursday was a day of anxiety for Inspector Fairbrother. He conferred with Superintendent Belcher in the morning, and Belcher, in an ominous tone of commiseration, remarked that it was a little unfortunate that Frank McGeen had been given his freedom before any attempt had been made to verify his statement. He pointed out that there were offenses for which McGeen could have been held, even if it had meant leaving him in York and letting the York police hold him. True, the superintendent was speaking with what the Americans call hindsight. He had not advised that McGeen should be held. He had let Fairbrother handle the whole affair, and now he could sit behind his belly and comfortably reflect that any subsequent censure by the Chief Constable would be Fairbrother's pigeon. Fairbrother did not whine about this attitude, even to himself. He expected it. When a mistake has been made in the police force, as in some other organizations, it is the devil take the one who is not adroit enough to shift the responsibility to someone else.

"But I suppose you can easily pick him up," said Belcher. "Did you put a tail on him?"

"No," said Fairbrother, quite crestfallen, "I didn't."

"Oh dear, oh dear," said the stout superintendent.

Fairbrother was doing what he could. He had put men out, canvassing bookmakers, runners, and informers. He hoped for good information, but would have been pleased to hear even a reliable whisper. He required news not only of wins enjoyed or losses suffered by McGeen, but also by Gunner Byles and Lew Frost. It was important for him to know whether those men had been winning money or losing money.

He did not feel more than vaguely hopeful. So far, not a breath of helpful information had come in. The street-corner bookmakers of Champion Road did not usually make books, in the sense of putting pen to paper. They were men exact in memory and agile in mental arithmetic. Scribbled betting slips, easily destroyed after the races, were their only written records. Once destroyed, the slips were conveniently forgotten, and would no doubt be inconvenient to remember.

Mr. Sands the coin expert was the first comforter of Fairbrother's tribulation. The inspector ventured to call him on the telephone at eight o'clock in the evening, to ask if any progress had been made. He was surprised to learn that Mr. Sands had completed his task. After a busy evening on Wednesday, and a hard day of traveling here and there on Thursday, he was exhilarated rather than tired. He had enjoyed himself, and he had personally weighed, in lots where possible, specimens of all the coins on Fairbrother's list. He knew the total weight of all the coins, and he was prepared to give evidence to that effect.

"Thanks an awful lot, Mr. Sands," said the inspector with deep sincerity. "I really can't thank you enough. Did you have a lot of trouble?"

"No. A few phone calls, and then some short journeys in my car. I knew just where to look, you see. I am well acquainted with the collections of my friends."

"Well, congratulations. It would have taken me about a fortnight to do it myself. What is the total weight of the coins?"

Sands mentioned his total. It was within a pennyweight of the weight of McGeen's gold bar.

"What is the weight of the bar?" he asked. Naturally he hoped that his computation would provide the police with the evidence they wanted.

Fairbrother started to tell him, and then changed his mind.

"It would be better if I didn't tell you that, Mr. Sands," he said. "If you don't know the weight of the gold bar, no defense counsel will be able to suggest that you weighed your thumb in your enthusiasm to make the two weights the same."

"I see what you mean," said Sands gravely. "The defense might be quite capable of making such an accusation. But if I still don't know the weight of the gold bar when I give my evidence, then they're bound to recognize my veracity. That was very thoughtful of you. Of course you have had a great deal of experience."

"But not with ducats and doubloons, Mr. Sands, so thanks again. Will you be at home tomorrow if I send a man to take a statement from you?"

"I'll be expecting him," said Sands.

That was the end of the talk. Fairbrother sat in thought for a while, then he got up and reached for his hat. In the main office he met Adkin, who appeared to have developed a flair for being available just when the inspector wanted a man. Adkin was nominally off duty: he had been told to go home at six o'clock. He had gone home, and he had returned. He had worked hard on the Gilmour job, and he wanted to be present if there were new developments.

"Are you afraid of missing something?" Fairbrother demanded.

"That's right, sir," was the cheerful reply. "I smell trouble. The right sort of trouble."

"Well, let's hope your nose isn't misleading you. Come on, we'll see if we can find Frank McGeen."

They did not call for a car. They went out on foot, and spent a fruitless half-hour seeking McGeen in places where he might normally be found at that time in the evening.

They walked back to Headquarters. "I'll have to put out the word," said Fairbrother. "Then we'll get a car and prowl round the streets."

He caused a message to be radioed to all ranks on duty in the city. Francis McGeen, wanted for interview in connection with the murder of Samuel Gilmour.

"We'll walk down to the garage," he said. "It'll be as quick as ringing for a car."

They went out of the building and walked along Crown Row. They had to walk some three hundred yards to the garage, past the frontage of the municipal offices and the main entrance of the jail.

Daylight was going, and the brilliant sodium lamps of Crown Row were illuminating the scene. Near the entrance to the jail a police patrol van was standing. Between the van and the entrance there was a group of struggling figures. "A lock-up," said Fairbrother, without much interest.

But as they drew nearer he quickened his pace. At the center of the swaying group was a man who looked like a giant in that light. No fewer than four policemen were holding him.

"I believe it's McGeen," said Adkin, with excitement in his voice.

"You're dead right," said Fairbrother tensely.

Somebody must have got a hurtful hold on McGeen, for the reeling group suddenly accelerated away from the van and, still closely integrated, crammed itself into the narrow doorway of the jail. It was followed by the van driver, carrying a policeman's helmet and holding the arm of a thickset man who appeared to be in physical distress. The man was Lew Frost.

When the two detectives reached the entrance, McGeen and his hostile retinue were halfway on the long, narrow passage which led to the charge room. Besides McGeen, the man they could see most clearly was the constable who had lost his helmet. There was blood running down the constable's chin, and he seemed to be angry. They saw this man finally lose his temper. He kicked McGeen behind the knees, and when McGeen sagged for a moment he thrust out a strong arm and rammed the side of the big man's head into the wall.

It was the sore side. McGeen roared with pain. He uprose in his fury and appeared to throw off policemen as a maddened bear might throw off attacking hounds. But the man without a helmet wasn't thrown anywhere. He banged McGeen's head again, and again. McGeen decided that he had better go where he was required to go. He staggered along to the charge room, with his police escort in close attendance. The police driver and Frost followed quietly.

Fairbrother and Adkin looked at each other. The inspector's eyes glittered with eager speculation. The detective constable was grinning broadly.

"Did you see Frost's nose?" Adkin asked.

"Yes, and I'm wondering if McGeen did it. If so, there might be a bit of something in it for us."

They went along to the charge room. They entered it at the same time as Smithson, the duty inspector, who had been called from his office. Fairbrother had time for a few hurried words with Smithson.

"If I seem to be interfering, George," he said in a low voice, "play along with me. I have a very good reason."

Smithson nodded. He entered the charge room and sat behind the desk, ready to accept or refuse the charge of drunk and disorderly, assault on police, or whatever it might be. Fairbrother and Adkin entered quietly and remained near the door.

Smithson listened inscrutably while the arresting officer briefly presented his case. The two prisoners had been causing a disturbance in the narrow street behind the tavern named, appropriately enough, The Call To Arms. A small crowd had gathered. Some women had been screaming. As the arresting officer arrived on the scene he saw McGeen knock Frost down and kick him twice in the face. When the constable interfered, McGeen turned and struck him in the face. The constable ventured the opinion that McGeen was like a madman, and Inspector Smithson frowned, because the P.C. was excited enough to forget that in presenting a case no policeman should express an opinion unless asked for it. The P.C. went on to say that he fought with McGeen—"endeavored to restrain him" was his way of putting it—until the arrival of police reinforcements. While McGeen was being restrained the prisoner Frost sat on the ground, holding his head.

"H'mmm," said Smithson, when the tale was told. He pressed a bell button to summon the jailer, then he said: "Any idea what the trouble was about?"

Frost raised his drooping head. He removed a bloodstained handkerchief from his face and remarked in a thick voice that the trouble was about an unprintable woman.

"He was interfering with my wife," said McGeen.

Frost retorted to the effect that McGeen was legally separated from his unmentionable wife. He added that the gory female animal could not bear the smell of her shockingly illegitimate husband. It was all copulating jealousy, he said. "I was only talking to her," he concluded, "and look what he done to my face. What a bloody pal!"

The terrible words rang sweetly in Fairbrother's ears. He moved forward, and peered down into Frost's injured face. "This man ought to go to the Dispensary and have his nose seen to," he said with just the right touch of stern solicitude. "He's losing too much blood."

Smithson nodded. "Get him charged," he said to the arresting officer. "The stipendiary magistrate will have to decide whether or not he has merely been the victim of an assault."

Frost was solemnly charged with behaving in a disorderly manner at such a time and date in Back Cross Street, and he replied: "He hit me first. I didn't even have a chance to defend myself." The constable made a note of the reply, and Fairbrother said quietly to the van driver: "Take him out, but don't go without me."

The pair went out. At a nod from Fairbrother, Adkin followed them.

The detective inspector said to Smithson: "I'll make myself responsible for Frost. He'll be in court in the morning, if he's fit to appear."

McGeen spoke up. The drink or the strong emotion which had started his violence was still working in him. He was still defiant, and reckless of consequences. "Don't think I can't see your game," he said to Fairbrother. "Creeping round Frost to make him sing for you. To hell with you. He'll tell you all he knows, and that's damn all. You're wasting your time."

Fairbrother's answer was a shrug. He left the charge room and went out to the van. He sincerely hoped that McGeen was wrong. Frost *had* to know something. This could be one of those slices of luck which make the difference between superintendents and inspectors, and between inspectors and sergeants.

The driver was in his seat. "Take it easy," the inspector said to him. "And go the longest way round. Our man isn't dying."

The driver said: "I get you, sir," and Fairbrother went round to the back of the van and climbed inside. He closed the door, and the van started on its journey.

"I don't like riding in these things," Frost complained. "You should've got me a ambulance."

"It wasn't worth it. You're not going far," Fairbrother replied. He took a clean, folded white handkerchief from his pocket and said: "Here, take this. And stop blowing your nose. That only makes it bleed more."

With no word of gratitude Frost took the handkerchief, and dropped the red-stained rag he had been using onto the floor of the van.

"A good-lookin' fellow like you!" said Adkin without a blush. "It's a shame. He's made your nose the shape of a bit of corrugated iron."

Frost said what he thought McGeen was, and fingered his nose tenderly. "You think he has?" he asked anxiously. "Won't they be able to put it right?"

"It's hard to tell. Broke in three places, from the look of it."

Frost made some more remarks about McGeen, and Fairbrother said: "You've had it with him. He says you'd shop him if you could, except that you don't know what day it is."

"He's the one who don't know what day it is. He won't do, when I've done with him. They don't have calendars in the jug."

"Now you're swanking. You don't know all that much."

"Oh, don't I? I've been biting his ear ever since last Saturday. Just the odd fiver now and again. Borrowed, you know. No blackmail."

"You didn't have to threaten him, then?"

"No. He kept asking me where I got my nerve from, keeping on asking him for money. I said I got my nerve where he got his cash. He said I didn't know nothing. I said: 'You keep on believing that.' I said: 'We sometimes like to take a walk on a fine Friday night.' I said: 'Just lend me a fiver and you'll die happy.' "

"And he lent it to you?"

"You bet he did. But he kept getting a bit more irritable, like."

"But you never told him what you actually knew?"

"No, I never atcherlly told him."

"Then it can't be blackmail. You're absolutely in the clear."

"I don't need a bloody copper to tell me that. And I'm going to stay clear."

It seemed that Frost might not be going to "sing" after all. His rancor needed reviving. Fairbrother could see only one way to do that.

"How did tonight's little do start?" he asked. "Were you only talking to McGeen's wife, as you said?"

"That's all. But I was doing all right."

"It was wife trouble, and not money trouble?"

"Happen a bit of both. I've had about twenty quid off him altogether, but today I'd got down to about six quid, and I knew he was starting to get low, too. I could tell by the way he acted. So I thought I'd better have another couple of quid while the going was good. I gave him the old tug of the sleeve, but he balked. He said he was browned off of supporting me. I said I needed support. I said I was the fellow who knew nothing, remember, and I wanted to stay that way. He said he'd think about it. I said he'd better, because I needed the green stuff. He gave me a very bad look, and sheered off somewhere for a meal. Didn't ask me to go with him, you notice. That was this afternoon just before tea, in a certain club we go to. It struck me then I'd better watch my step. Though I'm not frightened of him, mind you. I'd a-paralyzed him tonight if I hadn't a-slipped."

"So you didn't get any money today?"

"No, but I was going to have it. I wasn't going to be put off. After I'd had a bit of tea I went looking for McGeen. I didn't find him, but sometime after eight o'clock I met his wife in the Call To Arms. I've never had much to do with her, but I've always fancied her a bit. She looks like a warm 'un to me. Anyway, she gave me the nose-in-the-air treatment at first. But I noticed she was drinking common ale and I guessed she was hard up. That's the time to catch 'em, when they're hard up. So I ordered her a double gin. She asked me what was up with me, but she had the gin. I told her I was flush. She said seeing was believing. I said I'd show her my money when I knew what I was going to get for it. She said: 'So that's the way it is, is it? I didn't know you'd ever give a woman money.' I said I might make an exception if it looked like being worth while."

"As you remarked, you were doing all right."

"I sure was. I bought her some more gin and we started to make a night of it. She was good company, and I forgot about going to look for McGeen. But she was telling me about some of his little ways and we were having a right good laugh when he walked in. I think it must've been us laughing what made him mad. He went straight up to Amy and knocked her off her buffet. That was his mistake. When he turned on me, I was ready. I— well, I defended myself. The landlord—Tod Winter, the wrestler —vaulted over the bar and parted us. He whistled up his waiters and they slung us out, and then I had to defend myself in the street. McGeen was like a crazy maniac. He's still mad jealous of that wife of his."

Said Fairbrother: "He'll have the chance to cool down if I can get him right. It'll be a good thing for his wife, too. She'll be able to have her fun in peace."

Frost thought about that. He brightened a little. Then he said: "I want to ask you a question, off the record. If McGeen has some money what he's stole, and I sap him and steal this stolen money, does that make me a thief just the same?"

"It certainly does. Robbery with violence. With your record you'd get seven years."

"But suppose I said I only took it off him so's I could give it back to the proper owner?"

"You'd have to show some proof of that intention. If you spent the money, or withheld it, the excuse wouldn't be valid."

Frost nodded. He thoughtfully dabbed his nose with Fairbrother's handkerchief, and stared down at the floor of the van. The inspector, with a very slight surreptitious movement, made a sign to Adkin, who was seated near the door on Frost's side of the van. Adkin did not make any noticeable movement, but a notebook and pencil appeared in his hands. The light in the van was not very good, but it was good enough for him to write shorthand.

Frost had another query. "Suppose there was a witness, and he kept quiet, and then told the police later on?"

"No offense. The witness would be okay with the police. He'd have nothing to fear from them."

"Think the doctors'll be able to straighten my nose?"

"It's hard to say. McGeen has just about ruined it for you. And you weren't a bad-looking fellow, Lew."

Frost spat redly. Then he said: "Me and McGeen was in the Starving Rascal last Friday night. We was talking to two gimmers. He must've seen summat I missed, because when we come outside with these females he started backing out of things. That was funny, because he'd seemed right keen on one of these dames from the start. He upset the party all right. The wench what would've been mine, she said she'd stick to her pal. They cleared off and left us."

There was a short silence. Fairbrother did not speak. Adkin was still.

"When they'd gone," Frost resumed, "I asked McGeen what was up with him. He said he was sorry, but as a matter of fact he had a previous appointment with a woman whose husband worked on nights. I thought it was a rum do he hadn't mentioned this woman before, but I didn't say so. I said I'd totter off home, and I left him standing there like a cabby at a christening."

There was another pause, while Frost tried to find an unstained place on the handkerchief.

"He was standing outside that fish-and-chips shop in Timberhall Lane, just round the corner from the Rascal. The light from the shop gave him a long shadow, and as I walked away I could see it out of the corner of my eye. That shadow never moved. He just stood there, watching me, and it struck me then he was up to something he wanted to leave me out of. So I went into the tripe shop and stood there reckoning to wait to be served. McGeen couldn't see me, but I could see his shadow. He stood there a good two minutes, watching to see if I would peep out at him. Then he moved, and I nipped out of the shop into the next door's doorway, which was dark. I could watch him then. He was walking away. He turned round a couple of times and didn't see nothing. He didn't turn round again, so I started to follow him."

Frost paused again. The police van had rolled very gently to a stop. They were at the Dispensary. "Traffic lights," said Fairbrother.

"We should be nearly there," said Frost, but he went on with his story. "Well," he said, "McGeen went home. I thought I'd been wasting my time, and I was thinking of going home myself when he came out again. He set off back the way we'd come. I had to duck round a corner middling sharp, or he'd a-walked into me. I followed him back, and then I lost sight of him just when he got to the Starving Rascal. He seemed to disappear there. I daresn't go any further, so I turned along the little cross street there, which runs parallel to Bagdad Street. I took the second alley and came to Bagdad Street, and I stood in the doorway of that little grocer's shop at the corner of the alley. Still I couldn't see nothing of McGeen. I thought he'd either gone into the Rascal or else I'd lost him completely. I was fair nonplused. I didn't want to lose him. I knew he was on some game."

Frost stopped to dab his nose. His face was now quite covered with blood. He was a dreadful sight.

"I waited," he continued. "I saw Sam Gilmour's daughter come out of the Rascal and get into a taxi what had come. She was going to a dance, from the look of her. Then the last of the taproom customers came out, or at any rate they looked like taproom customers. A minute or two after that Abe Farley came out and slammed the door behind him, just as if he'd dropped the latch. He walked off, and I was thinking of doing the same when I saw McGeen. He was standing in the dark in that big loading bay at Champion Foundries, straight opposite the Starving Rascal. He lit a cigarette and I saw his face. That cigarette is going to cost him plenty. But for that I'd never a-spotted him.

"Well, he waited and I waited, and I didn't light no cigarette. I heard eleven o'clock strike, and there weren't as many people going up and down Timberhall Lane. Then about five minutes after it had struck eleven somebody came out of the Starving Rascal and pulled the door shut very quietly. I couldn't recognize this bird like I recognized Abe Farley, because he started coming in my direction, with his back to the light at the corner. And he soon went out of sight. He turned the corner into the alley parallel to mine, between me and Timberhall Lane."

Frost paused again, and this time it was a dramatic pause. He was coming to the climax of his narrative, and in spite of his injuries he was to some extent enjoying himself.

"What do you think happened?" he said. "No sooner was this geezer out of sight than McGeen came out of his hole on the run. He was running on his tiptoes as hard as he could. He went down Timberhall Lane, taking a parallel course to this stranger. I went down my alley, also parallel, and when I came to the corner of the cross street I peeped round very cautious like. McGeen was coming tiptoeing on the cross street, to intercept the other bloke. He got there in time. He stood just near the corner, squeezed back against the wall, but I could see him against the lights of the lane. Then the fellow came along, and at the corner he must have looked my way first, because he didn't try to duck when McGeen sapped him. He just went down flat on his face, clean out of time. And he never saw who hit him. It was a neat job, I'll say that much.

"Well, that's what happened. McGeen knelt down beside the bloke and rolled him over to go through his pockets. He was in a sweat, 'cause he kept looking this way and that all the time. He was soon on his feet and away, and I went along to see who he'd robbed. It was Gunner Byles, and he had a revolver stuck in his belt, so I reckon McGeen had been lucky to get home with his first smack. I didn't touch Gunner. I knew there'd be nothing left in his pockets and I didn't want the gun because it might be hot enough to get me into trouble. I just cleared off and left him."

Fairbrother relaxed with a long, silent sigh. "So now we have the whole picture," he said. "Somebody did see Gunner sneak into the cellar during Tom Casey's beer dispute. McGeen saw him, and waited outside to relieve him of his plunder. Gunner committed a murder and didn't get a cent out of it."

"I think McGeen would have left him alone if he'd known he'd done a murder," said Frost.

"Maybe," the inspector murmured thoughtfully. He looked at Frost and said: "Even when Gunner got you with a bottle you knew he was a murderer."

"That's so. But I thought I'd better keep my mouth shut so long as McGeen was in the money."

"All right, Lew. Thanks for the information. I think we must be at the Dispensary. We'd better let them have a look at your face."

The face in question was twisted into some sort of grin, and malice was there. "You're in a hurry now," the injured man said. "You're wanting to go and drag in Gunner Byles. Well, I hope you catch him."

"What do you mean?"

"I happened to see him watching while me and McGeen was being put in the van by that crowd of coppers. He wasn't laughing. I thought that was queer."

"You think he's tumbled to something?"

"Does he know about McGeen's gold bar?"

"Yes."

169

"Then he knows who sapped him. He'll think I'm in it as well. When he saw us get locked up for fighting he had the breeze up. He'd be afraid one of us might talk. You won't find it so easy to catch him. He'll be on his way out of town."

chapter

sixteen

Fairbrother did not spend any more time with Lew Frost. He left Adkin in charge of him, with instructions to take him to the jail after treatment, or to stay at his bedside if he was detained in hospital. The inspector returned to Headquarters in the van, and this time he told the driver to take the shortest route at all possible speed.

Elated at this happy climax in his day of professional tribulation, he pondered whether or not he would phone Belcher at his home and tell him what had happened. He decided that he would not phone. He would wait until Gunner Byles had been arrested. He would present the superintendent with a cleared case and a prisoner.

He did not share Frost's belief that Gunner would flee from Airechester, but he was determined to cover all possibilities. He put out an express message to all districts, requiring the arrest of Gunner for murder. With that done, he got hold of every C.I.D. man he could find. He sent his men out in pairs. He wanted this to be a C.I.D. arrest, for the credit of himself and his department. They had one advantage. At least one man in every pair knew Gunner by sight. The majority of the men in uniform did not know him.

The time was ten minutes past nine. The plainclothesmen who had been detailed to follow Gunner around reported by radio that he had been out earlier in the evening, and that he had returned home at twenty minutes to nine. He had not come out again.

The news gave Fairbrother his first feeling of uneasiness about Gunner. He realized that a mistake had indeed been made: an error of omission. Gunner's private entrance had not been covered. It was unusual—it was almost unnatural—for Gunner to go home an hour and twenty minutes before closing time on a fine evening when he had money to spend. It indicated that he had gone home simply to get rid of his following of policemen, and that he had gone out again by his secret exit. If he had taken the trouble to do that, then he had some nefarious activity in mind. Or else he was running away.

With Sergeant Nolan and two detective constables, Fairbrother went to Champion Road. He found the insecure warehouse window which Bill Knight had described to him, and he left the two constables to guard it. Then, taking Nolan with him, he went into Hudson House by the front door. The place seemed to be deserted. All the lodgers were out, which was not surprising, and all the Byles family seemed to be out, which was very strange indeed.

Then Mrs. Byles came down the stairs, dressed for the street.

"Hello," said Fairbrother. "I was beginning to think there was nobody at home."

"There soon won't be. Our Rosem'ry's gone to the pictures. Our Junie's at the Starving Rascal, and that's where I'm going."

"I notice you don't mention Gunner."

"I was waiting for you to mention him. You don't expect *him* to be in at this time of night, do you?"

"He came in at twenty minutes to nine."

"Did he? Well, I was in the kitchen then, and I never saw him. Is that who you're after?"

"Yes."

"That'll be three times in a week you've arrested him."

"No. I never mentioned the word."

"Are you mentioning it now?"

"I'm afraid so, Mrs. Byles. I'm going to charge him this time."

That hit her. She had to lean on the stair rail. The corners of her hard mouth sagged. "You're going to charge him with—murder?"

Fairbrother stepped forward. "Are you all right?" he asked with concern. "Can I get you something?"

Her head came up. She stood erect. "You didn't answer my question."

"I'm not obliged to. Besides, you're his mother."

"Does that touch your finer feelings? I can take it."

"Well, all right then. I'm going to charge him with willful murder."

This time she did not flinch. "You're sure he did it?"

"I'm just as sure as I could be, Mrs. Byles."

"In that case," she said, moving to pass the two policemen, "you'd better find him. I've got my other children to look after."

She was walking toward the front door. "I shall have to search the house for him," Fairbrother said.

"Search where you like," she answered, without turning her head.

She went out. Fairbrother and Nolan looked in all the rooms downstairs, then they went up to the first landing. The inspector found Gunner's room. The door was not locked. He entered, switched on the light, and pulled the bed away from the wall. He groped in the cavity behind the skirting board, a proceeding which made Nolan's mouth drop open. The cavity was empty. Gun, gloves, jimmy, key and money had been taken away.

"I'm afraid he's scarpered," Fairbrother said.

The remainder of the search was a formality. Fairbrother found the door which led to the unoccupied premises next door. It was locked.

He and Nolan went back to headquarters, to wait for news. The inspector sat in his office and thought about Gunner Byles. Gunner had about twenty-five pounds in cash. That was not a great deal. Possibly he would try to increase it. Fairbrother picked up the telephone and dictated a special vigilance message for all ranks in all departments, even the motor patrol. A close watch was to be kept on all lock-up property, especially near the center of the city.

At ten o'clock there was news. Sometime between nine and ten there had been three attempts with a one-inch jimmy or case opener at the rear of some good-class shops in Boundary Street.

One of the attempts had been successful. A smart leather-goods shop had been entered and the till had been rifled.

A few minutes later came the news that the sum of thirty-four pounds had been taken from the leather shop. Fairbrother wondered if that would be enough for Gunner. Fifty-nine pounds in all. It still wasn't a great deal of getaway money, though men had been known to get away on less. He did not think that Gunner would get away, however much money he had. All railway stations and bus stations were under observation, and the motor patrols were stopping all main road traffic on the outskirts of the police district.

Meanwhile, in the city, closing time had come, and searching detectives had ceased to stalk in and out of public houses and billiard halls. Now, they watched the late-evening crowds and the supper places, and such dubious clubs as would admit a man like Gunner.

At Headquarters, no more break-ins were reported. Fairbrother began to be fairly certain that no more would be reported. He believed that Gunner was now trying to get out of the city. Lew Frost had been right for once in his mistaken life. Gunner knew that Frost or McGeen or both of them had waylaid him and robbed him of his murder gains last Friday night. Then he had seen them fighting, and he had seen them arrested. He had some experience of such affairs, and he feared that there would be wild recriminations. Through the reckless desire of one hooligan to get the other into more trouble, his own name might be uttered. Eventually the police might piece the true story together. These were possibilities which Gunner's jumpy intuition had made into certainties. He had foreseen the event, and he had decamped. But he was not yet out of the city.

Bill Knight spent the latter part of that Thursday evening at the Starving Rascal. He had intended to stay away, not wishing to be involved in any more unpleasantness, but curiosity drew him. He wanted to see how Junie and Gay were getting on together.

He entered the inn at nine o'clock. The place was only moderately busy. Abe Farley and the man from the brewery were acting as waiters. Gay, in a very smart dress, was behind the bar.

Junie, also wearing a smart new dress, was behind the bar with her. Apparently both girls had felt the need to be looking their best for this occasion.

Bill, as he took his accustomed place at the bar, could see that Gay was not allowing Junie to serve customers. She was giving the girl no chance to become interested in her work. Junie stood about, waiting for something to do. She picked up empty glasses, and washed them and polished them, and then waited until there were more empty glasses. Once, when Gay was pumping beer with furious energy and efficiency, a thirsty customer invited Junie to fill him a glass of beer. After an embarrassed but by no means timid glance at Gay, Junie picked up a glass and reached to a pump. Gay immediately stopped what she was doing, and took the glass from Junie's hand, and filled it.

Junie, very naturally, sought to relieve the tedium by moving along the bar to talk to Bill. Gay, busy at the time, noted the move with a swift sidelong glance of dagger-like sharpness. Bill felt uncomfortable, and rather sorry for Junie.

"How are you getting on with it?" he asked her, for the sake of something to say.

Junie's chin came up, and she gave a very slight toss of her shining blonde head. There was neither defeat nor humility in her glance as she looked at Gay. "I'm doing as I'm told," she said. "And I'm learning about women."

Bill began to wish that he had followed his original intention of staying away from the Starving Rascal. The trouble here was deeper than he had thought. But it appeared that Junie could stand up to it. It was possible that she might, eventually, be more than a match for Gay. Well, she had had a tougher upbringing.

Then Abe Farley came from the taproom shouting orders. He remarked that he was getting busy. A few customers had left, but more had entered. He lifted half-a-dozen pint glasses from his tray, and put them aside on the bar. Junie went to take them and wash them. Gay swiftly filled Abe's orders, and moved along the bar to Bill.

"It's awful," she said. "I don't think I can go on with it, having her in the bar."

"I expect she's doing her best," said Bill feebly.

"Whose side are you on?" Gay asked sharply.

"You know I'm on your side," he said. "But I still don't see why you should take such a dislike to the kid. She's harmless."

"That's what you think," Gay retorted.

Bill was searching his mind for a tactful rejoinder when two tall, hard-faced young men came into the bar and looked around. They also looked in all the public rooms and in the men's toilet. Then they went out.

"Coppers," Bill said. "They seem to be looking for somebody."

Gay nodded without interest. Detectives looking for somebody were no rare sight in a Champion Road pub. Her manner made Bill realize that, and he did not speculate as to the identity of the wanted man.

Then Mrs. Byles appeared at his elbow, and Gay moved away. He slipped from his bar stool and offered it to the woman. She got her haunches onto it, not without some grunting and puffing, and then somewhat tardily she said: "Thanks."

In normal circumstances Bill would have been mildly irritated by her arrival, but now he was relieved. "I suppose you've come to see how Junie is getting on," he remarked.

"Right first time. She doesn't seem to be working herself to death."

Bill made no comment about that. Let Ma Byles find out for herself what was happening. He ordered a whiskey, which Gay reluctantly served.

"I'll pay," said Mrs. Byles.

"No. I'll get this one."

The woman assented with an absent nod, and then she said: "Those fellows who went out as I came in. Were they two D's?"

"I think so. Looking for somebody, I suppose."

"They're looking for our Gunner. They're after him right, this time. Fairbrother is going to charge him with murder."

Bill was silent, thinking about Fairbrother, and Gunner. He could not feel sorry for Gunner. He was glad, glad that this was the end of the investigation and the end of his own life as a police spy. At last he would once more be able to look all men in the eye and tell the truth without fear or favor.

"Do you feel bad about it?" he asked.

Mrs. Byles shrugged, but Bill, knowing her better these days, thought that her apparent indifference was hiding considerable suffering.

"I don't feel good about it, at any rate," she said. "He's my lad, after all. He's a no-good. He never was any good. But he's my flesh and blood. I can't say I like to think of him swinging at the end of a rope."

Bill had no words to say, so she went on. She spoke with unusual emotion for her, but in another woman her tone would merely have evinced a slight bitterness. "When he were a kiddie I used to think the world of him," she said, "even though he were a little devil even then. A little cruel devil. But when he started to grow up he hurt and disappointed me so often that I had to sort of give up having any feeling for him. It was a kind of self-defense. He'd have ruled the house like a Turk and beggared us all, sisters an' all. I had to harden against him and stand up to him. He didn't like it. He used to call me some horrible names. He didn't love anybody, anybody in the world but hisself. I don't think he could love anybody. The one thing he never dared do was strike me. Not because I was his mother, but because he knew I'd turn him out of the house if he did that. He's robbed me scores of times, and robbed his sisters. Robbed 'em of their little bits of things they treasured. Oh, he's been a bad 'un, a bad 'un."

She stopped, and looked around with a puzzled frown, as if she were trying to remember why she was there. Only Junie, from the middle of the bar, and Bill, beside her, were looking at her. Only Bill could hear her regretful words.

"Anyway," she said, her voice hardening. "It looks as if he's had it. He's going to finish up at the place he's been heading for all his life. He's always been terribly interested in folk who've been hanged, reading these reaped-up murder cases in the Sunday papers. Well, now he'll be one of 'em hisself. And he deserves to be, if he murdered Sam Gilmour for what he could get out of the till. I should worry about him. He'll swing for killing Sam, and I'll inherit Sam's money and property. That's blood money for you."

Bill reflected that now she sounded more like herself: the flinty-eyed, flinty-hearted Ma Byles who could keep a rabble of Irish and Polish lodgers in order. This was the Ma Byles who would shortly become known to the popular press and its readers. The world would never really know how she felt about her son's crime.

Junie put down her glass-polishing cloth and came to them. Her mother said: "Why don't you shape yourself and draw some beer?"

"You keep out of this," said Junie unexpectedly. "You got me here with your interfering. What I do when I am here is my business."

Mrs. Byles looked surprised, and then she smiled dryly. "Starting to fight your own battles, are you?" she queried. Then she said: "Eeh, Bill, you've done summat to this lass. You've changed her. She's daft about you, and it's a good job you're an honest lad. I only hope she'll be able to settle down all right when you've left us."

"When he's left us?" Junie asked, unable to conceal her dismay at the mere mention of Bill's departure. "Where's he going? He can keep on stopping with us, can't he?"

"He can if he wants, love," said the mother. "But don't be kidding yourself. Bill's different to us. He's been brought up different and he sees things different."

"I can be like him," said Junie. "I can look at things his way. I can be respectable like he wants. I am respectable. And when I've earned some money working here I'll be dressed as smart as anybody. I chose this dress myself, and I look as smart as little Miss Oity-Toity here."

Bill admitted to himself that she was right. She was as smart as Gay. Or nearly as smart. Nobody, in his opinion, could be quite as smart as Gay.

But Mrs. Byles said: "Don't be kidded, love. Don't delude yourself. Then you won't be too badly disappointed."

As she spoke, the woman's glance slid to the neat figure of Gay, as if she would compare the two girls. Bill looked at Gay, too. She was smart, all right. As trim as a racing skiff. Her figure was perfect. Not so promising as Junie's, he had to admit. Both girls had perfect figures in their different styles, but Gay's was more sort of taut. It nearly had angles. It suddenly occurred to him that she would have very sharp elbows by the time she was forty. She was one of the sort who would dry up rather than put on a few pounds of comfortable flesh. He did not like thin women. His gaze moved to a dimple on Junie's elbow.

Anyway, he thought, a man doesn't go for a girl just because of her figure. The face was very important. Now Gay's face . . .

Gay's jaw was set with displeasure as she furiously pumped beer. Bill knew that was because of the presence of two of the Byles family. She certainly had a temper, and she could keep it up. Well, temper and sustained anger went with character. Character, that was what a man looked for in the girl of his choice. Gay had good looks and character. She would make a man a good wife, keep him up to the mark, stop him from back-sliding, make him get on in the world.

Young Junie, now, she was too happy-go-lucky for her own good. She was a nice kid, all right. A sweet disposition but no character worth mentioning. She'd pamper a man. Even in re-pose her longish but by no means bony face was a mirror of good nature. It was one of those faces which would grow even hand-somer as she matured. It would stay in good shape. She would still be a bonny woman when she was fifty.

But she wasn't in Gay's class, Bill decided. Gay was superior to her. His mother would approve of Gay.

"Can't you make up your mind?" Mrs. Byles asked him coolly.

Bill was startled. "Why? What about?"

She grinned at him. Her cynical composure indicated that she was quite normal again: no longer thinking about Gunner. "We'll have another drink," she said. "This time I pay."

They had another drink. Bill knew that for the sake of good relations with Gay he ought to go away from there and return at some time when Junie was not present. But he lingered. He was still there at twenty-six minutes past ten when everyone except Junie and Mrs. Byles had gone home. Mrs. Byles was waiting for Junie. Bill was waiting to be alone with Gay, so that he could put matters right with her. He thought, now that there was a warrant out for Gunner, that he could take the risk of explaining everything to her.

It was twenty-five minutes past ten when Abe Farley and the brewery man went home, and they did not latch the outer doors because Bill and Mrs. Byles were still on the premises. It was a few seconds after that when John Harper came groping cautiously down the stairs. It was twenty-six minutes past ten when Junie finished the washing up and Gay took the last glass from her and put it in its place behind the bar. And it was twenty-six minutes past ten when Gunner Byles walked into the inn by the side door.

Once again it had happened, the traditional thing. The murderer had returned to the scene of his crime.

chapter

seventeen

Gunner came in quietly. He was unperceived until he stepped from the side passage into the stronger light beside the bar. If he was surprised to see Bill and his mother and sister still there, he did not show it.

He had the Webley .45 in his hand, and his voice was steady and confident as he advised everyone to remain perfectly still. John Harper stepped toward him, peering shortsightedly. Without looking at him, Gunner pushed him aside. The old man staggered away and rolled over a stool.

Junie and Gay, behind the bar, were both standing near the till. Gay turned suddenly, as if she intended to run to the farthest end of the bar. She turned so suddenly that she hit the till hard, near the base, with the heel of her hand. The till did not ring, but a drawer flew open.

"Leave that till alone!" Gunner snapped, sour and resolute. "I'm coming round there."

"Don't be a fool, Gunner," his mother said. "Don't make things worse than they are."

Gunner did not even look at his mother. He was watching Bill, who had started to walk toward him. "Stay where you are," he warned. "This gun is loaded, and I'll shoot you if you come near me."

179

"You won't shoot anybody with that gun," Bill said. "Give it to me."

"I'll shoot you, you bastard," said Gunner. "Get back!"

There was no doubt that he would shoot. This was a different Gunner. During the last hour or two he had been facing up to some very bitter facts, and he was coldly desperate.

But Bill advanced confidently. He reached for the gun. Just as confident in his own way, Gunner removed his thumb from the cocked hammer and pressed the trigger. The gun roared.

Junie had been staring with a sort of horror at the thing which she saw when the flat bottom drawer of the till flew open. She had not been aware that the till had such a drawer, with such a thing in it. She had not been allowed to touch the till. But when Bill began to move toward her brother her gaze left the till and, wide with alarm, followed Bill.

When Gunner fired, the thunder of the explosion was convincing, and the air was filled with a cloud of solid particles which looked and smelled like gunsmoke. Bill got a stinging portion of that discharge in his face, a contingency which the ballistics expert had overlooked. He was temporarily blinded, and his lunge for the revolver miscarried as Gunner sidestepped. He staggered blindly past Gunner, who turned to face him. Bill also turned, and through a mist of stinging tears he saw his man. Then he was blinded again. Quite coolly, no doubt supposing that Bill was already badly wounded, Gunner had fired at him a second time.

The sound of the shots mingled with the screams of Junie. She had been screaming for Gunner not to shoot. After the first shot she snatched up the automatic pistol from the drawer of the till and pointed it in both hands, and screamed that she would shoot Gunner if he fired again. When he fired his second shot, she pressed the trigger of the automatic, but it was immovable. Nothing happened though she pressed the trigger with all her strength.

Having settled with Bill to his own satisfaction, because at that range he could not have missed, Gunner turned to go to the till. He saw Junie pointing a pistol at him, and he fired without hesitation. The roar of his gun was followed by the sharp crack of the automatic. One of Junie's thumbs, seeking purchase as she pressed desperately on the trigger, slipped onto a little catch on the pistol butt. The catch moved easily, and the pistol went off.

The crack of the pistol, so different from the revolver's roar, was followed, except for the drifting gunsmoke, by absolute stillness in the room. Gunner had staggered back two paces. He stood then for a second or two, like a man too surprised to move. Junie's bullet, unluckily aimed, had caught him square on the forehead. He stood thus, with a hole in his head, then his knees buckled and he fell on his back.

When Bill got the dust and tears out of his eyes he became aware that a pair of strong young arms were giving him support which he did not need.

"Bill, Bill!" Junie was frantically imploring. "Are you hurt? Are you all right?"

"Yes, I'm all right," he said, shaking out his handkerchief and applying it to his watering eyes. Then he looked around. The room was blue with acrid dust and smoke, which was just beginning to settle. Over by the window, getting shakily to his feet, was John Harper. On the floor in the middle of the room was Gunner, lying on his back with one hand raised to shoulder level and the other, still holding the gun, across his body. Over at the end of the bar Mrs. Byles was still sitting on her stool. She had one elbow on the bar and she was resting her forehead on the fingers and palm of her hand. Her eyes were closed. The other hand was pressed to her heart and she was sobbing almost silently, at breathing intervals, like someone in the throes of severe internal pain. Behind the bar was Gay, and she was staring in horror at Junie.

"She killed her own brother," said Gay. There was no sympathy in voice or expression: only horrified condemnation.

From that moment, Bill Knight was a young man without any immediate plans for marriage. A girl could have too much character, and too much respectability. He still had no clear idea of what had happened, and he looked at Junie for confirmation of Gay's extraordinary statement. She was still concerned with him, asking him if he was all right. She seemed unable to believe that he was not injured. He was about to tell her that Gunner's revolver had been loaded with blanks, but the habit of discretion restrained him. "He missed me," he said.

Then he saw the pistol lying on the bar, and he remembered the sharp crack of the shot which had killed Gunner. He began to understand. He remembered the pistol in the till, and he remembered Gay's movement which had opened the till. Junie had picked up the pistol and fired it in an attempt to save his life, and she had killed Gunner. For which Gay condemned her, instead of thanking her. That was carrying a natural dislike a little too far, Bill thought.

Nobody in that room had any doubt that Gunner was dead. Nevertheless, Bill examined him. While he was doing so, the full realization of what she had done came to Junie. She began to weep bitterly. She went to her mother, and her tears brought the comfort of tears to the older woman. They wept in each other's arms.

Bill, using the several simple tests which he had learned in the police ambulance class, came to the conclusion that Gunner was quite, quite dead. It was not a doctor who was required, but the C.I.D. He looked up, and saw Gay still watching, with nothing but outraged horror in her expression. He met her glance coldly, and got up from his knees, and went to the telephone.

He dialed the police number, instead of 999, and he asked for Inspector Fairbrother. He had to wait a little while, because the inspector was himself engaged on the telephone.

While Bill waited, he thought about Junie. She must never know, he decided, that to save him from an eyeful of dust she had taken her brother's life. He thought that the matter of the doctored bullets need not be made public. It would not affect an inquest verdict in any way. He believed that Fairbrother could arrange it with the coroner, if the coroner had any human sympathy at all.

He thought about himself. He would become well-known, now, in Champion Road. Men who would otherwise have forgotten him would now be eager to remember him and discuss him. Could he, then, start to walk about the town in a policeman's uniform, to be pointed out as the police spy for whose sake a girl had killed her own brother? That was another fact which he would ask to be suppressed. Only three or four men in

Airechester knew that he was a policeman. He would resign, and ask for secrecy from them. There was no need, now, for him to give evidence at a trial. He would give evidence at Gunner's inquest as a laborer, unemployed, of no fixed abode. Then poor Junie would never know that he had been a policeman. She would not break her heart by thinking that she had shot her brother in order to save a detested copper.

He wondered what he would do after the inquest. He could go back to his old job in Sheffield: when he had left, he had been told that he could go back at any time. Or he could transfer to another police force, so long as they did not ask him to do any more pub-crawling jobs. London perhaps; the Metropolitan Police. In a big force like that he could lose himself, because nobody would be interested in Bill Knight who had made a bit of a stir in Airechester.

He would have to think about it. He would have plenty of time to think about it.

And what about Junie? He had a feeling half uneasy, half pleasant, that wherever he went, she would follow. Thy people shall be my people, and thy gods, my gods. Even if he joined the London police, she would think it was the right thing if he did it. Character? Well, he didn't know. She was certainly a good kid. One of the best.

≫≫ If you've enjoyed this book and would like to discover more great vintage crime and thriller titles, as well as the most exciting crime and thriller authors writing today, visit: ≫≫

The Murder Room
Where Criminal Minds Meet

themurderroom.com